Pulse humming, Kristen came face-to-face with the man who'd arrested her the night before.

"Is there a problem, Chief?"

"Alex, please."

He was wearing a uniform today, looking unbelievably good in stark black. She almost wished she could see the soft gray of his eyes through his dark sunglasses. Not wanting to be attracted to him, she swallowed hard. "Okay, Alex, do you have a problem with me?"

"Why would you think that?"

"This is the second time today you stopped in front of the store like you were casing it. Or maybe you're expecting me to be doing something not to your liking. Maybe you just want to arrest me again."

The way he was staring at her so intently, as if he wanted to say something but was reluctant, made her mouth go dry.

Then a slow easy grin lit his face. "Will you have dinner with me?"

Kristen swallowed hard. She'd had a purpose in moving to Sparrow Lake, and it certainly wasn't romance. No matter how tempting this man in uniform was, getting involved would just complicate things.

Dear Reader,

Lynn Patrick is a writing team—Linda and Patricia being our real first names.

Linda's middle sister liked to quilt. While Linda was visiting the small town in which she grew up, her sister took her to a specialized quilting store with creative projects hanging on the walls, yards of fabrics, and friendly local personnel who also offered classes on weekends and evenings. She found the place inspiring and, though she's a city person now, she couldn't help imagining the story of a burned-out urban dweller returning to her roots to find love and happiness.

Linda's sister also had small twin granddaughters, some of whose escapades inspired scenes in *Home to Sparrow Lake*.

We hope you fall in love with these characters just as we did. And be sure to look for us on Facebook!

Lynn Patrick

HARLEQUIN HEARTWARMING

Lynn Patrick

Home to Sparrow Lake

HARLEQUIN® HEARTWARMING™

Recycling programs
for this product may
not exist in your area.

ISBN-13: 978-0-373-36634-7

HOME TO SPARROW LAKE

Copyright © 2013 by Patricia Pinianski and Linda Sweeney

Printed in U.S.A.

LYNN PATRICK

is the pseudonym for two best friends who started writing together a few decades ago. Linda is a professor with a reading specialty, and Patricia writes as Patricia Rosemoor. Together they enjoy creating worlds that are lightened by the unexpected, fun and sometimes wonderful vagaries of real life.

Books by Lynn Patrick

HARLEQUIN HEARTWARMING

SHALL WE DANCE
THE MARRIAGE ASSIGNMENT

HARLEQUIN SUPERROMANCE

343–GOOD VIBRATIONS

SILHOUETTE ROMANCE (as Jeanne Rose)

26–THE PRINCE OF AIR AND DARKNESS
55–HEART OF DREAMS
64–GOOD NIGHT, MY LOVE

HARLEQUIN INTRIGUE (Patricia Pinianski writing as Patricia Rosemoor)

707–VIP PROTECTOR
745–BOYS IN BLUE
785–VELVET ROPES
791–ON THE LIST
858–GHOST HORSE
881–RED CARPET CHRISTMAS
924–SLATER HOUSE
958–TRIGGERED RESPONSE
1051–WOLF MOON*
1047–IN NAME ONLY?*
1101–CHRISTMAS DELIVERY
1128–RESCUING THE VIRGIN*
1149–STEALING THUNDER*
1200–SAVING GRACE*
1261–BRAZEN*
1292–DEAL BREAKER*
1345–PUREBRED*

*The McKenna Legacy

For Linda's sisters and their families, where we got some great and also fun details for this story.

CHAPTER ONE

BEING BONE TIRED for a change felt good.

Kristen Lange knew she was driven when it came to work, and it had been nearly a year since she'd had the opportunity to satisfy her type A personality. But thanks to Aunt Margaret, she'd spent a long day going over Sew Fine's records to acquaint herself with the business. She knew nothing about shops that sold quilting materials and offered quilting classes. But she was a quick learner.

When her eyes began to water and she couldn't stop herself from yawning, she knew it was time to call it quits. There was always tomorrow.

She checked her watch. One in the morning. Sheesh, it already *was* tomorrow.

Enough. Even a type A needed some sleep.

And food, her noisy stomach reminded her. She remembered having lunch halfway through the day, and she'd meant to order in dinner, but she'd been so preoccupied going over the store's accounts and various orders—mostly handwritten on scraps of paper—that she'd simply forgotten she needed to eat. Her growling stomach was doing a fine job of reminding her. When she got back to the house, she would have to raid Aunt Margaret's refrigerator.

She closed down the computer and searched under the desk for her high heels. Designer shoes were her weakness, but four-inch stilettos weren't meant to be worn for so many hours, and she'd taken them off once the store had closed for the night.

Yawning again, she shoved her swollen feet into her shoes and headed for the back door, where she shut down the store's lights.

She was so tired she might not bother with the fridge after all.

It wasn't until she'd closed the door and heard the automatic lock click into place that she realized she'd left her purse—*and keys!*—by the register inside.

Drat! She couldn't get into her car. Now what was she supposed to do? She guessed she could walk home—crawl nearly a mile was more like it—but then she had no keys to the house. They, too, were inside the locked store. She didn't want to wake her aunt, who'd stayed home all day trying to fight off a sinus infection, so she figured she'd just have to find some way back into Sew Fine.

Unfortunately, the windows facing the alley were too high. She could reach them, but there was no way to get herself in a position to climb inside from the ground. And, of course, the store had an alarm system. But if she could figure out how to get in through a window, she could quickly drop to the floor and shut down the alarm, which was next to the back door.

The downtown area of Sparrow Lake was nearly deserted at night, so who was going to hear?

Kristen looked around for something to climb on. The Dumpster would get her high enough, but it was shoved to one side of the building, not directly under the window.

Too tired to cry, she made an unhappy face and then got to work.

If, a year ago, someone had told her that she would be stuck in her small hometown, living on her aunt's charity, trying to make sense of a business that she didn't understand, she would have laughed at the sheer ridiculousness of the idea. Now here she was, dressed in a designer business suit and heels, pushing a Dumpster along the back of a building so she could climb on top of it to break in.

You can't go home again.

That thought had been echoing through her

mind since Aunt Margaret had invited her to do so. At the moment, she wondered if she'd made the biggest mistake of her life by trying.

Kristen wearily set the Dumpster in place and struggled to get on top of it. Good thing she still worked out. Only three tries and she hiked herself up with her arms like she would to get out of a swimming pool. Throwing her upper body forward, she grabbed onto the side of the Dumpster and squirmed sideways until she could get a knee under her.

One look down at her filthy, snagged suit told her it was ruined.

What else could go wrong?

Kristen got to her feet and checked the closest window. Of course it was locked tight. Groaning, she checked the other window, knowing what she would find before even trying to open it.

Wearily, she assessed her options. She could walk that mile and sleep on the front porch swing, or she could sleep atop the Dumpster. Neither idea appealed to her.

So she told herself that a girl had to do what a girl had to do, and, with apologies to Christian Louboutin, picked up one of her precious shoes and used it to break a single glass pane, immediately setting off the alarm.

Nearly on her last nerve, she gritted her teeth

at the shrieking sound that pierced the night, and after taking a furtive look around to make sure no one was out there with a shotgun aimed at her, used the heel of the shoe to clear the glass so she wouldn't cut herself. Then she stuck in an arm and found the lock. Once she released it, she opened the window and raised the sash. The sill was about three feet higher than the Dumpster, and she was wearing a tight skirt, so it would take some fancy maneuvering to get inside.

After making certain there was no glass on the sill, she hitched her skirt high and started to climb in when, half in, half out of the window, she was nearly blinded by a brilliant beam from a flashlight below.

Then a deep voice said, "Lady, you're under arrest."

Speechless, she froze.

The light moved up and down over her, and the man added, "You know, you really ought to dress more appropriately when you're robbing a place."

Okay, *that* struck her last nerve.

POLICE CHIEF ALEX NOVAK appreciated the length of leg he got to admire for a moment before yelling, "Come on down now!" above the still-screeching alarm.

"You don't understand!" the woman hanging on the window sill returned.

"I understand you're trying to break into the place."

"Because my keys are inside!"

"Sure. Like I haven't heard that one before."

"How do I know you're a cop? You're not wearing a uniform," she said, looking over her shoulder at him as she balanced on the sill.

"I'm not on duty."

"Then why are you being such a pain in the—"

"If you don't come down voluntarily, I'll have to come up to get you. I don't think you want that."

He could hear her muttering under the sound of the alarm, but she slid her legs back down to the Dumpster. He admired them all the way up to her thighs revealed by her skirt catching on the window sill. She muttered some more and he thought he heard a rip when she freed the material.

Then she turned to glare down at him. She appeared a little crazed, with tufts of dark blond hair sticking out around her face emphasizing her outraged expression.

"I can't believe you have nothing better to do than cruise alleys in the middle of the night!" she shouted over the blaring noise.

Alex clenched his jaw. "I heard the alarm go off and knew someone was up to no good!" He flicked a switch on his radio and connected with the night desk at the station. "Call Margaret Becker and tell her there's been an attempted break-in at Sew Fine. Someone needs to come and turn off the blasted alarm."

"No, don't call her and wake her!" the woman protested. "I can turn off the alarm if you let me get inside."

Figuring that would give her the opportunity to give him the slip by going out the front way, he said, "Just come on down."

She grabbed up her shoes and moved to the edge of the Dumpster. "Your arresting me is absolutely ridiculous."

His irritation level shot up a notch. "Casting aspersions on my job isn't going to win you any points."

He could see her face clearly now. One cheek was smeared with dirt, but it was her sour expression that detracted from her softly rounded cheeks, thick-lashed blue eyes and full lips. A sour expression aimed at him.

Even so, he stretched out his free arm. "Let me give you a hand."

She ignored it and got herself down, planting both stockinged feet in the alley. She started to put on her shoes, then stopped and straightened. She was a few inches shorter than he, but if she was wearing those stilts, she could meet him eye-to-eye.

"You're not going to put those on?"

"After planting my feet in muck?"

Her way of saying "are you crazy?" Her voice went up so high that it, along with the alarm, scraped down his spine.

"C'mon." He took her arm and led her to the edge of the alley where he'd left the patrol car.

"You're not even going to ask me to explain first?"

"Explain all you want at the station."

"But Margaret Becker is my aunt!"

"That remains to be seen."

He really should handcuff her, but she looked close to tears, and he thought things might not be exactly as they'd first seemed. He'd never seen her around town before, but if Margaret truly was her aunt…

The raucous alarm was driving him crazy.

Nope. This wasn't the place to have any kind of conversation. And he did want to talk to her. A woman wearing designer everything breaking into the back of a store was the most intriguing thing that had happened around here in the two years since he'd moved to Wisconsin from Chicago.

Opening the rear door of the squad, he said, "Get in and watch your head."

CHAPTER TWO

KRISTEN HAD EXPECTED a small-town police station would be deserted at night. She was surprised to see a couple of uniformed officers talking to the woman at the desk. Their conversation ended immediately and the woman said, "I called Mrs. Becker, Chief. She said she would get over to the store and shut off the alarm right away."

"Thanks, Janet."

Kristen tightened her jaw. "My aunt has been sick. You shouldn't be bothering her, *Chief.*"

"Not here."

She felt the gazes of the two officers follow her and the cretin as he led her toward the rear of the station. He escorted her into an office. The brass plate on his desk read Police Chief Alex Novak.

"Sit," he said. "Please."

Too exhausted to protest, Kristen dropped into a chair.

How had her life gone so wrong?

She'd lost her job, her savings, her home.

And now *this* new humiliation.

"If you're going to arrest me, just get it over with." At least that way, he would throw her in a cell with a cot and she could get some sleep. Undoubtedly he would take unflattering photos of her and then fingerprint her.

"First things first," he said. "How about you give me that explanation now."

Great. She could have cleared this up at the store if only he would have listened. "As I said, Margaret Becker is my aunt. I'm working at Sew Fine now—"

"I've never seen you around town."

"Because I just moved here from Chicago a few days ago."

"Chicago, huh?" His thick eyebrows shot up. "Do you have some kind of identification?"

She glared at him. "I do, actually. In my purse! Which I accidentally locked in the blasted store!"

"No need to shout…what did you say your name was?"

"Kristen Lange."

"Lange." His expression shifted slightly. "Hmm."

"Well, I wouldn't have the same name as Aunt Margaret. She's been married a few times." Three times, actually. Divorced twice, and then widowed three years ago."

"Actually, I was wondering if you were related to Brian Lange."

"He's my kid brother." The police chief knew Brian? Why? Brian had only returned to Sparrow Lake from California a month before she'd come home. "And Heather Clarke is my younger sister."

Heather was the only sibling who had lived in Sparrow Lake all her life. Kristen had left for school at eighteen and had gone on to a job in Chicago. She'd come back to Sparrow Lake for visits, of course, but she'd never intended to live here again. She'd had big plans for her future and had never wanted to feel like the failure she obviously was.

"Funny," the police chief said. "You don't look like Heather or Brian."

"They resemble Mom. I've been told I look like our father."

His gaze narrowed as he gave her face an intent once-over. "I don't remember another Lange."

"Because he hasn't lived here for more than a decade."

She wasn't about to explain that their irresponsible father had walked out on his family, leaving his wife to fend for herself and three children. Two years ago, Mom had remarried and her husband's new job had prompted a move to California for them and Brian, who'd been in high school.

"So you're living with Margaret."

"Temporarily."

"Working for her."

"Temporarily."

"Not married?"

Resenting being grilled, Kristen frowned. "What does that have to do with anything?"

His eyebrows flicked and he seemed to be smothering a smile.

"I was wondering why you're living with your aunt."

"What business is that of yours?"

"Just trying to get all the facts, ma'am."

Kristen sat back in her chair and fell silent. Now that she was able to see him clearly in the light, she realized he was a good-looking man, probably in his early thirties. He had dark hair, gray eyes, a slight cleft in his chin and a smile that would be nice if it wasn't plastered sarcastically on his face.

Was it her imagination, or was Police Chief Alex Novak being just a little too personal here?

Her gaze went to his left hand—no ring— and then back to his speculative expression. He knew her aunt. He knew her sister. He knew her brother. *So let me go home, already.*

"Are you going to arrest me or not?"

"That all depends."

"On what?"

"On whether Margaret Becker will vouch for you." He looked beyond her. "And there she is now."

"Aunt Margaret?"

Kristen twisted around in her seat and saw her aunt at the front desk, talking to the woman named Janet. Still dressed in what Kristen thought of as satin lounging pajamas, Aunt Margaret had merely put on a pair of sandals and thrown a light wrap around her shoulders for modesty before leaving the house. Neither Janet nor the officers who greeted her before going out the door seemed to think her manner of dress unusual.

Suddenly, Aunt Margaret marched toward the police chief's office, her face set in a frown. To Kristen's great relief, she saw the purse she'd left in the store in her aunt's hands. Also to her relief, her aunt looked fine, not sick, after all.

"Alex, what is going on?" Margaret shifted her attention to Kristen. "Hello, honey." She handed over Kristen's purse. "What a terrible thing to have happen on your first day working for me."

"So, this is your niece?"

"Of course she is, Alex. Who else would she be? Can't you see the resemblance?"

Kristen smothered a smile. If there ever had been a resemblance between them, her aunt's spiked red hair and penchant for bright colors like the orange-and-teal print of the pajamas she was wearing kind of smothered it.

To her irritation, although he was wearing a straight face, Alex said, "Yes, of course, Margaret. Your niece looks just like you."

Aunt Margaret beamed. "Well, we're going to be off now. Time to get some sleep. Come on, Kristen, I'll drive you back to your car."

"Hey, wait a minute—"

Aunt Margaret stopped dead in her tracks, narrowed her gaze on the police chief and added a slight chill to her tone. "Wait for what, Alex? You don't have a problem with my niece, do you?"

"Uh, no, of course not."

"Good. Then we'll see you later."

If Kristen wasn't so tired, she would have laughed at the frustration on Alex Novak's face. Whatever he'd been maneuvering for, he was disappointed.

That thought made her feel just a little better after he'd added more stress to her already disastrous evening.

"YOU'LL FEEL BETTER after you have something to eat," Aunt Margaret promised as they entered the house through the kitchen entrance.

Kristen wasn't so sure of that. Trying to deal with the police chief on top of her awful first day at the store had stressed her out enough for a month. "Maybe I should just go to bed."

Her aunt was already in the refrigerator. "Never go to bed hungry. Have a little something." She pulled out a covered container. "Macaroni and cheese?"

"All right." Kristen couldn't resist an old favorite comfort food after all she'd been through that night. "But just a little."

She fetched a small bowl from a cabinet. She couldn't remember the last time she'd had mac and cheese, maybe not since she'd been in school. It wasn't the kind of dish she would have sought out in multi-ethnic Chicago, but in Wisconsin, it seemed perfect, Wisconsin being the cheese state and all.

"Just sit," her aunt said, taking the bowl out of her hands and pulling a spoon from a drawer. "It'll only take two minutes to heat up in the microwave."

Kristen gladly sat on a stool at the marble-topped island and watched her aunt move around the huge designer kitchen she so rarely used.

From the outside, the classic French Normandy stone manor was entrenched in the landscape, as if it had overlooked the lake forever. The inside had been renovated by the previous owner—the kitchen and baths were only fifteen years old—but the style was still quite traditional. Too traditional for the artist in Aunt Margaret.

Kristen loved the house, but she didn't feel at home here, not even in the huge guest suite. In addition to her bedroom and walk-in closet, she had a nice-sized sitting room and a spa-worthy bathroom. The guest suite was nearly as big as her own apartment had been, she thought morosely, remembering how the bank had foreclosed on her condo after she'd used up most of her savings.

"Here you go, honey." Aunt Margaret set the bowl and a fork before her. "Eat up. Then you can get some sleep."

"Thanks."

Kristen's mouth watered at the smell. Of course her aunt had overloaded the bowl with food, and she couldn't possibly eat it all this late. She slid a forkful into her mouth and just let it melt there before swallowing. It tasted so good it nearly made her toes curl.

Her aunt slid onto a stool across from her. "There's something I wanted to talk to you about. I have an early meeting at the university tomorrow."

Kristin took another forkful. "A faculty meeting?" And another.

"Actually, it's with my dean. I'm turning in my resignation."

Surprised, Kristen asked, "Why? I thought you loved teaching."

The bowl was half-empty. She ought to stop now.

"I do love teaching, but I'm tired, honey. Teaching full-time and running the store have worn me out. I haven't had the energy or time to do the things I want."

"But Heather is managing the store now." Her aunt was still teaching quilting classes and stepping in to work the store if someone called in sick, but that was nothing compared to managing the place.

"Your sister is a hard worker. I'm very grateful that she stepped up. But teaching full time…" She shook her head. "Even though I will resign, I can still be an adjunct in the department and teach a sketching or painting class a semester. It's the students I love. What I don't love is committee work. Thank goodness that as an adjunct I won't have to go to all those boring meetings anymore."

Kristen couldn't imagine being without something to do every moment. Then again, her aunt had decades of that behind her. Nearing seventy, she deserved to slow down if she wanted. She simply didn't act like a senior citizen. Didn't look it, either. She kept her hair the same bright red it had always been, and she must be using some incredible skin products, because the only wrinkles she had were the welcoming smile lines around her striking hazel eyes.

"What will you do with all that extra time you'll have?" Kristen asked, deciding that maybe she could have one more bite of the luscious mac and cheese.

"For one, I would like to make some plans to travel. And I want do something with this house to make it more livable."

"Aunt Margaret, this place is great as it is," Kristen said, though it was starting to look a little shabby in places and needed quite a bit of maintenance.

"You know, I've been wanting to transform it with color."

Ever since her husband, Donald, had died, Aunt Margaret had threatened to paint the walls bright colors and perk up the whole place with pieces of art, but she hadn't done anything yet.

Not even normal maintenance. The only room her aunt had ever redesigned was her studio, and that must have been shortly after she'd married Donald and moved in with him.

"Sounds great," Kristen said, putting the last forkful of food in her mouth. "We'll have to talk more about it tomorrow when you get home." Unbelievably, she'd finished every morsel. Tempted to lick the bowl clean, she restrained herself and took it and the fork to the sink, rinsed them and set them in the dishwasher. "Aunt Margaret, about the store window—"

"Don't worry about it, honey, it's easily fixed."

"If you'll tell me who to call, I'll take care of it first thing when I get to the store."

"All right. I'll put the name and number of my handyman right here on the counter before I leave for the university in the morning. And I'll call Heather, too, so she won't be shocked."

"Great." Kristen yawned, then kissed her aunt's cheek. "Now I need go pass out."

Which is exactly what she did upon entering her room. She didn't bother stripping down any further than removing her dirty suit jacket and skirt. She didn't take a shower. She was falling-down exhausted. Thinking she could take care of any mess tomorrow, she simply turned off the light and fell face-forward onto the bed.

The moment her head hit the pillow, she was asleep.

ALEX SAW THE light go out on the east side of the house. Kristen Lange's room? The patrol car's engine running, he sat on the road a hundred yards from Margaret Becker's home, a small mansion compared to most homes in this community.

He hadn't meant to come this way tonight, but heading for home from the station, he'd stopped at a convenience store for some food for Spike, a stray cat he'd been taking care of, then found himself taking the long way around the lake. He'd tried convincing himself that he was checking on the Lange kid, Kristen's brother. But he didn't figure he would find Brian skulking around at this hour.

He had to admit it was the woman herself who interested him right now. Kristen Lange didn't seem like a typical small-town girl coming back to her roots. Although *he* wasn't exactly small town, either.

Maybe it was the Chicago connection that drew him to her. There were aspects of the big city he didn't miss, but there were others he did. Plus, most of his family still lived in Chicago. Unless it was rush hour or construction season, it was only a ninety-minute drive away, so he got back to see them often enough.

Still, the women here were softer, less likely to give him a run for his money. They didn't have that edge that attracted him. He needed a challenge in his life that had nothing to do with work, and Kristen Lange was spicy enough to make him anticipate their next encounter.

MARGARET POURED HERSELF a glass of lemonade and sat in the small bay window off the living room overlooking Sparrow Lake. She and Donald had spent many pleasant evenings together there, just talking and enjoying the view. After two bad marriages that had ended in divorce, she'd finally found her soul mate in Donald. When she'd lost him, she'd bought the quilting store and had thrown herself into managing it, in addition to teaching, to fill the empty spaces in her life.

But now her life wasn't so empty.

When Heather's husband had been killed in Iraq, the poor girl had been devastated. She'd also been left with twin toddlers. Margaret had given her niece a job at Sew Fine and all the emotional aid she had needed, and now Heather was like a daughter to her. Her nephew, Brian, had moved back from California to go to college in Wisconsin, and she'd opened her doors, giving him a place to live and a part-time job at the store. Finally, Kristen had come home after more than ten years, though her niece thought it was simply to recoup and regroup before going back out into the dog-eat-dog business world.

Margaret had plans for Kristen. She'd feigned sickness so that her niece would immediately get wrapped up in the business end of Sew Fine. Smiling at the thought, she toasted the lake that held Donald's ashes.

"I'll always love you, my darling," she whispered. "And I'll see you again one day, but for now I have to move on and discover new possibilities."

Margaret was thinking how nice a new man in her life would be.

As hard as it was for a strong and usually independent woman to admit, she had loved the excitement of a romance. Her first two marriages had been fun and exciting until they weren't anymore, the reason she'd ended them. They'd been short-lived, but she had nothing to regret.

And then she'd met Donald.

Margaret sighed. She would never meet an-

other Donald, of course. But maybe someone nice to keep her company once in a while
wouldn't be too much to ask.

That, and new possibilities for her lovely
niece, who had become too serious, too driven
and too obsessed with the idea of being a failure
ever since Margaret's younger brother, Sam, had
abandoned his family.

CHAPTER THREE

"YOU WERE TRYING to do what?" Heather asked, as she stared up at Sew Fine's broken window. Then she took a good look at Kristen and snickered. "Dressed in your designer duds? I would have paid to see that."

"It wasn't all that funny, believe me. Especially not when the police chief caught me."

"Alex caught you?"

Alex? So her sister knew him on a first-name basis. And from the sound of Heather's voice, she was highly amused by the idea of Alex having the upper hand.

"He's an impossible man. Wouldn't listen to a word I had to say until he got me down to the station."

Heather snorted. "Did he *handcuff* you?"

"Get that suggestive tone out of your voice! There was nothing even vaguely fun or amusing about what happened to me. Alex Novak is a bully."

"Really," her sister drawled.

Kristen took a deep breath and silently counted

to ten. Heather was being Heather, trying to drive her nuts, just as she had since they were kids.

They were adults now, and Heather had matured in other ways, managing the business and working toward a college degree while being a great mother. Matured, except for the way she presented herself. She still wore mostly jeans, sweatshirts or sweaters and running shoes. Her fine-boned face was make-up free other than a swipe of lip gloss, and her long, thick, light-brown hair was pulled into a ponytail. Still loyal to her late husband's memory, Heather might dress this way on purpose, Kristen thought. Even so, Heather was attractive now, but with a little work she could be stunning. Then again, stunning would be hard to maintain while running after five-year-old twins.

Pulling the note Aunt Margaret had left from her pocket, Kristen said, "I need to get the window fixed. I already called this Chuck Hansen before leaving the house, but he hasn't returned my call."

"Maybe he ignored it because you called from your cell and he doesn't have that number."

"Maybe."

While Kristen made her call from the store phone, the first customer of the morning entered and engaged Heather.

Not so happily, Kristen had to leave a second message on Chuck's cell.

"Hi, this Kristen Lange again, calling about the broken window at Sew Fine. I should be here all day, so as soon as you get this, I would appreciate a return call. Thank you."

The handyman didn't need to know who broke the window or why, though she wouldn't be surprised if word had already gotten out and was spreading around town. She could imagine the *Chief* taking delight in sharing the tale with his buddies.

She saw him in her mind's eye, snarky smile pulling up the corners of his mouth....

The bell above the front door tinkled. Kristen looked that way to see another customer come in and start browsing through fabrics.

Then a black-and-white vehicle outside the store caught her attention. Kristen blinked. That was a patrol car. So why was it sitting there, as if the officer behind the wheel had an eye on the store?

Who exactly was out there? The police chief himself?

What in the world did he think he was doing, casing the store?

She started toward the front door, but before

she could get close enough to check, the squad car pulled away from the curb and drove off.

She didn't want to think about the man who had been so miserable to her in the middle of her crisis, anyway, Kristen told herself. She would concentrate on business. She went to the rear of the store—the "office" area—and sat at the desk. She started the computer, thinking to pick up where she'd left off at one in the morning.

Aunt Margaret had asked her to familiarize herself with Sew Fine and see if she had any ideas on how to grow the business.

Three years ago, with a newly earned MBA, she'd gotten a position in marketing with Chicago Lifestyle, a small sporting goods company. In less than a year, she'd been promoted to director of marketing and had helped double sales. But when the economy had taken another dip the following year, the company had "reorganized" and she had been out of a job.

Doing Aunt Margaret's bidding was actually her kind of thing and allowed her to keep her talents sharp while looking for a real job.

The store itself was huge. Bolts of fabric and notions took up one side of the space. On the other side of the aisle were a dozen long tables with sewing machines, doubled to face each other, so women taking classes could chat. Sample quilts and smaller quilted pieces hung on both walls, making the store warm and inviting.

Working that long day yesterday had given Kristen a pretty good overview of how the business worked.

Sew Fine was open six days a week with late hours on Tuesdays and Thursdays for quilting classes. And there were two classes on Saturdays, one for kids, the other for teens. Training them to be lifelong customers, she thought. Great long-tail marketing idea there.

The store seemed to be doing a comfortable business for the number of people employed. Heather was the only full-time employee. Gloria Vega and Louise Powell each worked twenty hours a week, and Kristen's brother Brian ran errands and cleaned up in the store two or three hours a day. The advanced quilting class was taught by Aunt Margaret. Kristen wondered if she would continue teaching now that she wanted to retire, or if they would need to find someone to replace her.

The profit after paying the staff definitely could be better for Aunt Margaret. She would get a pension from the university, of course, but that huge house of hers probably chewed up her cash on a regular basis. She'd used the money Donald had left her to pay off the mortgage and the exorbitant taxes. And as Kristen had already realized, the house needed work.

No doubt this was the reason her aunt wanted some ideas about growing the business. Aunt Margaret might fear she would have to sell the house if she couldn't raise the store's income. Having lost her own home to the economy, Kristen wasn't about to let that happen to someone she loved, a senior citizen who deserved to retire in comfort and security.

The first thing she could do was to get a better sales system in place for customers who called in orders. Now, whoever answered the phone wrote the customer's name and what she wanted on a piece of paper. Kristen looked through the box of scraps that held unfulfilled orders. An archaic and fallible system. She would start by installing a simple computer program so the person taking the order could enter the details. Then someone should be assigned to checking orders and fulfilling them on a specific day every week. Regular customers would be on file, as well, and their information automatically brought up via a database. The same database could be used for mailings.

"Aren't your eyes crossing from being on that computer so many hours yesterday?"

Kristen started. Both customers had left the

store, and Heather was standing over her. "They are a bit tired." Having managed little more than six hours sleep, she *was* tired. No late night, working or otherwise, for her today.

"So take a break. We've hardly had a chance to talk since you got here."

"It's not like we haven't talked in ages," Kristen said, thinking of their weekly Sunday-night phone calls.

"But now I can see you."

"Okay, okay." Kristen smothered a yawn. "I need coffee anyway."

Heather poured two cups. "You seem to be taking to working here."

Kristen didn't want to get her sister's hopes up. "It's only temporary, you know. Until I get on my feet." She took her mug from Heather. "Then I'm going to start job hunting again."

That was the agreement she'd made with Aunt Margaret. She would work here while sending out her résumé and driving into Chicago for interviews. If she could get them.

"You're going to look for a job in Chicago?" Heather asked, her voice filled with disappointment.

"That *is* my home."

"Not anymore."

"You mean, not at the moment." Kristen sipped

her coffee, willing it to give her extra energy to get through the day.

She was hoping to be back in a new job and a new Chicago apartment before winter. Surely that would give her enough time to help grow Sew Fine into a more viable business.

"What have you got against living here?" Heather demanded. "I miss you. Aunt Margaret misses you. And now that Brian is back, *he* would miss you if you left again."

"Wait a minute. Isn't Brian supposed to be working this morning?" Kristen had thought he could sweep up the broken glass.

"Brian doesn't always keep to schedule."

"And you're okay with that?" Heather was the manager, after all, Kristen thought.

"He is very helpful, Kristen. He'll do anything I ask of him."

"When he's here."

"So I give him a break. He's had a hard couple of years since Mom remarried and moved to California."

"Losing his friends in the middle of his freshman year of high school must have been difficult," Kristen admitted.

"Not to mention he lost his job. Mom used to call him the man of the house. You remember that, don't you? Even as a little kid, he took on a lot of responsibility, so he wouldn't let her down. Well, maybe you don't really know, because you went away to college so soon after Dad left. Mom was so proud of Brian. Mom thought it was great that he didn't have to keep that responsibility anymore when she married Mike, but I'm not so sure."

Kristen understood completely. "Brian lost his identity." He must have felt as if he had failed their mother. Just as Kristen had failed at the career she'd so wanted.

Now Kristen felt even worse about Brian than she had before. Their kid brother could probably barely remember having a father in his life, and then when their mother had remarried, he hadn't taken to his stepfather. According to Mom, Mike and Brian had been continually at odds. No doubt Brian resented having a man tell him what to do if he'd considered himself the man of the house all his young life. Her mother had mentioned increasing problems with Brian and decided the only way to make the kid happy was to let him go to college in Wisconsin.

According to Aunt Margaret, Brian could do no wrong. The change in address had seemingly made the difference. Now if only he would get to work on time.

And if only she would get a new job even better than the one she'd had.

Kristen said, "You can all come down to Chicago to see me for more than a day or two, you know. And I can come back here more weekends than I did before. It's not that I don't like Sparrow Lake, because I do, but there's no opportunity here for me to prove myself."

"You always had more drive than anyone I know. Except for Mom, if in a different way. She was always working, too."

"To support us," Kristen reminded her. "You know Mom didn't have a choice. She didn't have a career when Dad left. She had to take whatever job she could get."

Which for years had been two and three part-time jobs all at once to make ends meet. Kristen had vowed then to get an education that would provide her with enough security so she never had to scrape by. She would never be a failure like her father, who couldn't seem to succeed at anything, not even at having a family. Losing her job, then her savings and finally her home had been humiliating to someone with her work ethic.

She *had* to get back everything she'd lost. It was a matter of pride.

She just needed a time-out first.

"Have you heard from Jason?" Heather asked.

Okay, he was one thing she'd lost that she *didn't* want back. "No, why would I?"

"You were together for nearly three years."

"And I was fooled into thinking he loved me." At least, that's what he'd told her. "When you care for a person, you support them, good times or bad. He didn't want to hear about my job search or my fear that I would lose my condo when I went through my savings. He wanted me to be the same bright, busy *working* woman who supported *him* emotionally."

Eventually, he'd simply moved on to someone less complicated, though of course the way he put it was *I'm doing this for you because you're using me as a crutch and you need to stand on your own two feet.*

Right.

Soured on relationships, Kristen would focus all her energies on rebuilding her career. She'd always known she had to learn to rely on herself, and nothing in her experience had changed her mind.

ALEX PARKED IN his spot in front of the police station and hurried inside to meet with Officer Owen Larson. After his late-night adventure, Alex had slept in. On the way here, he'd stopped in front of Sew Fine for a moment. He hadn't been able to help himself. Part of him had wanted to go in and see if Kristen Lange was as feisty as he remembered. He hadn't been able to put her out of mind.

He stopped at the desk. "Is Owen in?"

Before the receptionist could answer, Owen called, "Over here!"

Alex waved and walked back to the desk where Owen was checking his smartphone. His buddy was twenty-six but looked closer to sixteen with reddish hair, freckles and a wiry body that had little discernible bulk. Looks could be deceiving. As slight as he appeared, Owen had incredible muscle strength, could bench press his own weight and dead lift even more. He was fast on his feet and could jump a fence without hesitating. He'd been the star of the high school cross-country team and a champion in college.

"You're late," Owen said. "What's up?"

"Late night."

"So I heard." Owen set his phone down, but he kept one eye on it.

"Expecting a call?" Alex asked.

"A text."

Alex didn't have to ask from whom. Owen and his new wife, Trina, had to text each other love notes all day. As long as Owen wasn't behind the wheel of a patrol car when he did so, that was fine with Alex. Owen had become his good friend in the two years since he'd left the city and moved to Sparrow Lake, and he'd even been best man for Owen's wedding a few months back. Though he was younger than Alex, Owen seemed to have his life far more together. Owen now had a wife he loved and plans to start a family.

"So what's with you and Margaret's niece?" Owen asked.

Alex frowned at him. "I caught her breaking into her aunt's store, and I brought her in for questioning."

"I hear there was more to it. A little something special going on between you two?"

Wishful thinking. Alex hadn't had anything going on with *any* woman for far too long. "Who's making up stories now?"

"Janet. She said the way you looked at the Lange woman and the tone you used when you spoke to her made them all think there was more to the story than you were telling."

"They just need something juicy to chew over. A new woman in town fits the bill."

"I might believe you, but—"

"What?"

"That expression on your face now. I know

you too well, buddy. You may not have anything going yet, emphasis on the *yet,* but you're sure thinking about it."

Owen meant well, and he wasn't wrong, but Alex wasn't about to start talking about a woman he didn't even know yet.

"Any new reports about the pranks being pulled around town last night?" Alex asked.

"Not last night." Owen sighed. "At nine-fifteen this morning, the fire truck showed up at the library to find someone had pulled the alarm. Of course there was no fire. Not even a wisp of smoke."

Alex shook his head in disgust. "I wonder where Brian Lange was at nine-fifteen." And he wondered if Brian's sister could tell him. That might be a sticking point in getting to know her better.

"If we could catch Brian and Matt and Andy in the act—"

"We could put the fear of jail time in them before they go too far."

They talked for a bit about the situation with the boys running wild. Something bad had been brewing in this area of the state since the summer before. Alex had heard rumors of drug trafficking, and there had been a few armed robberies in nearby towns. He wasn't about to let anything like that go down here in his town.

Sparrow Lake was pretty much crime free. So far.

Owen got to his feet. "I'd better get back to work or my boss might fire me."

Alex grinned and gave him a thumbs-up. But once the officer left the station, Alex found himself brooding over the problem.

Since Brian Lange had moved back to town the month before, he'd been hanging out with two high school students a year younger than he was. Alex had seen the three of them together, and to his way of thinking, the local boys idolized the California transplant and would do anything to impress him. Since his return, all kinds of odd events had started happening. Pranks that made people angry. The three boys had been sighted several times in the areas where pranks had been pulled, although no one had actually seen them in action.

Nothing serious. Yet.

And Alex wanted to make sure it stayed that way by nipping trouble in the bud.

While on the job in Chicago, he'd seen terrible things happen to kids because no one got in their way when they started down the wrong path. Things that destroyed their futures. Things that took away any future they might have at all.

That was the reason he'd left Chicago. He'd been part of a gang unit in the Chicago Police Department, and they'd been dealing with a crime in progress. A crazed, drug-ridden kid had fired at his team and then had pointed a gun straight at Alex. Instinct had kicked in faster than he'd had time to blink, and he'd fired his own weapon. He'd been in the right. Had done exactly as he'd been trained to do. After the investigation, he'd been exonerated. None of that mattered, not even the fact that the kid had survived.

Alex had kind of gone crazy after that.

Haunted by the what-ifs, he swore he wouldn't let the kids here, in his town, get on such a self-destructive road when he could steer them down a more positive path before it was too late.

Feeling down just thinking about Chicago, he went to his office and tried to bury himself in paperwork, but he simply couldn't concentrate. He needed a distraction, something to take away the dark cloud that hung over him. Something to make him smile.

A few minutes later, he found himself in his squad car heading back to Sew Fine.

CHAPTER FOUR

"You were scheduled to work at nine this morning," Kristen told Brian when he finally strolled in the door just before noon.

"I was? Oh, sorry. The time must have slipped my mind."

He gave her an innocent expression, yet Kristen couldn't tell if it was genuine. He was still a kid, though, and needed some guidelines.

Kristen sighed. "Maybe you should add your work schedule to the calendar on your phone."

"I'll do that." Brian kissed her on the cheek. "Sorry, sis."

Okay, how mad at him could she be? Instead of chastising him, she gave him a big hug.

"What was that for?" he asked.

"I just missed you, is all." She'd missed a lot of things while he was growing up, as Heather had reminded her.

His answering smile lit up his big blue eyes. He would be handsome if only he would grow out his faux-Mohawk haircut. The sides were sheared short and the top was spiked, making his already narrow face seem thinner. Not that she would make any suggestions in the haircut department and chance hurting his feelings.

Brian asked, "So what do you want me to do first?"

Not having wanted to leave the shards of glass from the window on the floor any longer, she'd swept them up herself. And after her talk about Brian with Heather, she'd gotten a better idea of how she could make him feel like a more important member of the Sew Fine team—by giving him more responsibility. Heather had enthusiastically agreed.

So Kristen asked, "How would you like to be in charge of fulfilling orders for the store?"

"What? You mean be a clerk? I don't know anything about quilting."

Kristen jiggled the box of orders written on scraps of paper. "I mean fulfill these. We need someone to be in charge of phoned-in orders, to make sure they all go out once each week."

"You want me to be in charge of something?" Brian sounded surprised.

"Why not? This is a family business, and you're part of the family."

"Yeah, okay. What do I do?"

"Round up the items being ordered. If you need material cut, or you need to know what an item is or where to find it, ask Heather or Gloria. You'll get the hang of how the store is organized fast enough. When you have everything in an order, package it and go on to the next one. When you complete all of the orders, sort them into store pick-up or mail. Then you can run the orders that need to be mailed over to the post office."

Brian grinned and nodded. "I can do that."

"Great. I'm installing a computer program so future orders will be more organized, but in the meantime, good luck with these." She handed him the box.

Not looking in the least daunted, Brian took the handwritten orders over to one of the class tables and started sorting through them. Maybe having actual responsibility would make Brian feel more needed at the store, and encourage him to keep to the hours he was scheduled.

She'd assured her brother that he would quickly learn how the store was organized, something she hadn't yet explored. She needed to know exactly what they were selling so she could get some marketing ideas. With that in mind, she decided to stretch her legs and take a more thorough look for herself.

Heather and Gloria were both busy with customers. As had happened yesterday around noon, the customers seemed to multiply, no doubt taking advantage of their lunch hours. So, thinking to get a more thorough idea of their product lines and whether or not they could display goods more effectively or perhaps offer some kind of incentive to customers, Kristen decided to check out the stock on her own.

Closest to the office space were shelves of books and videos about quilting. A half-dozen colorful baskets held samples of the patterns that were stored in a file cabinet. Notions—rulers, cutting tools, pins and needles, and spools of thread—took up the center of the store. And brilliantly colored fabrics were displayed closest to the windows to take advantage of the natural light. It was only when she was admiring some batik prints that she noticed a black-and-white patrol car stop next to the curb directly outside the store.

Pulse humming, she ducked down to take a better look at the driver...just as Police Chief Alex Novak looked back.

Was he checking up on her?

Without thinking it through, Kristen left the store to find out. Through the windshield, she could see that his expression changed, as if he hadn't expected a confrontation. And then, appearing resigned, he got out of the vehicle. She came face-to-face with him curbside. His feet were still planted on the street, while she was on the higher curb, so they were actually eye to eye. Not that she could see the soft gray color of his eyes through his dark sunglasses.

"Is there a problem, Chief?"

"Alex, please."

He was wearing a uniform today, looking unbelievably good in stark black. Not wanting to be attracted to him, she swallowed hard. "Okay, Alex, do you have a problem with me?"

"Why would you think that?"

"This is the second time today that you stopped in front of the store, as if you were casing it. Or maybe you're expecting me to be doing something not to your liking. Maybe you just want to arrest me again."

The way he was staring at her intently, as if he wanted to say something but was reluctant, made her mouth go dry. Was he really not going to explain himself? The way he was staring at her was so...so personal.

Her pulse quickened, and she was about to demand an answer, when he said, "When I drove around back, I noticed the glass in that window was still missing."

"And?"

"I wondered why."

"And I've been wondering why Aunt Margaret's handyman hasn't returned my calls. Three of them." She couldn't help sounding a little exasperated. "That's why. So is having a window with no glass illegal in Sparrow Lake?"

"Just risky. You never know who might try to crawl in through an open window."

Heat rose along her neck as she remembered the way he'd caught her the night before. Did he enjoy embarrassing her? She thought so.

"Thanks for the observation, Chief, but as long as it's not illegal…"

She didn't finish the statement. His eyebrows flashed upward over the tops of his sunglasses, and he looked as if he wanted to say something more. But in the end, he gave her one of those sarcastic smiles that irritated her and touched the front of his cap before backing off.

"Have a good day, ma'am."

She stood there, feet glued to the curb, as he got into the patrol car and drove off. No man had ever made her feel so uptight before. What was with that? Tension gradually flowed out of her body, and she retreated back inside the store.

Now what had she been doing before she'd seen Alex out there? Oh, right, taking a mental inventory of the store's wares. Her mind had gone blank. Instead of product, it was filled with

Alex Novak's face. The way his mouth always seemed ready to curl in a smile. Or was it a smirk? She shook away the image and forced herself to concentrate on work.

Happy to see that Brian was gathering items to fulfill those orders, she went back to the office area to search the internet for the computer program that she wanted to install.

Glancing back to Brian, however, she hesitated. Rather than working, he was now reading something on his cell phone. She knew he was into the whole social networking thing. He was always checking his phone and sending off messages to his friends. Nothing wrong with that—all the kids and many adults did it—but he was supposed to be working now. About to say so, Kristen stopped when Brian slipped the cell back into his pocket and got to work on an order.

Okay, then. Back to work for her.

She had the ability to concentrate even in the midst of chaos. Sew Fine was fairly calm compared to the office she'd last worked in. As she clicked on internet links to check out several potential programs, she heard the entrance door opening and closing, customer questions being answered about the pros and cons of using patterns as opposed to kits, soft laughter coming from someone at the other end of the store. Nothing affected her concentration.

Not until a jarring noise came from directly behind her on the other side of the back wall, as if someone was stomping on loose boards.

Kristen tried to ignore the noise, and for a moment it went away. Then a rough, grating sound scraped straight down her spine.

"What the…?"

She turned to see movement on the other side of the broken window. Had the handyman simply shown up and started the job without telling anyone? But wait…the person wielding a tool that scraped the frame was dressed in black.

Suspicion made her hackles rise. Lunging out of her chair, she made for the back door and threw it open only to find Alex, a rectangle of glass in hand, standing on the Dumpster. He was trying to set glass into the empty window pane.

"What do you think you're doing?"

He gave her a quick glance before returning his attention to his task. "You're welcome."

"I didn't thank you."

He sighed. "I figured you wouldn't, but that doesn't stop me from being polite."

Realizing she'd let her temper best her when it seemed he was simply trying to do her a favor, Kristen took a big breath to calm herself. What was wrong with her? She never used to be like this. Then, again, she'd never run into an Alex Novak before. Now he was using some kind of a tool to push little pieces of metal into the frame, undoubtedly meant to hold the glass in place.

"Look, I'm sorry," she said and meant it. "You just...well, kind of startled me, is all."

He glanced her way again and grinned. "You weren't ready for me, huh?"

Not sure any woman would be, she asked, "Did Aunt Margaret call you to take care of the window?"

"No one had to ask me." He rolled a cord of white stuff around the glass frame and used the tool to press it in place. "I could see you needed a little help. You couldn't get Margaret's handyman to return your calls, and I assumed you wanted the place locked up and the alarm set tonight."

"Well, yes, of course."

He used another tool to remove any goopy stuff off the glass. "And I don't want to have to respond to a burglary in progress, so I'm taking the easy way out."

Kristen realized he was done when he jumped from the Dumpster and landed next to her. And she realized she'd sounded ungrateful for a charitable act.

"Well, thank you, Alex. I mean that sincerely."

He set the sunglasses back in his hair and cocked his head, his gray eyes going soft as they swept over her face. It put a knot in Kristen's stomach.

"You'll have to get someone to paint the compound and touch up the frame. Wait a couple of days, though, so the compound has time to dry out."

"Okay."

"In the meantime, I'll take a look at your alarm system, make sure it'll work now."

Kristen followed him inside and watched as he pulled a chair under the window and stood on it. Glancing around the store, she realized that no one was paying them any mind. Alex checked something attached to the window frame then stepped down.

"Looks all right," he said, returning the chair to where he found it.

"Well, thank you again."

She noticed his attention was elsewhere. He wore a speculative expression. Alex seemed to be focused on Brian, who was still working on filling those orders. Undoubtedly he was surprised to see a teenage boy working in a store frequented mostly by women.

When Alex turned his gaze back to her, Kristen said, "If there's ever anything I can do for you—"

"There is." A slow, easy grin lit his face. "You can have dinner with me."

Though her pulse fluttered at the thought, she frowned in response. "Dinner?"

"You know, that's when you eat to satisfy those hunger pangs in the evening hours."

"Um, I don't—"

"Eat?"

"I was going to say that I don't think it would be appropriate."

"Which part?"

"My dating you to pay you for fixing the glass."

"That's not exactly what I was asking you to do."

"What, then?"

"I just want to get to know you better."

Tempted, Kristen swallowed hard. She had to admit the police chief had more going for him than she'd first thought and not just in the looks department. He might be a little snarky at times, but he was a well-intentioned person. His fixing the window had been very thoughtful. But she'd had a purpose in moving to Sparrow Lake, and it certainly wasn't to find a man. She wasn't going to be here that long, anyway. A few months at most. Getting involved romantically would just complicate things.

Alex cleared his throat. "About dinner?"

"I appreciate your interest, but I don't think it's a good idea under any circumstances."

His expression went neutral when he asked, "Any particular reason?"

Realizing she might have offended the man again, Kristen assured him, "It's not you, Alex. I simply have too much on my plate right now to be indulging in any kind of extracurricular activities."

"Wow, that sounds sad."

"What's sad about my being focused?"

"On work?"

"Aren't you focused on *your* job?" Which he ought to be, considering he was chief of police, Kristen thought.

"Within reason. But…hey, I didn't mean to make you uncomfortable. I'll just leave now."

"Good… I mean…all right. And thanks again."

If he heard her, he didn't respond, simply headed out the door.

And Kristen quickly deflated. Turning back to her computer, she realized Aunt Margaret was standing there, had probably caught the whole show.

"Aunt Margaret, I didn't realize you were coming in this afternoon."

"I just came back from my meeting with the dean."

Indeed, Aunt Margaret was dressed more conventionally than usual in a skirted suit. Of course, she'd added a purple-and-blue flower-print blouse and matching earrings.

"So what are you doing here?"

"I just thought I would check in to see how things were going." Aunt Margaret arched her eyebrows. "Which seems to be in an interesting direction for you."

Desperate to get her aunt talking about anything but Alex, Kristen asked, "How did your meeting go?"

Her aunt gave her a look that said she knew Kristen was avoiding. Then she said, "Dean Whitiker was very cordial, and of course he understood that I needed time to do other things."

"So you'll still be able to teach a few classes if you want?"

"He seemed amenable to the idea." Her aunt looked up. "I see the window is fixed. What time did Chuck get here?"

"Actually, your handyman never got back to me."

Appearing surprised, Aunt Margaret asked, "Then how—"

"Alex."

"Really. The chief of police fixed our store window? And how did that happen?"

Kristen explained, telling her aunt about their earlier encounter and then Alex's showing up to replace the pane of glass.

"I do believe he's sweet on you."

"Is not!"

Her aunt laughed. "You're certain of that?"

"Well, it wouldn't matter if he was." Kristen threw herself back into her desk chair. "I can't get involved with anyone from Sparrow Lake."

"Why ever not?"

Hearing her aunt's indignant tone, Kristen thought she was on a roll, insulting people when she didn't mean to. She tried to explain in a non-confrontational way. "I have nothing against anyone here, but you know I'm leaving as soon as I find a new job in Chicago. I have to get my career back on track." She would show everyone that she could do it. Her former bosses, the business associates who'd no longer had time for her, the friends who'd come to her emotional aid but had looked at her with pity. "I don't believe in long-distance relationships. They never work out."

"Relationships are more important than careers, sweetheart."

"You couldn't prove that by me."

"Just remember that a job can't take you in its arms for a hug when you need one."

Her aunt, the romantic, Kristen thought. Aunt Margaret might have found her true love in Donald Becker, but Kristen hadn't forgotten how Jason had abandoned her in her hour of need.

Much the same way her father had abandoned his whole family.

THOUGH SHE'D SWORN she was going to leave the store early that evening, Kristen ended up hanging around long enough for one of the quilting classes to start. Gloria was teaching a beginner/intermediate session in the back and there were five women seated around the large table there. Kristen knew two of the women, but the others had probably moved to town after she'd left for college.

"This is Margaret's niece, Kristen," Gloria told them, her dark eyes bright. "She's here to help her aunt with the store."

Kristen nodded at Nellie Martin, an elderly woman wearing large black-framed glasses. She owned the consignment shop a couple of streets over. "Hi, Nellie, it's good to see you again. I've come to love consignment stores." She'd frequented a couple in Chicago where she'd gotten most of her designer duds at a significant discount.

"Well, then, drop by and we'll get reacquainted," Nellie told her.

Kristen moved on to the next woman at the large table, a mousy little middle-aged woman in a gray dress. Emily Auerbach was the mayor's wife.

"How nice that you take classes here," murmured Kristen, to which Emily merely nodded with a tight smile.

Emily always had been more than a little eccentric, as Kristen had realized when she was a kid. On Halloween one year, Emily had posted "Keep Away" and "No Candy Here" signs on her lawn. The next year she'd decorated. No signs. Still, one of Kristen's friends had insisted Emily was a real witch, and all the kids had avoided her.

Gloria introduced her to one of the new women in town—Shara Lessley, a beautiful young African-American woman with a headful of tiny braids. The other was Laurie Jamison, a thin redhead. Kristen tried to connect descriptions with names so she could remember them. Even so, she would be lucky if her tired brain recalled anyone.

"Are you an artist like your aunt?" Shara asked.

Kristen shook her head. "Good grief, no. I'm a businesswoman." She admired the gorgeous metallic printed fabrics Shara was working with. "Is that a quilt?"

"It's going to be a quilted wall hanging."

"You ought to learn to quilt," Nellie told Kristen. "It's not that hard. Just work on a simple square to begin with."

"Or a place mat or pillow covering," Gloria agreed. "I like to see a quilter take on a whole project to begin with, even if it's small."

"I don't know," said Kristen with a laugh, happy to realize the women were dedicated to their craft. Her aunt had told her that at least one person from Sew Fine's classes won a ribbon at the county fair every year. "I've never so much as taken up a hem. I don't think sewing is one of my talents."

"Nonsense, everyone can sew if they try." Gloria raised her brows. "And knowing something about quilting could help you with the business end of things. Why don't you sit down and join the class?"

"That would be wonderful," added Shara, the others nodding in agreement. "We could use some new blood. We've been hanging out together for a couple of years now."

Then it was more like a quilting circle than a class, Kristen decided. She didn't want to stay any longer, especially not tonight. However, she agreed to at least drop by the class again next week. Before she left, Gloria plunked a prepackaged kit of color-coordinated strips in her hands.

"What's this?"

"Just take them home and play with the fabric, the colors and the designs."

Kristen objected, "Well, I can't just take this. I have to pay…"

"Don't worry, I'll write the kit down for the records, Ms. Businessperson," Gloria told her.

"Well, okay…"

"Try it, you'll like it."

Gloria sure could be a compelling salesperson, Kristen admitted, heading home. Sew Fine was lucky to have her. Kristen even opened the package of material strips and spread them out on the bed before she went to sleep. In shades of blue and turquoise and contrasting green, they certainly were pretty. But not only was quilting out of her sphere of knowledge, it took too long to finish anything.

Longer than she would be in Sparrow Lake.

ALEX WASN'T ONE to give up easily when he wanted something. And it seemed he wanted to get to know Kristen Lange even more than he'd originally realized. Just trying to have a simple conversation with her was a challenge. He could only wonder what spending time with her would be like. Undoubtedly, she would dispute everything the way she had when he'd caught her breaking into Sew Fine.

If she knew about his current investigation, she wouldn't be happy. And if she had accepted his dinner invitation, he would have felt obligated to tell her about it, considering her brother was involved.

Not that Brian Lange seemed like a bad kid.

Alex had seen how hard Brian was working in the store. And he'd heard Margaret sing the kid's praises more than once.

So why was Brian looking for trouble with Matt Stapleton and Andy Eccles?

Nellie Martin had been the first to make a formal complaint. Someone had mixed a rainbow of clashing colors and styles on the consignment store's mannequins. One was wearing lingerie on top of its outer clothing, while another sported a purple feather boa over what appeared to be a raincoat. He'd had to force himself to keep a straight face on that one. Women's styles were so crazy at times, he hadn't even been certain that mischief was afoot, and Nellie wore a pair of what seemed to be fairly strong glasses. He'd wondered if the aging woman simply had trouble with her eyesight and had dressed the mannequins in dim light, then had been horrified to see her work the next day. After all, there hadn't been a break-in—Nellie had admitted she'd left in a hurry and may have forgotten to lock up.

But then the other calls started coming.

Old Mr. Fergus had risen one morning to find two panels of his picket fence had been pulled out of the ground and were lying neatly on his front lawn. What was he supposed to do? He was too old to put them back himself, and he couldn't afford to hire someone to do the work.

Feeling sorry for the old guy, Alex had asked for volunteers at the department to help the man, and both Walt and Jack had agreed to put the fence back together again. While Alex's officers worked, Mr. Fergus had speculated on who could have done the deed. He'd seen Matt and Andy and "that new boy" hanging around outside at dusk and had thought nothing of it at the time. But after the fence incident, he had wondered, making Alex wonder, too.

A speculation that had put the spotlight right on the trio as the incidents—and sightings of one or more of the three teenagers—had increased. Alex could only figure they were bored and looking for ways to entertain themselves. If he could actually catch them in the act, he could put the fear of the law in them, force them into choosing reparation and community service or make them go before a judge, something he really didn't want to do. He simply wanted to change their direction into a more positive one before things got out of hand. Then he would have no choice. He would be forced to arrest them.

Truth be told, the night before he'd been going down the alley behind Sew Fine looking for signs of mischief.

Alex hadn't been at all prepared to find it in Brian's sister.

What a conundrum. He'd wanted to catch Brian in the act; he simply wanted to *catch* Kristen.

Two goals at odds with each other.

Though he'd known Kristen for less than twenty-four hours, he was certain that, if he arrested her brother, she would have nothing to do with him.

What to do?

CHAPTER FIVE

ALEX DIDN'T APPROACH her for a date again, but in the next few days, Kristen swore she saw him more than anyone other than her aunt or siblings. No matter where she was—home, store or just walking through town—she saw Alex cruise by her in the patrol car.

Slowly.

She didn't know whether to be annoyed or flattered.

Then she found herself looking for Alex every time she was out on the street. And sometimes she looked out Sew Fine's windows to see if she could spot a patrol car anywhere around.

That's what she was doing late one morning the following week when her sister joined her at the window.

"What are you looking for?" Heather asked, scanning the area outside the store.

"Oh, nothing. I was just stretching my legs."

"Huh. You've been doing a lot of that the past week."

"I get tired of sitting so much." Not wanting

to talk about her paranoia over Alex, Kristen started back to the office area.

Right on her heels, Heather said, "Then get away from that computer and start working in the store."

"I only know a little about quilting."

"You can learn more. That's why you're taking Gloria's class, right?"

"I'm not exactly *taking* it. I'm just checking things out. If I understand the classes and what they provide for customers, I can market them better."

"Whatever. It's a smart move. You never know, you might be ready for Aunt Margaret's advanced session in no time."

"That's very hopeful of you." Kristen laughed. "I'm not quite ready for art quilts yet." She thought about her aunt's retirement. "Is Aunt Margaret going to keep teaching here at the store now that she's retiring?"

"As far as I know, she wants to continue."

"But what if we expand and there are more people for classes?"

"We can hire more teachers."

Knowing her sister had made some beautiful quilts, including one for her, Kristen asked, "Would *you* want to do a class?"

Heather blanched. "Are you kidding? I'm already working full-time and going to school part-time. And somehow I have to make extra time for the twins every day. If I was going to do anything else, it would be outside. I can hardly take care of my own garden."

Which Kristen knew was important to her sister, who was studying to be a horticulturist, specializing in sustainable landscapes.

"Relax, already. I was kidding, Heather. Like you say, we can get more teachers."

"There are several women who come here who have been quilting forever."

"Then why do they keep taking classes?"

"To socialize. They've turned it into more of a quilting circle. Everyone brings potluck. So the women eat and talk and work on their quilts. Sometimes they choose to work on group projects. You know, if someone is having a baby or getting married."

Reminded of Jason, the man she'd thought she would marry, Kristen turned away, saying, "Sounds like they have a good time."

If not *her* idea of a good time, she thought, walking back to her desk. Before her personal financial crisis, she'd enjoyed going to plays and museums and dinners with her friends. Which went to prove how much she *didn't* belong in a small town. She didn't mind observing a few classes but she didn't want to be part of a quilting circle—she wanted her old life back.

And right now, she wanted to eat. It was lunchtime, and she wasn't about to miss another meal. Grabbing her shoulder bag, she set off through the store to the front door. "I'm going to grab some lunch," she told Heather. "You want me to bring something back for you?"

"Thanks, but I brought a sandwich."

Kristen knew she should have done the same, but she hadn't even thought about it. A holdover from her old life where she'd had lunch out every day. She couldn't afford to keep doing that, so she needed to make sure the fridge was stocked with things she could eat. And no more mac and cheese for her or she wouldn't fit into her secondhand designer suits, which she would need to wear on interviews. In the meantime, she decided to check out the family restaurant directly across the street.

Thinking she should have a salad, Kristen mused about what kind of dressing she would get as she checked the street for moving vehicles before crossing in the middle of the block. A siren went off nearby, but she paid it no mind as she tried to decide if she should eat in or take her meal back to the shop.

"Miss Lange, wait a minute!"

Her foot froze on the curb.

She knew that voice.

Turning, she saw Alex Novak getting out of his patrol car. He'd switched off the siren, but the light bar was still flashing. Her pulse fluttered at his approach.

"Chief," she said, responding in kind to his calling her Miss Lange. "What can I do for you?"

He was pulling out an official-looking pad and a pen. "You can cross at the corner next time."

"What?"

"You were jaywalking."

He had to be kidding. "This isn't the big city!"

"No matter. There's a town ordinance against crossing in the middle of the street. That's why we have those nice white lines at every corner, to give you a safe place to cross."

"But I *was* safe," she said reasonably. Maybe if she kept her voice moderate and friendly this time, he would back off. "There weren't any vehicles coming. I checked. In fact, there aren't any now." Town traffic was moderate at its worst.

"I'm afraid you're going to have to pay a one-dollar fine anyway." He started filling out the ticket.

"One dollar?"

"Yep."

Reason lost out to irritation. Why was he

doing this? And how did he happen to be here at the exact time she went out to get lunch? Was he trying to persecute her because she wouldn't go out with him? Is that why she'd seen his patrol car crawl by so often over the past week? So he could find a way to irritate her for refusing his invitation to dinner?

Crossing her arms, she glared at him. "I won't pay it." She wasn't going to throw away even one dollar because he had an issue with her decision to not see him. "This is ridiculous."

"Let me get this straight. If I write a ticket for one dollar, you won't pay it?"

"Absolutely not."

"You're sure?"

"Positive!"

"All right, then." He actually smiled as he pulled out his handcuffs and indicated she should hold out her hands.

"I will not."

"Right now, you've only committed an infraction subject to a small fine by jaywalking. But unless you cooperate, I'll have to add resisting arrest to the charges. Then you'll have to go before a judge."

"Oh! I never—"

"Me neither."

Kristen was horrified. Townspeople were stopping to watch the spectacle, and they were tittering at her plight. She recognized several people she knew, including Emily Auerbach. Undoubtedly the mayor's wife would make a big deal of this. And Heather was standing in front of Sew Fine, her expression alternately shocked and amused.

Indignant, Kristen held out her hands, and Alex locked the handcuffs around her wrists, then said, "Now if you'll come with me…"

She tucked her chin into her chest so she wouldn't have to look at any of the bystanders and rushed toward the patrol car. He opened the back door and put his hand on her head. She ducked away from him and clunked the side of her head on the metal frame.

"Ouch!"

"I was trying to avoid that happening," Alex said, but he was grinning at her.

Refusing to be baited, she slid into the backseat of a police car for the second time in less than a week. She couldn't believe he thought this was funny. Or anyone else. She heard the chuckles and joking comments around her. Small towns were supposed to be friendly. Kristen choked back a sound of frustration as the patrol car moved down the street, past residents who were trying to get a better look at her.

She simply wasn't feeling the love.

He didn't know what made him do it.

Alex knew he was going to hear about this—probably from everyone, including the mayor—but he didn't care. He hadn't been able to figure out another way to get to know Kristen better, and when he'd seen her cross the street illegally he just hadn't been able to help himself.

"Comfortable back there?"

Kristen made a rude noise in response.

"The jaywalking infraction and fee are listed on the town books," he told her, lest she think he was making this up.

Owen had explained that it was to protect seniors and kids, the violators most vulnerable to getting hit by a moving vehicle. Neither seniors nor kids wanted to part with their dollar, so jaywalking had gone way down after the possible citation went on the books. Alex had never enforced the law before, but he hadn't been able to resist doing so. Now, at least, he had Kristen's full attention.

"Where were you going when you crossed illegally?" he asked.

"To the restaurant directly across from Sew Fine. I had no idea you had a rule against it."

"It wasn't a rule against your getting something to eat."

"Well, you didn't let me, did you? So you're

honestly going to take me to the station because I won't pay the fine?"

"I never said that."

"Then where are you taking me?"

"To do a little community service."

"Entertaining you is considered community service?"

He laughed. "Nope. That's just a bonus."

A minute later, he pulled up to the Sparrow Lake Community House, a two-story building with terraces on both levels overlooking the lake. Opening the rear door of the vehicle, he helped Kristen get out, then he removed the handcuffs.

She rubbed her wrists as if the metal had chafed them. "I don't understand what we're doing here."

"Good works. Your alternative to paying the fine. I hope you don't object to that, too."

She frowned at him but followed when he headed for the entrance to the building. He went straight to the kitchen, which was at the end farthest from the lake. Two gray-haired women wearing dresses and sensible thick-soled sandals were filling one of three cardboard boxes.

"Kristen," Alex said, "Have you met Nellie?"

"Of course. I used to live here, remember. How are you doing, Nellie?"

"Pretty well. It's nice to see you again. Though I thought you were coming by my consignment store."

"Don't worry, I'll make it there soon."

Alex relaxed a little.

Kristen was smiling as she informed him, "I know Louise, too. She works part-time at Sew Fine."

"Kristen!" Louise's dark face lit up and she laughed with delight. "You're here to help Alex deliver the meals! Bless your sweet heart."

"Yes, the meals," Kristen said, moving closer to take a better look at the filled boxes.

"We have a couple of dozen seniors around town who aren't as mobile as some of us are," Louise explained. "So a bunch of us with too much time on our hands take turns providing them with a good meal every day."

Nellie said, "We call this the Sparrow Seniors Soup Kitchen."

"Not that we actually serve soup," Louise quickly added.

"We do sometimes."

"Only in the winter, though."

The women looked annoyed with each other until Kristen said, "This is really wonderful of everyone involved."

"And wonderful of Alex to fill in for our driver at a moment's notice." Louise shook her head. "Poor Bernie called in sick an hour ago and we didn't know what we were going to do since Nellie doesn't drive anymore. And I never learned."

Still wondering how anyone not living in a big city got by without driving, Alex said, "No problem." His gaze lingered on Kristen's face. For once, she wasn't frowning at him. "I'm glad to help out. That's a great thing about living in a small town, having a sense of community that the big city doesn't have."

He noticed Kristen's lips tightened a tad. Then she relaxed and asked, "What can I do?"

Louise handed her a clipboard. "Here's the list of homebound seniors and their addresses. It also tells you if there's a special meal. A few of our seniors are vegetarians. And one couple keeps kosher. All of their lunches are marked and are in this smaller box."

Looking over the list, Kristen said, "Okay, I can keep track."

Alex placed the smaller box on top of a big one. "I'll be back to get the other box in minute."

"No need," Kristen said. "I can get it."

She impressed Alex by picking up the box as if it weighed next to nothing. "You work out."

"Just keep that in mind," she muttered, leading the way out of the kitchen.

"Bye-bye," Nellie called after them.

"And thank you both," Louise added.

Alex followed Kristen, admiring the way her hips swayed gently. Rather than a suit, she wore a dress today, something less rigid and more feminine in a print—blue on white, the blue the same shade as her eyes. And her strappy heels made her legs look long and gorgeous.

When they got to the patrol car, Alex said, "Let's just put these in the backseat." He wedged the boxes against the vehicle and opened the door.

She slid her box inside. "Where am I supposed to sit?"

"Next to me."

"In handcuffs?"

Alex juggled the boxes and got them both in the backseat. "Not if you continue to be cooperative."

She gave him a searching look. "How long did it take you to come up with this plan?"

"What plan?"

Raising her eyebrows, she grabbed the clipboard and walked around the squad car. Alex swallowed his smile as he slid into the driver's seat. She was a smart cookie. He wasn't surprised she'd figured him out.

Now he had to find a way to keep her from thwarting his attempt to get to know her better.

CHAPTER SIX

KRISTEN WOULD NEVER admit she was enjoying herself in Alex's company, but there it was. Halfway through their deliveries, she had already seen parts of town she didn't remember. She'd also seen some nice people she remembered from the old days and felt good about doing something positive for the elderly who couldn't do for themselves.

Apparently, Alex hadn't hesitated in taking over for the regular driver. His generosity of spirit touched her. She was having a real feelgood moment because of him. She couldn't remember the last time she'd done something so spontaneous and for such a good cause…not that she'd had much choice in the matter. But still…

"I hear Margaret is retiring," Alex said.

"She turned in her resignation at the university a few days ago."

"About time she took it easy. She's…um…a lot like you."

Surprised, she said, "I'm nothing like Aunt

Margaret. She's so creative. She has an artist's soul. I'm very practical and boring."

"Boring?"

Kristen waited for a verbal shot from the police chief, but he simply let the word hang in the air between them.

Then he said, "I wasn't talking about what you do but about how you do it. From what I understand, Margaret has been filling her every moment, mostly with work. Sound familiar?"

"Okay, so I admit I'm a type A. What's wrong with that?"

"Nothing. But people can be ambitious and competitive about fun things, too."

"I'm not sure I know how to have fun."

Having an adventure like this was unexpected and a little strange. So was giving up control to someone else. And yet, letting someone else be in charge for once gave her a taste of freedom that she enjoyed. No decisions to make, even if for a short while. She couldn't help but respect Alex.

She gave him the address for the Gerbers, who were the next people on the list and a couple she knew. A few minutes later, he pulled up in front of a house that showed its age. The siding didn't look bad, but paint peeled from the porch steps and the windows. In addition, the grass was overgrown and the flower beds needed tending.

"Wow, this place could use some work," Kristen said.

"Make a note of it on your list."

"Why?"

"We're starting a community service program for first-time offenders. We're looking to help people who can no longer do outside work for themselves and can't afford to hire anyone."

"Sounds like a great idea."

"I'm glad you approve," he said.

Kristen started. Expecting to see that snarky smile, she was surprised that Alex actually *did* appear to be pleased. Why her opinion was important to him, she couldn't imagine.

"As long as you don't mean you're starting the community service program for me." She narrowed her gaze at him. "You don't, do you?"

He grinned. "Not unless I catch you jaywalking again."

Biting back a smile, she checked her list. "We need to deliver three meals here. Two regular and one vegetarian."

"You get the vegetarian and I'll grab the other two."

Glad to get out of the vehicle—she'd merely been a passenger until now—Kristen opened one rear door as Alex opened the other. She dug out a vegetarian meal and then looked up. He was smiling at her. She couldn't stop herself from smiling in return.

She let herself enjoy the moment as she followed him up the five steps to the door.

He rang the bell.

Movement at the corner of her eye made Kristen start. A silver-haired woman was staring through parted curtains out the window. Kristen raised the container of food to show her. The curtain closed, and a moment later, the door opened.

"A couple!" the woman exclaimed. "Well, that's a first. Is that Kristen Lange?"

"It is, Mrs. Gerber. Good to see you again."

"You, too." Mrs. Gerber looked from Kristen to Alex. "Aren't you two cute together!"

"Thank you, ma'am," Alex said politely. "Would you like me to carry the food to your kitchen?"

"Nah, Herman needs the exercise." The woman turned to yell, "Herman get off that couch and come get lunch!" Then she turned back to the porch and gave Kristen and Alex a sweet smile that made her face look like crumpled paper. "Herman and I have been married for sixty-three years. How long have you two been together?"

"About an hour." Amused by the woman's mistake, Kristen explained, "We're not a couple."

"Oh, really? You have that look about you. Doesn't she, Alice?" she asked, as a silver-haired look-alike—her sister—stepped next to her.

"What look, Betsy?"

"Like they're a couple in love." Betsy yelled again, "Herman!"

"Coming! Give a guy a minute, would you?"

The two women beamed at them until Kristen started to grow uncomfortable. She was thankful when Herman finally came to the door. Completely bald, he looked at them out of rheumy eyes.

"I'll take those," he said gruffly as Alex handed him his boxes and Kristen put hers on top. "New delivery people, huh?" He didn't seem to recognize either of them. "Thanks. Real nice of you."

With that, he turned and shuffled away.

"Yes, thank you both," Alice said.

"I still think you two belong togeher," Betsy added, making Kristen practically run back to the patrol car.

She slid into her seat and pretended interest in the list when Alex opened the driver's door and got behind the wheel.

"Quite the characters, aren't they?" he said.

"Uh-huh."

"Are you uncomfortable?"

Though heat surged up Kristen's neck, she said, "No, of course not. Why would I be?"

"Why, indeed?" Alex murmured, as he started the engine.

Kristen gave him the next address, then said, "I wonder how old they are."

"Depends on how young they were when they married. Could be mid-eighties. Herman looks older."

"Sixty-three years. That's amazing. I've never met a couple who've been together that long before. Relationships usually don't last."

"It all depends on the couple. My parents have been together nearly forty years. You just need to find the right person."

"Well, that's the trick, isn't it?" She'd thought Jason was the right guy for her and look how wrong she'd been. "People can fool you."

Feeling Alex's questioning stare, Kristen looked away from him out the side window. She didn't want to talk about the man who'd disappointed her, who'd ditched her when things got rough, so she was relieved when Alex didn't press her.

She checked her watch. Good grief, she'd been gone for nearly an hour already, and she hadn't even called her sister to tell her what was up. Heather had seen Alex haul her off, though, so it wasn't as if she'd just disappeared. She left her cell where it was. Explanations could wait until she got back to the store.

The final few deliveries went faster than she'd expected. Alex kept the conversation on general topics about the town. Then he headed the patrol car back toward Sew Fine, and Kristen girded herself to be tormented by Heather. Undoubtedly her sister would have her own suppositions about Alex's arresting her.

To KRISTEN'S SURPRISE, the moment she walked into the store, she was attacked by a five-year-old ball of energy dressed in bright yellow.

"Aunt Kristen!" Addison said, wrapping her arms around Kristen's legs. Her blond hair was poking in every direction around her beaming face.

Kristen tweaked her niece's ponytail. "Hey, Addison, I thought you and Taylor were at day camp." Fortunately, Heather had been able to enroll both girls all day, five days a week.

Addison let go of Kristen and gave her a big, big sigh. Her expression turned serious and her blue eyes held a touch of sympathy. "Taylor told a boy to stop bothering her and then she punched him and Mommy had to come get us. Mommy gave her a time-out." She pointed to the back of the store.

Indeed, Taylor sat in a chair, arms folded over her little purple-clad chest. Her expression was stormy and she was kicking her legs in the air.

"Oh, dear, how long is the time-out?"

Addison shrugged. "She got up twice, so Mommy finally told her to sit there until she had permission to get up or there would be *consequences*."

Kristen bit the inside of her lip to keep from smiling. The twins were always so dramatic. And naughty. Especially Taylor, who was the little leader of the duo. They were also sweet and loving.

Seeing her sister coming toward them, Kristen thought how lucky she was to have the girls.

"Uh-oh, here comes Mommy," Addison sing-songed while slinking away.

"So you're back," Heather said. "Finally. Have a nice lunch?"

Kristen's stomach growled. "Um, I never had a chance to eat."

"What in the world were you doing all that time? Did Alex really arrest you?"

"You wouldn't believe what we were doing."

"That good, huh?" Before Kristen could deny anything had gone on between her and Alex,

Heather said, "I need to ask you for a favor. Taylor is being impossible today. I think she might be coming down with a little cold. I can't keep the twins here." Her gaze zeroed in on her mobile daughter, who was running through an aisle of fabric, touching each bolt as she went. "Addison, honey, walk please." She turned back to Kristen. "I've just been waiting for you to return so I can take them home."

Heather looked beat, Kristen thought, even as she asked, "If you go, who is going to be in charge?"

"You, of course. Unless you want to call Aunt Margaret in to work."

"No, no, let's not bother her." Kristen's stomach did a little somersault. "I can ring up purchases, but I don't know how to help customers find what they want."

"Gloria is here now. Louise will be here shortly. Whatever you can do to help them will be fine. And if you have a problem, just call me."

"Okay." Hopefully there wouldn't be a problem and everything would go smoothly.

"Thanks." Heather sighed and waved Addison over. "Let's go get Taylor."

"Bye, Aunt Kristen." Addison held her arms up for a hug.

Kristen pulled the little girl to her and kissed

her cheek. Then Addison ran off ahead of Heather to her twin.

"C'mon, we're going home!"

"No! I wanna stay here!"

"Taylor, you have a choice," Heather said in an unbelievably calm voice. "You can either stay here until tomorrow morning, or you can home with us and relax with your stuffed animals. Which do you want to do? It's your choice."

Surprised by her sister's ultimatum—would Heather actually leave the store without Taylor?—Kristen waited as the little girl thought it over, kicked her legs, then stood up. Apparently, Heather knew exactly how to handle the twins. Then again, Kristen had always known her sister was a great mom.

As they left by the back door, Heather waved with a relieved expression. Her sister had too much responsibility for a twenty-three-year-old, Kristen thought. If only Scott hadn't died in Iraq. Heather and Scott had been crazy about each other from the first time they'd met in high school. Heather had been a freshman, Scott a junior. By the time Heather had learned she was pregnant, Scott was in the Army. They'd gotten married just a week before he'd been shipped off to Iraq. He'd come home from his first tour, but unfortunately, he'd been sent back, never to return.

Kristen thought about her short-lived discussion about relationships with Alex. Even when two people were madly in love and right for each other, there were no guarantees for the future.

"I HAVE A PLAN," Brian said. "You know that big old house with the wraparound porch and the gigantic garden a block east of Main Street?"

"Sure do," answered Andy Eccles, a grin splitting his freckled face.

Brian walked along the lake path with his buddies as they did every chance they could late at night. He'd sneaked out after Aunt Margaret and Kristen had gone to bed.

The biggest of the boys, tall with a little extra bulk around the middle from too much food and general lack of activity, Matt Stapleton asked, "You mean the one with the stupid garden statues?" He shuffled along, puffing, as if just walking was too much of an exertion for him.

"A bazillion of them." Matt's complete opposite, Andy danced as if hip-hop music played constantly in his head under that mop of curly red hair. He was a scrawny kid, and his raggedy clothes threatened to fall off him.

"What if we move them around?" Brian

mused. "You know, like put the deer statues on the other side of the house. And take all those rabbits and frogs and squirrels out of the garden and put them in a big circle on the flattest part of the lawn. What do you think, guys?"

In reality, the idea was as stupid as most of the pranks they'd pulled. Not that they'd actually harmed anyone's property.

As usual, both boys were looking to him for guidance. Andy and Matt were both about to be seniors in high school. They were practically the only kids around this summer that he knew from before he got moved to California because of his stepfather's job. For whatever reason, the duo saw him as a leader, and he liked the feeling of having some say in things again. No one else had listened to his opinions in the past four years.

"Woo-oo!" Andy danced some more. "What are we waiting for?"

They set off toward Main Street, Andy making sounds as if he was singing. More like howling, Brian thought. As usual, Matt followed—he was highly influenced by his much smaller friend and didn't seem to have a brain of his own.

Then again, Brian knew *he* was acting like he didn't have a brain, either. He didn't care, though. He had no one to impress but these jugheads. Mom wasn't here and his sisters and aunt didn't seem to see him for who he was. Well, maybe Kristen, at least a little. When she had asked him to take charge of phoned-in orders at the store, he'd felt as if someone needed him.

Too bad it was too little, too late.

The big old corner house came into sight. Brian stopped and held his hand up so the others would stop, too.

"Make sure no one's watching first."

"Who's gonna be watching at one in the morning?" Andy asked.

Matt added. "Don't see no one."

Neither did Brian.

"Okay," he whispered, moving forward. "Let's do it, but quietly!"

They crossed the street and went straight to the middle of the yard alongside the house where a family of metal deer stood guard. The deer were fairly heavy. Andy grunted as he tried to budge one.

"Matt and I can move these," Brian said. "Why don't you go get those rabbits out of the garden?"

He and Matt combined forces to lift the big buck and carry it around to the other side of the house. They went back to get the doe, carrying her together, as well, and then returned to each pick up one of the much smaller fawns.

When Brian noticed Andy standing in the

middle of the garden, his back to them, not moving anything, he hesitated. "Andy," he whispered, "you okay?"

Andy nodded but didn't say anything.

With the weirdest feeling crawling down his spine, Brian left the fawn and walked over to see what was going on with his scrawny friend who had gone past the flower bed and into the vegetable garden. Coming around to one side, Brian saw that Andy was stuffing something in his mouth. Then Andy bent over and twisted a tomato off the plant in front of him.

He was eating? Now?

"Andy, what are you doing?" he whispered frantically. "The longer we stay here, the more likely we'll get caught!"

"Okay, okay!"

But Andy didn't move out of the vegetable patch. He stuffed the tomato in a pocket and grabbed another and a couple of green peppers, as well. He shoved one in his pocket, the other in his mouth. Brian wondered how he could do that without washing the vegetable first. Yuck!

Andy picked up a rabbit statue and carried it to the flat, open part of the lawn. In the meantime, having moved the remaining fawns, Matt hurried over and started moving the smaller animals, letting Andy tell him where to place them. They arranged the sculptures in circles beginning with rabbits on an inside ring, moving to frogs, then squirrels. They also placed a few geese on the outside, their heads looking at the center.

Andy chortled. "Hey, this is like a crop circle. They'll think aliens were here."

Brian had to grin. Andy must have seen one of those TV specials about mysterious events. He found a big, dumb-looking garden gnome and placed it in the center of the circle. "And this is their leader."

Brian didn't miss the fact that Andy finished the pepper, went back to the vegetable garden and pulled a zucchini from the vine and started chomping on that.

What was wrong with him? How could Andy eat so much so late at night? How could he eat so much and stay so skinny? And why was he so into vegetables when most guys would rather have a juicy burger?

It was then it hit Brian. Andy was hungry. Not normally hungry, but ravenous, as if he hadn't eaten for days. Was that why Andy's clothes were falling off him? Because he didn't have enough to eat? He'd never said anything about being hungry before. He had parents. At least Brian thought he did.

Realizing they were done moving the lawn

ornaments around, he whispered, "Good job! Let's get out of here."

He'd have to find out what was going on with Andy. Aunt Margaret's refrigerator was always full....

They were barely off the property when Brian heard a vehicle coming down the street. He looked back. A black-and-white.

"Cops!" He was already running. "Don't follow me!" he ordered the others. "Go in different directions!"

He sped down the sidewalk as fast as he could go, aware that the cruiser behind him had picked up speed. He feinted to the right, ran across a lawn and headed for the backyard.

When he heard a deep male voice shout, "Stop right there!" he panicked and looked for a place to hide.

A car door slammed. At the back of the property now, knowing the cop was after him, Brian took off down the alley.

Where to hide?

He couldn't get caught. Couldn't go to jail.

Halfway down the alley, his chest twisting into a tight knot, he spotted a small stand of trees pressed up against a four-foot-tall picket fence. He didn't stop to think, simply slowed and hopped onto the fence, then grabbed a low branch and hauled himself up into a maple tree. He climbed a bit higher into the canopy and flattened himself against the trunk.

The slap-slap of leather on pavement followed. The cop slowed and stopped just yards away. Brian swallowed hard. He didn't dare breathe. Didn't dare move. This wasn't just any cop after him. Even with only the moon as light, he recognized the guy.

The police chief.

His heart was beating so hard that surely Chief Novak could hear it. But the man below looked around, muttered something in a low voice and backed off.

Brian didn't breathe again until he heard the cop's footsteps fade away.

CHAPTER SEVEN

"MRS. GRANT CALLED first thing," Janet said when Alex walked into the office the next morning. "Apparently our pranksters were up to no good again. They moved her lawn ornaments all over the place."

"Yeah, I figured."

Before Janet could ask him to explain, he went back to the break area to find Owen pouring himself a cup of coffee. Though it was Saturday, the citizens of Sparrow Lake still needed protecting. The officers took turns working a weekend a month, and Alex almost always checked on things. At least, when he wasn't fishing.

"Hey, Alex, what's up?" Owen asked.

"Nothing good."

"Ah, you heard about Mrs. Grant's garden bunnies."

"I didn't just hear about them," Alex said, pouring coffee into a mug. "I almost caught one of the pranksters last night."

"Who?"

"Brian Lange. Fast kid. He got away from me."

"So you want me to go to the house and pick him up?"

"No. The thing is, I didn't see him do anything." Alex took a slug. Exhausted from the last week of prowling around town late at night, looking for the gang of three, he needed to mainline that coffee to wake up. "I spotted them a couple of houses away from the Grant place. But they split up and ran. After I lost Brian, I went back and realized that those deer Mrs. Grant loves were on the wrong side of her property. I figured that's what they'd been up to. I just can't prove it."

"So what are you going to do?"

"The only thing I can do." The one thing that was going to ruin what he finally had going with Kristen. "I've already tried talking to Margaret Becker about her nephew, but she circumvented the conversation by telling me what a great help he was to her. She had nothing but praise for him, so I knew she didn't want to hear it. I'll have to talk to the person in that family who doesn't seem to run on emotion. I'm going to talk to his sister."

"Oh, you mean the one you hauled in here last week?" Owen asked with a knowing smile.

"The same."

"She's not going to like it, either."

"No, but I think she'll listen."

Alex feared Kristen wasn't going to like *him* again, either. And just after he'd won her over. Well, at least a little. Connecting with her yesterday while delivering those meals had been the best time he'd had since moving to Sparrow Lake.

Alex thought over his options.

He could pick up Brian and his buddies and try to scare them straight, but that wasn't a long-term solution. Once they got over being chastised, they might just get sneakier. He needed to get to the people who had influence over them, to figure out what was missing or wrong in their lives, and then maybe he could make a difference.

As to involving Kristen...

She couldn't have had many dealings with her brother for years, not with her in Chicago and him in California. Still, she was his sister, and family had power. Brian needed some guidance before he crossed a line, and Alex decided that was more important than his own personal life.

No matter the outcome for him, he had to involve Brian's sister, because it was the right thing to do.

He could only hope that Kristen would be

reasonable and work with him to find a way to divert her brother's negative energies toward something good.

"ARE YOU SURE you want to paint the front door such a bright color?" Kristen asked as she looked down into the paint can.

"Absolutely," Margaret said. She stooped to stir the paint and eyed Kristen's navy pants and white T-shirt. Not a speck of vivid color on her. Her niece was too conservative for her own good. "This will make the entryway pop."

Kristen raised her eyebrows. "A chartreuse front door. Okay."

Margaret laughed and dipped her paintbrush into the can. "It's spring green, not chartreuse, and it's a happy color. Lighten up, Kristen. Expand your vision of our world." She loved that her niece had volunteered to help, but she wished the creative gene hadn't passed Kristen by. "I've never wanted to be like everyone else, and I've been unhappy with this white door for a dozen years now, ever since I married Donald and moved into his place. He told me to paint it whatever color I wanted, but I never did. It's about time I'm finally doing something about it."

Margaret brushed color onto one part of the

panel and admired the bright yellow-green, similar to the capris and flowing shirt she wore.

"I'm surprised you waited this long, Aunt Margaret."

As if reluctant to be part of this, Kristen carefully dipped her own brush into the paint and started working on the trim.

"Donald was as conservative as you are, sweetheart," Margaret said. "This was his house long before we married, so I kept things the way he was used to. I had my studio and my art. He had the beautiful home he'd always wanted. We were both happy compromising. After he died, I thought to make some changes, but I kept myself so busy I didn't have time to take pleasure in the little things."

"Hmm. You're saying I'm like your late husband, but Alex thinks I'm like you. The keeping-busy-every-minute-of-the-day part, anyway."

Heather had told Margaret about Alex arresting her sister for jaywalking yesterday. But for some reason Kristen didn't sound angry or defensive when talking about the man.

"So now it's Alex, is it?" Margaret mused.

"That *is* his name."

Kristen didn't look at her, kept her gaze on her paintbrush as if mesmerized. Margaret smiled.

The charming police chief had undoubtedly gotten to her niece. Very, very good in the scheme of things. The more Kristen had to like about living in Sparrow Lake, the less reason she would have to go back to Chicago.

"So, Kristen, when are you seeing Alex again?"

Her niece gave her a look that was probably meant to show she was annoyed, but informed Margaret that Kristen wasn't so sure of herself.

"I'm not *seeing* Alex. Well, unless I jaywalk again, and he happens to be around, I guess."

"I heard about that and about your delivering meals to seniors instead of paying the fine. Why didn't you just pay? It was only a dollar."

Kristen shrugged and kept painting. "Alex rubs me the wrong way. He got my back up."

Delighted, Margaret dipped her brush again and attacked the door with renewed enthusiasm. She hadn't planned on Alex. He was simply a bonus.

She and Kristen worked together in harmony. Despite her niece's own preferences, Margaret made a big deal about the entryway now looking perfect. They'd just finished when she heard a vehicle pull up to the curb and turned to see a familiar patrol car.

And couldn't help the smile that blossomed in response.

"Oh, look at who's here," she said as Alex left the vehicle. "The police chief himself." She couldn't help teasing her niece. "Are you sure you didn't do anything illegal this morning?"

"What?" Stooping to put the lid back on the paint can, Kristen glanced over her shoulder and lost her balance. Luckily she caught herself, but not before getting chartreuse paint on her hand. "Great." After wiping her hand with a paper towel, she shoved the hair out of her face and stood.

To Margaret's amusement, Kristen was finally wearing some vivid color where she'd touched her cheek.

"Ladies, good afternoon," Alex said, giving Kristen a penetrating look.

Kristen narrowed her gaze on him. "You're not here to arrest me again, are you?"

"Uh, no. I was just driving by and decided to be neighborly."

"Oh, how nice," Margaret said. "Kristen, why don't you offer Alex a cup of coffee."

Kristen frowned at her. "I don't think that's a good idea."

"I don't, either," Alex said. "But I wouldn't

mind your taking a ride with me. I want to show you something."

"A ride?" Kristen echoed.

"You know, sitting in the passenger seat of my squad for a while." His brows arched. "You must be familiar with the concept."

Tension seemed to zap back and forth between her niece and Alex. Margaret busied herself cleaning up.

"C'mon, take some time off," Alex said. "You don't have to be 'on' every minute."

"He's right, Kristen," Margaret said. "You should go."

"But Aunt Margaret, I cleared my calendar to help you paint today."

"And you did a great job. Didn't she, Alex?" Margaret indicated the brilliant-hued entryway.

He nodded. "Very, um, colorful."

"See," Kristen croaked. "Aunt Margaret needs me."

"Actually, I don't, sweetheart. We're through for now. So there's nothing keeping you from going and having a nice time with Alex." When Kristen stood there like a deer caught in the headlights, Margaret leaned over and whispered in her ear. "It's good for business to be friendly with the local authorities. Please go for me."

Kristen heaved a sigh. "I suppose I could go."

Alex indicated she should lead the way to the patrol car.

Margaret didn't miss the way he swept his gaze over her niece, or the way he insisted on rubbing his thumb over her cheek to rid her of that little smear of paint before opening the car door for her.

Watching them drive off, Margaret hummed happily to herself as she gathered the paint can and brushes and took them around back to the garage.

"SO WHAT IS this all about?" Kristen asked, suspicious of Alex's motives. At least he hadn't handcuffed her to get her in the car. Still, she was certain Alex had an angle. She simply couldn't figure out what it was. "Why ask me out for a drive?"

"I wanted to show you something and talk to you about an important matter."

She'd been forced into this outing by Aunt Margaret, Kristen thought. Her instincts had been to stay as far away from Alex Novak as she could. She didn't need to complicate her life, and she figured that's exactly what Alex would do to it if she let him get to her. Something that could definitely happen.

Though he was driving the patrol car, he

wasn't in uniform today. He was even more handsome wearing charcoal-gray trousers and a lighter shirt of the same gray as the eyes that fed her nerves when he glanced at her.

"What exactly are you doing for your aunt at Sew Fine?" Alex asked.

"She wants me to find ways to increase traffic and sales in the store. For one, there aren't any brochures, something I just started working on. Then they can be distributed to whomever will display them either here or in surrounding towns."

"Sounds like a plan. I take it this is your area of expertise."

Alex's interest in her work relaxed Kristen a bit. "I was head of marketing for Chicago Lifestyle, a sporting goods company, for more than a year."

"But you left that job in Chicago to work for your aunt?"

"I didn't leave it." She tried not to sound bitter. "I was downsized."

"That's happened to a lot of people. Sorry."

"Yeah, me, too. I worked very hard to get my MBA and to build my career. I was on a fast track for a couple of years. Great job, beautiful condo with a lake view. There simply was no fighting the reality of a depressed economy."

"So you lost your job. The condo, too?"

She nodded. "Among other things. I never thought I would be a failure." She wasn't going to tell Alex about Jason, though, about how he'd been more annoyed by her troubles than supportive. "I couldn't find another open position that paid anything close to what I'd been making. And I couldn't get a full-time job at lower pay, because the people hiring were afraid I would leave at the first opportunity."

"Probably you would have."

"Probably. And there was a prevalent attitude at the time. Too many employers wouldn't hire people who didn't already have jobs."

"That's crazy!"

"But a reality. It has always been easier to get a job when you already have one, but this market took the problem to new heights. I had to settle for a series of part-time jobs just to limp along. I'm very grateful to Aunt Margaret for offering me both a break from my situation and a challenge that lets me keep my hand in, working to grow a business. I needed a break from all the stress so I could create a strategy. And this way, when I apply for a new job, I'm no longer unemployed."

"You're ambitious and intelligent," Alex said, voice filled with admiration. "You'll figure out what you really want from life and get it before you know it. Things can turn around for you on a dime."

"Thanks. I hope you're correct."

Alex was being surprisingly sympathetic, which made her feel connected with him. Kristen was getting the idea that, after their rocky start, Alex actually liked her. She had to admit she liked him more than made her comfortable.

"Starting over can be difficult." Alex slowed the squad car. "I respect that you're determined to rebuild your life. Not everyone does that in a positive way."

An odd thing to say, Kristen thought. "What do you mean?"

"Some people react to change negatively, do things that aren't smart. Sometimes they even do things that aren't legal."

He pulled the car over to the curb and put it in Park. The way he was looking at her made her uncomfortable.

"Someone you know?" she asked.

"No, Kristen, someone *you* know." His voice caught for a second like he was reluctant to finish. Then he said, "Your brother."

"Brian? He's just a kid starting out in life. He's a little immature, but he'll grow up fast enough after he starts college at the end of summer."

"If he doesn't do something to ruin his chances first. Do you know his friends?"

Disturbed by the turn the conversation had taken, Kristen said, "I think Brian hangs out with some kids he used to know before moving to California."

He nodded. "Andy Eccles and Matt Stapleton. They're not bad kids, but they do get into trouble, and lately they've been close to crossing the line."

"What does that have to do with Brian?"

"He's been close to crossing it with them."

"I don't believe Brian has been doing anything wrong."

"Has he been acting strange lately? Disappearing for hours without an explanation? Going out late at night—after curfew—without telling anyone?"

Kristen stiffened. So that's why he'd wanted to get her alone. She'd known he had an angle, and it was one she didn't like.

"Wait a minute. This is why you asked me out for a drive? So you could make accusations about Brian?"

"So I could talk to you about your brother before I have to arrest him. I spotted the three boys on the street at one this morning right here."

"In front of the Grants' place?"

"Right. I asked them to stop so I could talk to them. They ran instead."

"They probably weren't doing anything wrong."

"Take a good look. Does anything look strange to you?"

Frowning, she looked out the house with its myriad lawn ornaments. Mrs. Grant had always loved placing statues of animals all over her yard. "Looks okay to me."

"Except the lawn ornaments are all moved around. Mrs. Grant was very upset when she called it in this morning."

"What?" She nearly choked on that. "You're all bent out of shape over a harmless prank?"

"Not one prank. They've been playing pranks on the townspeople a couple of times a week for the past month, Kristen. I want it to stop before those pranks get out of hand. Or before someone gets hurt."

Kristen opened the passenger door. "I don't have time for this nonsense."

Though she started to get out, Alex caught her arm and said, "If you care about your brother, you'll make the time."

Her pulse flitted through her at his touch, but she told herself it was because she was angry, not because she was attracted to him.

"You should be looking for real criminals to

arrest," she told him, "not people who are simply guilty of being new in town."

With that, she jerked her arm free and stalked off.

"I DIDN'T EXPECT you back so quickly," Aunt Margaret said when Kristen stormed into the house.

Kristen's irritation had escalated on the fifteen-minute walk home, but she put it in check for her aunt's sake.

Should she tell her or not?

Kristen was tempted to share the police chief's motives for getting her alone, but Aunt Margaret was so cheerful, she decided not to ruin her aunt's mood. Still, Kristen was disturbed by what he'd told her. What if Brian was getting into trouble? She would keep their conversation to herself, but maybe she could find a way to probe her aunt for information without giving away Alex's accusation.

Kristen followed her into the kitchen. There, to her surprise, her brother and one of his friends sat at the island, the surface of which was littered with containers of leftovers, mostly empty now. The friend was scrawny, but his plate was full and he was chowing down like there was no tomorrow.

"Oh, hi, Aunt Margaret. I hope you don't mind that I invited Andy to lunch."

"Of course not. This is your home, too. Brian."

"Hi, Mrs. Becker," the kid said through a mouthful of food.

"Andy, this is my niece Kristen. Brian's sister."

"Hmmph." He acknowledged her with his mouth full.

"Uh, we're done now, though." Brian slid off his stool and smacked Andy in the arm. "C'mon."

"You're not done until you clean up after yourself," Kristen said.

"Oh, right."

Brian scooped all the empty containers together and dumped them on the counter, opened the dishwasher door and stacked them. His friend Andy continued to chomp on a piece of chicken. He kept his head down as he ate, didn't look at anyone. Kristen gave him the once-over while Brian cleaned off the island. The kid was scrawny—how could someone so little eat so much? His clothes were too big, as if he was wearing hand-me-downs. His shirt and cutoffs were threadbare, if clean.

Pulling off a piece of paper towel from the roll, Brian handed it to Andy and said, "Let's go to my room."

"Yeah, okay."

Andy was a little weird, but he didn't seem like a troublemaker. Still, Kristen couldn't help worrying. Could Alex have been right about the boys? While Brian seemed fairly mature for his age, he wasn't adult-level responsible. He did a good job at Sew Fine…when he was there.

She turned to her aunt. "About Brian—"

"Your brother is such a sweetheart!" Aunt Margaret beamed. "He needs a little prompting, but he truly has been the most wonderful and helpful companion since he moved in with me."

Thus ended the conversation about Brian possibly getting into trouble.

Too bad Kristen couldn't forget about it.

CHAPTER EIGHT

HE'D AWAKENED BEFORE DAWN.

Alex had been tempted to take a hammer to his alarm clock until he suffered the next onslaught, an ambush by Spike, who suddenly realized it must be breakfast time. "Okay, okay," he muttered, setting the big fluffy cat down on the floor. The stray he'd been feeding had moved in, fattened up, and decided who was boss.

Groggily, Alex turned off the alarm and managed to sit up. He staggered out to the kitchen and fed Spike, then remembered why he'd set the alarm so early. He and Owen had made plans to go fishing with John McClintock, owner of McClintock Boat, Bait and Tackle. He'd better dress quickly.

An hour later, there he was, travel mug filled with hot coffee in one hand, fishing rod in the other, sitting in one of John's boats in the middle of the stocked lake. If they didn't get too many small ones they'd have to throw back in, they would take their booty back to John's store and cook fish over the grill on the patio for breakfast. It wasn't the fishing in itself that attracted Alex, but the camaraderie with his friends in addition to spending some time in nature. They were in a beautiful setting, in the middle of the lake, with stands of trees between the mansions and businesses at the water's edge. The lake's clean, deep water made it perfect for sailing or swimming or waterskiing.

At this time on a Sunday morning, however, there wasn't a whole lot of movement on or in the water. Alex had seen no more than two other fishing boats in the distance. No swimmers. He loved the sense of early morning peace. Well, usually. Fishing with the guys was an enjoyable venture, one to which he looked forward.

As if Owen knew that Alex was fighting to keep from nodding off, he said, "Drink your coffee. You'll feel better."

"I'm never going to feel better," Alex groused. "Not until I get, like, twelve hours of continuous shut-eye."

John laughed. "You're just a young whippersnapper. Wait till you get to be my age and wonder where the ability to sleep went."

"What are you? Fifty-six?"

"Closer to seventy-six," John said. "Actually I'm going to be seventy-two."

With thick salt-and-pepper hair and a lightly

lined face, John looked a decade younger than his years, maybe because, after retiring from a suit job in Milwaukee, he'd taken to his Sparrow Lake vacation home full-time. Then he'd bought the store and made his version of an idyllic life come true.

Alex was wondering what that felt like when he heard a faint buzzing. Owen put his fishing pole between his knees and pulled his cell phone from his pocket.

"Trina?" Alex asked.

"Yep." Owen's thumbs were going as he texted something in return. "She just woke up and wanted to tell me she loved me."

Thinking he knew the woman he'd like to have text *him,* Alex couldn't help but tease his friend. "Newlyweds!" He rolled his eyes so John could see.

John laughed. "Wish I had a beautiful woman who would text me about anything. You're a lucky man, Owen Larson."

"Don't I know it."

"It's been nearly seven years since she died, but I still miss Karen." John sighed. "What about you, Alex? When are you going to find you a woman?"

"When I win the lottery," he joked.

He'd had a woman in his life for a short while.

Rather than learning how to deal with the stress of being a cop's wife, Emma had left him. Said she couldn't stand the chances he took and wanted to end it before they brought kids into the world.

He'd been married for all of five months.

Now, nearly three years later, he'd finally found a woman he wanted to get to know better, but he feared that Kristen was never going to speak to him again, even though he'd been trying to help her brother.

"You know you're not too old to find someone else," Owen told John. "There are lots of mature women around here who don't have a man."

"No one around here much interests me," John said. "Except maybe one." He looked out across the lake at Margaret Becker's mansion. "But she would never give a boring old coot like me the time of day."

"Then find a way to interest her." Feeling a jerk on his pole, Alex realized he'd hooked a fish. "If you want to get to know her enough," he said, putting down his coffee cup, "you'll find a way to reel her in."

Good advice.

He glanced back at the Becker mansion.

Maybe he would take that advice himself and not give up on Kristen just yet.

WAS SHE DESTINED to see Alex everywhere she looked? Kristen wondered as she stared out the window on the other side of the kitchen sink. She was looking for that boat she'd spotted earlier, before the family had gathered for Sunday brunch. Family minus Brian, that was. It was nearly eleven and he hadn't yet joined them. At any rate, she'd been washing off fresh strawberries in a colander and had sworn she'd spotted the police chief in a fishing boat. It wasn't out there now, however. It seemed to have disappeared.

Had Alex been watching the house?

If so, had his interest been Brian?

Or her?

"Here are some more dirty dishes," Heather said.

Kristen moved to the side to let her sister put them into the sink but said, "I'll take care of them if you start putting away the food."

"Deal."

What was it with dishwashers, anyway? Kristen wondered as she turned on the faucet. It didn't matter how expensive the unit was, no matter the instructions, you always had to rinse off the dishes first if you wanted them clean.

"You haven't seen Brian, have you?" she

asked, raising her voice to be heard above the running water.

"No, not yet."

"Does he usually sleep this late?"

"How would I know?" Heather was wrapping a plate of leftover cut fruit with plastic wrap. "I'm not the one who lives here."

Heather sounded testy, making Kristen hold back the observation that she'd only moved in with Aunt Margaret the week before. As to Brian...he must have been out very late.

A reminder of Alex's accusation.

What had her brother been doing? she wondered, but figured there was no use bringing it up with her sister, who had been tense all morning, had actually lost her temper with the twins. Aunt Margaret had the girls now. They'd followed her to her huge, paint- and fabric-stocked studio where they could "create" something fun.

Heather had seemed relieved to have a rest from them.

Kristen finished loading the dirty dishes, added dishwashing powder and started the appliance.

Thinking to get her sister's mind off the girls, Kristen said, "You know, I enjoy working at the store more than I thought I would." A fact that surprised her. "Nice people. A whole lot less pressure than I'm used to."

"Uh-huh." Heather shoved a couple of cartons of leftovers into the refrigerator.

"Nice working conditions. No stress."

"Yeah, right."

Kristen caught Heather's sarcastic tone. What was wrong with her today?

"I was thinking of ways to improve Sew Fine's sales." Which was necessary for Aunt Margaret to have a decent retirement. "I wanted to talk to you about creating an online store."

"What?"

"That way, people who have been calling in orders could use it, and so could new customers who don't necessarily live in the area."

"I don't think that's a good idea."

"Why not? The sky's the limit, Heather. Customers could order from anywhere in the country."

Even as Kristen spoke, Heather's expression changed from disbelieving to downright anxious.

"No! It'll be on me to see that it works. I can't possibly take on something so complicated."

"No, no, I'll take care of setting it up, Heather. It's the best way to make the business grow."

"Grow? How many more orders?" Heather was so agitated she nearly dropped the plate of fruit meant for the refrigerator. "I don't think so, Kristen. I have my hands full now."

"Brian is already fulfilling the phoned-in customer requests. He can continue to take care of the orders when the internet site is up and running."

"Brian is going to start college soon." Heather's voice raised a notch. "Full-time. At the end of the summer! I can't count on him now. I'll never be able to trust him to pull it off then."

Kristen gaped at her sister. She'd never seen Heather so panicked. Her sister was the supreme juggler of work, family and school.

"Heather, is something wrong?" she asked.

"I can't take on anything more. I never should have agreed to be the store manager, but I knew how much Aunt Margaret wanted to retire and I needed the money for the girls. Everything I have to do…it's all too much for me!" Heather pushed a shaking hand through her hair and her eyes grew watery. "And now my sitter called about tomorrow night. She canceled. I'll have to miss a class, which will affect my grade. I'm scheduled to do a class presentation!"

"Hey, hey, calm down, please." Kristen had no idea the kind of pressure her sister had been experiencing. "You're not alone. You have family."

"If you're going to suggest that I ask Brian to take care of my girls—"

"I was going to suggest me."

"You?"

"Don't sound so shocked. I took care of you and Brian when we were growing up."

"But Brian and I weren't five-year-old twins."

"I know, I know. Taylor and Addison are little monkeys, running around looking for trouble."

"Believe me, they find it." Heather heaved a sigh.

Kristen put her arms around her sister and gave her a big hug. "I'll deal."

"You're sure you want to do this?" Heather suddenly sounded calmer than she had all morning.

"Positive. You can go to your class tomorrow night knowing that I'll have it all under control."

At least she hoped she would. That morning, the twins had been hugging each other one minute, sifting dirt into one another's hair the next. They'd gotten into all kinds of mischief before Aunt Margaret had finally lured them off to her studio.

Poor Heather. Kristen hadn't realized how so much responsibility had weighed on her younger sister. Heather suddenly seemed to be almost as badly off as their mother had been after their father abandoned the family.

Well, she was here for Heather, at least for now, Kristen thought. While she was still in Sparrow Lake, she would do whatever she could to make her sister's life a little easier.

A vow that bothered her later that day after Heather and the girls had left for home.

Knowing she needed to update her résumé before continuing her job search, Kristen pulled it up on her computer and added her work as a marketing consultant for Sew Fine. She would have to start sending résumés out soon. In this economy, who knew how long it could take her to find another job in Chicago? Or even an interview for a job.

She sat there staring at her résumé, realizing this was the first step to leaving Sparrow Lake. Leaving her family—the people who needed her—and she'd just gotten here. Aunt Margaret needed someone to make sure she could retire in comfort. Brian needed someone to make sure he wasn't getting into trouble. Heather needed someone to lift part of the burden of being a young widow with too much responsibility.

But what about what *she* needed? Aunt Margaret had agreed that Kristen would keep looking for something permanent while she tried to boost business for Sew Fine.

Since the day she'd received notice that Chicago Lifestyle was downsizing her, Kristen had felt a hole in her life that she hadn't been able to fill. Being told that she wasn't necessary to the company she'd helped expand in so short a time had truly been a humiliating experience, one she hoped never to repeat. She was determined to prove herself, to show them what a mistake they'd made in letting her go.

She did not want to be compared to her father, a man who had failed at everything he'd tried. True, most of the businesses he'd gotten himself into had been risky. But still...

So far, she'd proved nothing except how difficult it was to get a job when you were already out of work.

IT WAS ONLY early evening and Margaret was tired enough to stretch out on her bed, draped with gauzy material from post to post. Those twins were enough to exhaust anyone, even their mother, who was a third Margaret's age. Poor Heather. Margaret wished her niece could find a nice man to love her and her children. The girls could use two parents. Heather had been going it on her own for more than two years. Probably she didn't have the time to even think about dating again.

Worse, Kristen had the time and a nice man who was interested, but she didn't seem to want to let him into her life.

The phone rang, startling her out of her thoughts.

Reaching over to the nightstand, she picked up the receiver on the second ring. "Hello."

"Margaret? This is John McClintock."

"John." Odd, John had never called her before. "How are you?"

"I'm good. Um, I'm not sure if you know this, but I'm having a big fish fry at the shop next Sunday. The proceeds are going to fund a fishing camp for local kids."

"That sounds nice."

"I was thinking maybe you could invite your whole family. Your nieces and nephew and those two cute little girls. I'll bet those two rascals would like to learn to fish."

Undoubtedly they would. The twins were a lot like her—always wanting to try everything at least once.

"I'll see what I can do," Margaret promised.

"Listen, I have another reason for wanting you to come."

Margaret's pulse sped up a bit, and she sat up. Here she'd just been thinking about seeing someone new. Was John interested in her? She didn't know him well, but he'd always seemed like a very nice man.

"Yes," she said expectantly.

"It's my buddy Alex," John said. "He's a little soft on your niece Kristen, and she's a difficult one for him to get to know. He's gonna be at the fish fry, too."

"You want to set them up?" How silly that she'd thought the man was interested in her.

"I figured they didn't get a good start with Alex arresting Kristen and all. The fish fry would give them a chance to get to know each other better."

"It would," Margaret agreed. "I'll do it, John! I'll find a way to convince Kristen to come with me."

"Good. Good. I'll be looking forward to it."

"Same here."

"Okay." He sounded happy when he said, "See you next Sunday, then."

Margaret was happy, too. Conspiring with John McClintock to get Kristen and Alex together could be rewarding.

Not only would it be fun for her, if things

worked out between her niece and the police chief, it would give Kristen another reason to stay in Sparrow Lake.

To BRIAN'S RELIEF, Matt pulled his beat-up car over to the curb on a dark side street. It was well after midnight. Most houses around the area were dark, too. People in this town were already in bed.

"Why are you parking here?" Andy asked. "What if we need to make a quick getaway?"

"We're only a block from our target," Matt told him as he put the car in Park and removed the key. "This way, no one can place my ride at the scene of the crime."

Just hearing the word *crime* made Brian wince. Things were getting out of hand, and it was more and more difficult to keep his buddies from crossing the line.

"We're pranksters," Brian insisted. "Not criminals."

And not vandals.

They got out of the car, and Brian dragged behind Matt and Andy to the gas station, thankful that he'd talked them out of using that can of purple spray paint. Matt's idea. Brilliant. If they did get caught spray painting a building, they'd be arrested and thrown in jail. That's why he'd insisted on stopping at FamilyMart to buy a box of giant colored chalk, the kind kids used to draw lines for hopscotch and other games on sidewalks.

Only sidewalks weren't their target.

The gas station was.

"I still don't see why we couldn't use my paint," Matt said.

"That's what everyone would expect," Brian told him, trying to make it sound like what they were going to do was more interesting— cooler—when he was simply trying to avoid doing something he'd regret. You couldn't just wash spray paint off a wall the way you could chalk. "Think of us as street artists. We can tick off Mr. Hansen while entertaining the people in town who appreciate what we have to say."

His words were sounding hollow even to his own ears.

But once at the gas station, Brian relaxed and got into the prank. It was so late that no one was around to see them.

The building's walls were covered in stucco, so it wasn't as easy to use the chalk as he'd thought, but he'd always loved drawing, so he made the effort. He supposed he'd gotten that from Aunt Margaret.

Each of them had thought of something to say about energy reduction.

Andy drew an outline of a car hooked up to an electric pole and scrawled "Save the Earth, Buy Electric Cars." Matt drew a blobby guy wearing a mask with the words *Gas is Toxic* over his head. And Brian drew an intricate windmill and told the onlooker to "Save on Gas, Buy Hybrid."

"Cool," Matt said when they all stood back to admire their handiwork barely illuminated by a streetlight.

"People will be talking about this for a while," Andy said.

Unless the owner cleaned it off the building in the morning before anyone got a chance to see it, Brian thought. "Let's get to the car before some cop trolls the area." A cop named Alex Novak, he thought sourly.

They walked fast. Didn't run. No need to draw attention to themselves in case someone was looking out a window.

When they were all in the car, Brian drew a deep breath. What had he been so worried about? It had been fun and the whole town was going to see their handiwork.

"So what are we gonna do tomorrow night?" Matt asked.

"We can meet with these guys I know," Andy said.

Brian frowned. "What guys? You haven't told anyone what we've been doing, have you?"

"Nah, they wouldn't be interested in kid stuff."

"What would they be interested in?" Matt asked.

"Making money."

Brian had a weird feeling about this. "Doing what?"

"Don't know. That's why we need to meet with them."

Matt snorted. "I don't want some dumb job."

"Who says it's a job?"

That's what Brian was afraid of. "Forget about it. We don't need anyone messing up what we're doing now."

Neither of the other boys protested, but Brian feared this wasn't the last they were going to hear of the making-money deal. Pulling pranks was fun. Sort of. He didn't want to cross the line to dangerous.

CHAPTER NINE

ALEX ENTERED SEW FINE on Monday afternoon, his gaze automatically going to the rear of the store where Kristen sat at her computer. Ignoring curious shoppers, he headed straight for his target. He was halfway there before she looked up and saw him.

Kristen's expression closed, and by the time he got to her she was on her feet. Dressed less formally than usual, she wore wide-legged trousers and a pretty blue blouse the same color as her eyes. Her blond hair was pulled high into a sleek ponytail that made her look both elegant and casual.

"Alex. I didn't know you were a quilter."

He laughed. "Sorry, that's not my interest."

She narrowed her gaze on him. "Then why *are* you here?"

"Don't worry. I'm not here to make any arrests. I just want to help out a friend is all." Not to mention that he wanted to manufacture another opportunity to spend some time with her.

"Go on."

"His name is John McClintock. He's a nice man, retired from a demanding job. He now owns McClintock Boat, Bait and Tackle."

"*He's* interested in quilting?"

"Uh, no." Alex moved closer and lowered his voice. "I think he's interested in Margaret."

Her expression softened. "Really."

He could see that perked her up, just as he'd hoped it would. Her big blue eyes rounded, and she bit at her lower lip. He had to force himself not to stare.

Clearing his throat, he said, "John's giving a fish fry next Sunday. It's to support a fishing camp for kids."

"Yes, Aunt Margaret mentioned that last night."

"Good. You're coming, then."

"Aunt Margaret wants us both to go."

"What about you?"

"I told her I would see."

See about what? he wondered. Why did she hesitate? Was she so immune to having a little fun?

"If you agree," he said, hoping this would convince her, "then it'll be a slam dunk that Margaret will go. That will give her and John a chance to get to know each other better without expectations."

"Let me get this straight. You came here to ask me to go to a fish fry with Aunt Margaret so that your friend John can spend time with her."

"Exactly." He could see her mind spinning, searching for another angle. Alex kept a neutral expression when he said, "Margaret and John both lost their spouses a few years back. They probably could both use a little company once in a while. You admitted Margaret has done a lot for you. Surely you can do this for her, right?"

"Well…of course."

Apparently, she couldn't come up with an excuse *not* to go, and he would find a way to turn that to his advantage.

A grinning Alex said, "Great. It'll be fun. You'll see."

She seemed to choke a little before her gaze narrowed again. Her tone was dismissive when she asked, "Is that it, then?"

"For now."

Not wanting to blow what seemed to be a truce of sorts, Alex left without saying another word.

"AUNT KRISTEN!"

"Aunt Kristen!"

Kristen closed the front door of Heather's charming two-bedroom cottage and braced herself as the twins tackled her, nearly sending her flying backward.

Laughing, she stooped and gathered them to her to give them big hugs and noisy kisses on their chipmunk cheeks.

"Are you gonna take us to the park?" Addison asked. "I wanna go on the swings!"

"No! Let's make popcorn and watch *Princess Lara and the Butterflies!*"

"We watched that, like, ten times before, Taylor!"

"So? It's my favorite!"

Addison shoved Taylor. "Swings!"

Taylor shoved back. "Princess Lara!"

And Kristen stood there frozen for a moment, grateful when Heather entered the living room.

"Girls, girls, give your aunt some breathing room." She set her briefcase near the door. "Go pick out a book for her to read to you at bedtime."

"Yay!" they both yelled, running into the other room like miniature tornadoes.

Kristen laughed at herself. How could five-year-olds intimidate her? "So what do you think we should do tonight, Mom? Swings or movie? Or maybe both."

"Actually, I have another favor to ask. Would you mind taking the girls on a little shopping trip instead? FamilyMart is having a big one-day sale today and the girls need a few things."

Kristen forced a smile. "No problem." She hadn't counted on taking the twins anywhere in public. Just dealing with them in their own home was challenge enough. But if it would help Heather, of course she would do it.

"Great. I hope you don't mind switching vehicles, then. Easier than hauling the car seats from my SUV to your car."

"Right. No problem," Kristen said again.

Heather handed her an envelope. "Here's money and a list of what clothes they need with sizes. The clothes should be a little big on them. They're growing like weeds and these outfits have to last the whole season."

"Got it." Trying not to feel overwhelmed, Kristen tucked the envelope into her shoulder bag. "Go to class with an easy mind."

Heather nodded and hugged her. "Thanks. You're a lifesaver." Picking up her case, she called to the girls. "Addison…Taylor…I'm leaving now. You be good for Aunt Kristen."

The twins raced back to the entry to get hugs and kisses from their mother. Kristen thought her sister looked a little sad leaving them.

For a moment, Kristen thought of herself in this situation. She couldn't imagine not working. Still, she imagined she would be every bit as torn as Heather was.

Not that she was going to have to deal with being a mother anytime soon.

She wasn't even dating…no matter what people thought about her and Police Chief Alex Novak.

He had looked awfully cute, though, when she'd seen him that morning. And he'd actually been nice. More than nice, really. He'd been thoughtful enough to want to give his older friend and her aunt a chance to size each other up. There was more to him than she'd realized.

And his smile had been enough to make her breath catch in her throat.…

Once the front door was closed, she shook away his image and concentrated on her nieces. It took another five minutes to get them to the bathroom, dress them in clean T-shirts and strap them into their car seats.

FamilyMart was on the highway a few miles outside of Sparrow Lake. The twins alternately argued with each other and sang together, and in between asked her "how much longer," even though the ride was less than ten minutes.

It was with relief that Kristen spotted the FamilyMart sign and pulled into the lot.

Getting the girls out of the car, she held each

one's hand and cautioned them to stay with her inside the store.

That lasted for maybe five minutes.

Somewhere in the midst of looking over T-shirts, Taylor disappeared.

"Did you see where your sister went?" Kristen asked Addison.

"That way." Addison pointed.

"C'mon, let's go find her." Wielding the shopping cart with one hand, holding Addison's hand with the other, Kristen made her way back to the main aisle. "Tell me if you see her."

A moment later, Addison said, "There!"

Taylor stood amidst counters of stuffed animals, her little hand skipping over each head for a pat.

"Taylor, come back here, please," Kristen called.

The little girl glanced back at her, then picked up a black-and-white spotted stuffed horse before obeying. "Look what I got. It's Spotted Pony!"

Kristen humored her. "So it is. Very nice. But put it back so we can get those clothes for you."

Taylor's face wrinkled. "I want Spotted Pony."

"Maybe next time," Kristen said, even as crocodile tears rolled down Taylor's cheeks. Her chest tightened and she tried not to sound desperate. "Today we're just buying clothes."

"Don't *want* clothes! Want Spotted Pony!"

"*I* want clothes, Aunt Kristen," Addison said, her little face set in a smirk.

Kristen started. Was Addison trying to out-shine her sister for approval? "We'll get them in a minute, as soon as your sister puts the stuffed horse back on the table."

Her face set in a stubborn expression, Taylor threw the toy to the ground.

Kristen kept her temper with difficulty. "That's no way to treat a poor, sweet animal, and this one doesn't even belong to you."

Rather than trying to force the child to do something she probably would refuse to do, Kristen picked up the spotted horse herself and put it on the table where it belonged. Then she took Taylor's hand and pulled her back to the aisle—the little girl dragged her feet, of course—and placed the child's hand on one side of the cart.

"Hang on to that, Taylor. Don't let go."

Without prompting, Addison did the same, holding on to the other side and beaming at Kristen.

"Okay, girls, let's get back to the reason we're here."

How did her younger sister deal with the twins alone all the time? Kristen wondered. Ten minutes in the store and she was already exhausted. At least Addison was behaving herself.

She went through Heather's list, all the while keeping an eye on Taylor. At first sulky and uncooperative, the little girl got tired of being left out and was soon running around the table of T-shirts. It was all Kristen could do to get her to stop long enough to try them on.

"Can I have this one?" Addison asked.

"You can have whatever you want as long as it's a little loose on you," Kristen said.

By the time she had everything on Heather's list checked off, she was so frazzled she could hardly focus.

"Okay, we're done!" she said. "Taylor. Addison. Come on."

She kept up a good face as they headed for the cashier, but inside she just wanted to be home. Not that she could sleep until Heather returned. But she could get comfortable on the couch with the girls and read a book to them. That sounded like heaven.

The line was short and the cashier was quick. And Kristen was so grateful that she could actually imagine herself on that couch, feet up, head back, for a moment ignoring the girls squabbling.

Then it hit her as they exited the store. The girls *weren't* squabbling. That was an alarm ringing.

She hurried the twins to the SUV and strapped them into their seats after throwing the bags into the rear of the vehicle. She slid into the driver's seat as a uniformed security guard rushed out of the entrance and yelled, "Hey, lady, wait a minute!"

Glancing back toward the building, she saw another woman who'd followed them outside turn around.

Too tired to wonder what was going on, she took off.

She was just turning off the highway toward town when she saw the flashing lights of a police car behind her. Wondering who he was after, she pulled over to the right to let the vehicle pass.

Only it didn't.

The police car pulled up directly behind her, and a uniformed officer got out. *Oh, what now?* she wondered, rolling down her window. She recognized the officer from the night Alex had brought her into the station.

"Is one of the taillights out, officer?" she asked. "This is my sister's vehicle. I'll be sure to tell her right away."

"Sorry, ma'am, but you'll have to come with

me," he said. "You set off the store alarm at FamilyMart."

Horrified, Kristen said, "Me? Wait! I didn't do anything to set off an alarm."

"You'll have to tell it to the chief."

Kristen frowned. Had Alex put him up to this? And here she'd thought they'd called a truce that morning.

"Drive straight to the station," the officer said. "Just don't try to get away or there will be consequences."

"Consequences!" Addison chirped from the backseat.

Both twins were now acting like they were having a fun time, giggling and poking each other.

Feeling as if there was a black cloud over her, Kristen took a deep breath and drove. Consequences! What did the officer expect her to do? Take off for Mexico with two five-year-olds?

"I DON'T UNDERSTAND why the alarm went off," Kristen said.

Alex reached over to Addison and showed her the store tags. "Those sweaters look like the reason."

"Sweaters?"

Kristen took a good look at her niece. Addison was wearing two store sweaters she'd been trying on in FamilyMart. Kristen had been so frazzled she hadn't noticed.

"Oh, my goodness, I'm so sorry." She quickly got the contraband off her niece. "They were trying on sweaters and Addison must have forgotten to remove these."

"I didn't forget," Addison announced. "You said we could have what we wanted."

Kristen fought a rising sense of panic. "Look, I'll just pay for them now." That Alex was swallowing a smile didn't affect her, at least not in a good way. Her stomach was swirling, sending a weird sensation shooting through her. She couldn't stop herself from challenging him. "Do you enjoy bullying innocent people?"

"I'm not sure how innocent you can be when you have two sweaters you didn't pay for," he countered, his lips spreading into a big grin.

"You know, Chief, you should look into getting a job in a big city like Chicago where there are *real* criminals."

His smile quickly faded. "Okay, let's stop right there. I believe walking out of the store with those sweaters was simply a mistake. I just couldn't help myself from giving you a little grief. Sorry. And I'll keep this incident off the books if you take your niece back to the store and have her give the sweaters to the manager and apologize."

The stress that had been building in Kristen flowed right out of her. "Of course we'll do that, won't we, Addison? You'll apologize to the nice man at FamilyMart for wearing the sweaters out of the store." At least she hoped he would be nice about it. "We don't take things from stores unless we pay for them first."

Appearing stricken, Addison asked, "Am I bad?"

"No, honey." Kristen hugged Addison. "You just made a mistake. So you need to say you're sorry and you won't do that again."

"Okay."

Taylor hugged her sister, too. "You weren't bad, Addison. It was just a mistake."

Alex said. "I'll drive you all in my official patrol car."

Addison's screwed up expression cleared and both twins squealed with delight.

"Can we have the sirens on?" Taylor asked.

Addison added, "And flashing lights?"

"I'll see what I can do," Alex promised. He turned to Kristen. "That okay with you?"

Relieved that the crisis was over, Kristen said, "It's fine with me on one condition."

"Which is?"

"You figure out how to get the car seats out of the SUV and securely fastened in your patrol car. I have no clue."

CHAPTER TEN

LESS THAN A half hour later, Alex was happy the misunderstanding was straightened out. Addison had bravely made her apology through quivering lips and the manager had shaken her hand when he accepted it. Alex guessed the little girl finally realized she'd done something wrong. He felt sorry for the five-year-old, but he actually felt even sorrier for Kristen, who seemed worn out by the twins.

She was buckling in Taylor while Alex secured Addison, when Emily Auerbach walked out of the store. As usual, the mayor's wife wore a nondescript dress that looked as if it was thirty years out of date along with a sour expression that seemed frozen on her face every time they met.

Mrs. Auerbach gave them a piercing look. "Ms. Lange. Chief Novak. Arresting children now? Well, I never!" She shook her head, her hair-sprayed silver hair unmoving, and tsk-tsked as she passed. "I can't wait to see what Samuel has to say about this."

Alex didn't bother trying to explain. Mrs. Auerbach was an odd bird with even odder ideas. She seemed to like making something out of nothing. In the two years he'd been police chief, she'd made multiple complaints against various townspeople that had been a waste of his department's time. The mayor definitely needed to talk his wife down.

Again noting how exhausted Kristen seemed, he wondered how long she would be with the twins before Heather returned from class. Unless he stepped in, she would have to deal with the girls alone.

Ruffling Addison's hair, he said, "You know, you did such a great job making that apology, I think you deserve a reward for such good behavior."

"Reward?" Addison echoed, her little face brightening.

"I was thinking that maybe some ice cream—"

"Yay!" the twins yelled together.

From the open door on the other side of the vehicle, Kristen gaped at him. "Yay," she said, her voice flat.

They closed the doors and got into the vehicle.

A LITTLE DOWNTIME in the company of another adult who could help wrangle the twins gave

Kristen a chance to recoup. And Cherries On Top Ice Cream Shoppe was a cute little place she'd loved as a kid. They sat at a round glass table, the twins separated and sitting between her and Alex.

"Did someone at FamilyMart call 911 about the sweaters?" Addison suddenly asked.

Alex seemed surprised. "No. The guard called it in."

Kristen asked, "How do you know about 911?"

"Mommy told us," Taylor said.

"Mommy said it's for 'mergencies," Addison added. "She showed us how."

"Your mother is correct," Alex said. "Calling 911 *is* for emergencies. You only call it when someone is in trouble and needs help."

Both twins nodded, but Kristen wondered if they were old enough to understand what that meant.

Alex changed the subject. "So now that you have your new clothes, are you ready to start school next month?"

"Yes!" Taylor shouted. "Kiddygarden!"

"Oh, kindergarten." Alex sounded impressed. "That must mean you're what? *Four?*"

"Five!" Addison told him with a giggle.

"What are you going to learn?"

"To read!"

Taylor said, "I can read Spotted Pony."

"No, she can't." Addison rolled her eyes. "Mommy reads it to us so much that Taylor mem-rized it."

"Did not!"

"Did, too!"

For a moment, Kristen feared they would start another shoving match.

"You know what," Alex said. "I'll bet it's both. Memorizing words helps you remember them when you see and hear them at the same time."

"Oh." Addison licked the ice cream off her spoon.

That easily, Alex avoided a confrontation. Kristen was impressed. While the twins seemed to have energy, Kristen could tell they were tired, too. Alex had such an easy way about him when dealing with the twins that they actually behaved—well, so far—undoubtedly because they liked him a lot.

Kristen had to admit that she did, too. Why had she fought so hard against getting to know him? She enjoyed his company. Admired the way he thought about others. And he really was a fine-looking man. She was admiring his chiseled features when he caught her staring. His mouth curled into a slow smile that sent a jolt through her. The spoon she aimed at her mouth missed and chocolate ice cream dribbled down her chin.

Flushing with embarrassment, she grabbed a napkin, but before she could repair the damage, Taylor said, "Aunt Kristen spilled her ice cream!"

Not only did they laugh at her, but she heard snickers from somewhere nearby. And Alex was biting back his own laughter. In the end, she laughed at herself.

Alex's grin made him look even more attractive. "You should do that more often."

"Spill ice cream on myself?"

"No, laugh," Alex said. "You have a nice laugh."

Flushing again, she met his gaze and felt a real warmth inside. Why had it taken so long for her to admit she was attracted to him? From his actions, the attraction was mutual.

As if they were mentally in tune, he said, "I'm taking tomorrow afternoon off so I can go into Lake Geneva to pick up a window I'm having repaired."

She arched her eyebrows. "A window? Were you trying to break in somewhere?" she teased. "And why didn't you fix it yourself? I seem to remember you're good at that."

"And you have a good imagination," he said, grinning. "But it's a stained-glass window from a transom over my kitchen door. It's needed fixing since I bought the place. No one around here does that kind of work. If you can play hooky that afternoon, maybe you'd like to come with me for the drive."

That he wanted her company made her smile. It wouldn't be a long drive—less than an hour each way—but it would be pleasant to spend that time alone with him. Why not, then? Having one afternoon off wouldn't hurt anything. She looked at the twins. Alex had taken his own time to help her with them. She would make up the hours at the store during the rest of the week.

"All right. I'll go with you."

"Great."

The twins had finished their ice cream, and it was time to drop them off at home.

A half hour of relaxation and laughter had done her a world of good. Not to mention being able to look forward to a date with Alex. Holding hands with both girls as they headed for the patrol car, she realized she actually felt happy... a feeling that had eluded her for months while her life had spun out of control. But things were changing...shaping up...and Alex was partly responsible.

They secured the girls in their car seats and Kristen slid into the passenger seat. Relaxed, she sighed and laid her head against the headrest as Alex drove out of the parking lot.

"Thanks for your help tonight, Chief."

"Alex," he reminded her, finding her hand and giving it a warm squeeze.

Kristen felt happiness bubble up in her. "I meant your official help with the manager of FamilyMart. And thanks, *Alex,* for the ice cream break. I definitely needed to wind down."

He gave her a quick glance that warmed her inside again. "My pleasure."

She was so relaxed that she was actually wondering where this connection with Alex might lead when he said, "I don't know if you heard, but there was another incident in town last night."

His words chilled the smile right off her face. "Oh?"

"Yep. I didn't know about it when I talked to you before, but some teenagers used chalk to draw graffiti on the back wall of the old gas station at the edge of town. That's a little more serious than a harmless prank. The building is stucco and the chalk didn't wash out with a hose. The owner had to spend hours scrubbing that stuff off to get rid of it. He's really ticked."

Though Kristen was certain she knew the answer, she asked, "Why are you telling me about it?"

"Just wondering if you know where Brian was in the middle of the night."

Of course. Brian, again. This time she wasn't angry, the way she'd been the first time he'd brought it up. She didn't believe Alex made accusations willy-nilly. In fact, she was starting to worry there might be a basis to his suspicion.

Still, she said, "My brother was in his bed sleeping."

"You know that for sure?"

Actually, she didn't. She remembered a noise waking her. She hadn't been able to identify it and hadn't heard it again. She'd figured someone had gotten up to go to the bathroom or to the kitchen for an early-morning snack. It could have been Brian sneaking inside in the early hours.

Not that she was going to share that information with Alex. Not yet.

Somehow she was first going to have to find out if something was going on.

KRISTEN WANTED TO believe in Brian, but she was wary of his friends and couldn't help wondering if they were all responsible for the recent pranks Alex kept telling her about.

The problem was, how could she know for certain if her brother was involved?

By the time she got home, it was nearly eleven, and Aunt Margaret had already retired to her room. There was no sign of Brian, not in the living area, not in his room. She opened the door to check. The bed was as messy as the rest of the room, but there was no sign that he'd been there recently. The room was dark and still except for the light indicating his laptop was fully charged.

His laptop...

Kristen moved to the desk and stood staring down at the computer, torn between respect for her brother's privacy and worry that he was headed down a slippery slope. She didn't want to believe Brian was acting out, doing things that were questionable as Alex had indicated, but she would be a fool if she didn't consider that the police chief could be correct.

In the end, worry won.

Brian was always using his smartphone for social networking. She decided to try to figure out where that networking had led.

When she lifted the lid of the laptop, the monitor awoke immediately. She scanned the icons on the desktop and spotted a big BS in red. She knew that BS stood for BuddyShare Network, one of the new social networking sites. Hesitating only a second, she clicked on the program icon, half expecting she would need a password to get in.

To her surprise, she didn't.

Brian's recent life unfolded before her. Photographs and amusing graphics from the internet. A calendar that had his schedule at the store. That he'd taken her advice certainly surprised her. But the calendar also had some kind of coded entries that all took place at night.

Taking a deep breath, Kristen started to read the entries.

Nothing startling in the last few. It looked like a bunch of college students or soon-to-be college students were sharing the trials and tribulations of college life.

But in the left column, there was an item called PrivateTalk. And below that, a link that simply said SL.

Meaning Sparrow Lake?

Clicking on it, she saw there were only three buddies with code names. Brainiac, Hollowboy and Muscleman. Brainiac—Brian because he was the smartest? Hollowboy—Andy because he was so skinny? Muscleman—Matt because he was the big guy of the trio?

The last entry was from Hollowboy: *Meet at our usual time and place. Got some new ideas that'll be fun.*

So Brian had gone to the usual place, wherever that was. And what was the usual time? When had Brian left the house? It seemed to her that he must slip out after he thought it was safe—after she and Aunt Margaret retired for the night.

More importantly, what kind of ideas did Andy have? she wondered, as she continued to read down the page. There were several entries between the three boys that made the hair on her arms stand up.

Brainiac: *Ignore them.*

Muscleman: *Parents were invented to give us grief.*

Hollowboy: *We can do what we want, when we want.*

It was a little weird reading in reverse order, so Kristen went to the bottom of the page and read upward, in the order the messages had been relayed. The boys talked as if they thought they were hotshots, suggesting that they could fool everyone and as long as they didn't get caught, who cared.

Caught doing what?

Though she scrolled to other pages, she got nothing specific from the conversations. Just these vague entries about things happening and how they could have a good laugh.

Deeply upset, Kristen exited the program, and when the desktop reappeared on the monitor, she closed the lid.

Brian would never know she'd been snooping. She couldn't lose his trust or she might lose him. She had to talk to him, though, she thought, heading for the kitchen where she would lie in wait for him to come home.

She had to get through to her brother before he did something that he would regret, something he couldn't take back.

BRIAN SNEAKED INTO the house through the lakeside door, the same way he'd left. He tiptoed through the living room, careful not to knock into furniture the way he had the night before. He made it to the hallway before he heard a noise.

Pulse rushing, he stopped to listen. Nothing. He must have imagined it. No one was going to be awake in the middle of the night.

He continued on toward his room and was almost there before realizing someone was standing in his way. Just enough light filtered through the windows that he could make out her form.

"Kristen?"

"Brian. In the kitchen, please."

"I'm going to bed. I'm tired—"

"I'll bet you are. It's 3:00 a.m."

He shrugged and kept his voice casual like it was no big deal. "So what? I'm on vacation."

"Kitchen."

Brian wanted to argue, to push past his sister into his room, but he just couldn't. He turned and led the way, snapping on the kitchen lights, telling himself his sister didn't have any power over him. She'd been out of his life practically since he was a kid and she went away to school. Her being around now didn't make up for those missing years.

Besides, what could she do to him? He was practically an adult.

No matter what, Aunt Margaret would be on his side. At least he could always count on her.

Crossing through the kitchen, he tried to think about what he was going to say. Even if his sister didn't have any power over him, his stomach was churning.

Why wasn't Kristen saying anything? She was staring at him, and he prepared himself for an argument.

He sat at the island as far away from Kristen as he could manage. Still she didn't speak.

Finally, he mumbled, "I thought you wanted to talk."

"I do. I'm worried about you, Brian."

"Sure you are." Because she'd spent so much time with him before Mom got remarried and then moved him to California whether or not he wanted to go.

"Brian, we may not have been close distance-wise in the past few years, but that doesn't change anything. You're my kid brother and I love you."

Uncomfortable now, he muttered, "And?"

"And I don't want to see you making a mistake—"

"Well, just don't worry about me, Kristen. Another couple months and I'll be legal."

"I'll always worry about you, Brian. I only want good things for you. For all of us."

He wasn't going to let her get to him. He got up to leave, asking, "Is that it?"

Her "No, Brian, it isn't" stopped him. "You know there's a midnight curfew for anyone under eighteen. If you get picked up—"

"But I won't be."

"Brian, please. What could you possibly be doing out so late? This isn't a big city where things stay open all night."

"I'm just hanging with my friends."

"Where?"

"Around."

"That's not good enough, Brian. You can't keep doing this."

His pulse began to tick faster. Did she know? "Doing what?"

"You tell me."

"I don't have to tell you anything, Kristen. You're my sister, not my mother!"

"You want me to call Mom?"

"You wouldn't!"

If she did, Mom might make him fly back to California, and then he'd have to deal with the man she'd married again. Mike tried to act like he was his father...telling him what to do, how to act. In one fell swoop, Brian had gone from being the man of the house as Mom had told him so often, to being nothing but a kid who annoyed the new husband.

"Look, Brian, I don't want to be the bad guy here." Kristen stepped close to him and touched his cheek. "I just want to make sure you're safe and that you don't do anything foolish that will get you into trouble."

Brian clenched his jaw and pulled his head away. "I'm not in trouble!" And he wasn't falling for her nice routine.

It sounded as if she did know what he and his friends had been doing, but for some reason she wasn't saying so. So what if she knew? He hadn't done anything wrong. Not really. He and Andy and Matt had just been messing with people's heads. They hadn't wrecked anything....

"I don't want to see you get arrested," Kristen said.

"I haven't hurt anyone or stolen anything."

"What *have* you been doing in the middle of the night?"

"Nothing!" He tore away from her and headed for the door. "If you don't have anything else to say, I'm going to bed now."

"Brian, wait, please. If something is troubling you, if you need to talk, remember you can always come to me with anything."

Fat chance.

The last thing in the world he'd do was give his by-the-book sister ammunition against him.

CHAPTER ELEVEN

"It's a PERFECT day to play hooky," Alex said, when he opened the car door for Kristen.

Kristen admired the sleek black Jaguar convertible parked in front of Sew Fine. It looked like an older model, though it seemed to be in perfect condition. "Is this yours?"

"It is," he said as she slipped into the low passenger seat. "Why do you seem so surprised?"

"I've only seen you driving your patrol car."

He swung her door shut. "But now I'm off the job."

If he'd been on the job every time she'd seen him in the past week, he must be working as many hours as she was.

Kristen wiggled into the cushioned leather seat and buckled her seat belt, then glanced back at the store window where employees and customers alike watched. Heather's face pulled into a big grin. Her sister had practically done a happy dance when Kristen had told her where she was going that afternoon. Good grief, they were just picking up Alex's repaired window and having dinner before driving back to Sparrow Lake. It wasn't like this was a big deal date or anything.

Still, when Alex got behind the wheel, buckled himself in and started the engine, Kristen couldn't help the flutter of expectation that ran through her veins. His light brown hair brushed his sunglasses, making him look more casual than usual. And more attractive. For once, he'd completely shed his police persona. She liked it.

"You don't mind if I leave the top down, do you?" Alex asked.

"You're kidding. Don't you dare put up the top on such a gorgeous day!"

He grinned at her. "Just trying to be considerate. Some women don't like getting their hair messed up from the wind."

"Just drive." She was looking forward to feeling the wind in her hair.

A warm summer breeze rustled the air as they took off down the street and headed out of town. But when they passed a trio of teenagers riding furiously on their bikes, Kristen's excitement at having a fun afternoon warred with her continuing worry over her brother. Her stomach swirled as she thought about her early morning conversation with Brian. She'd tried to keep the conversation as nonconfrontational as she could. She hadn't wanted to accuse him of anything, rather had tried to get him to volunteer information.

And he hadn't bitten.

Had she approached her brother the wrong way? She wanted him to feel free to come to her, to tell her what was on his mind.

Wishing she could talk to Alex about Brian, she didn't know how to bring up the subject. She'd given him a hard time in the past when he'd tried warning her. Besides, Brian hadn't confirmed anything. Her brother's BuddyShare Network page worried her, but the boys had been vague about what they'd been up to. She'd found no proof of any actual wrongdoing.

They were on the highway headed for Lake Geneva before Alex said, "Are you okay?"

When he glanced at her as if to see for himself, she gave him a big smile. "I'm fine." A small fib. She shoved her worry about Brian to the back of her mind, determined to enjoy the afternoon no matter what. "Just relaxing and soaking up the fresh air, something I can't do in the shop."

It was a perfect day for an outing. Kristen was glad she'd dressed down—white capris, yellow sweater set and beige walking sandals. *Sorry, Manolo Blahnik and Jimmy Choo. Can't deal with your four-inch heels today.* Knowing she would want to explore Lake Geneva on foot—she hadn't been there since she was in high school but remembered it as a fun walking town—Kristen had decided to wear practical footwear, for once.

Alex turned on the radio. "Any particular music you like?"

A classic rock piece was playing.

"Great guitar. That's my kind of music."

Alex nodded. "Even if it was recorded before we were born."

Laughing together felt good.

So did talking about preferences—not only music, but movies and art. She was enjoying getting to know Alex a little better. They had more in common than she'd ever imagined. She couldn't believe how quickly the time passed. Before she knew it, they were in Lake Geneva and parking in back of a building a block off Main Street.

Glasstique took up the whole lower level, so it was large enough to display everything from stained-glass windows to hand-blown carafes to fused-glass jewelry. While Alex spoke to the owner, Kristen checked out the place. Aunt Margaret loved any kind of art, so Kristen looked for something that her modest budget would allow and found a thick, multi-colored glass teardrop that would look great hung in one of the windows that overlooked the lake.

She was taking it to the counter when the owner brought out the stained-glass transom for Alex's inspection, and Kristen had a chance to admire the piece with its beveled glass and leading.

"Gorgeous," she said.

"And a great job making it look new again," Alex told the owner, who placed it in a protective frame.

A few minutes later, they were back at the car, carefully putting their packages in the trunk.

"Walk or drive to the lakefront?" he asked.

"Walk. That way I get to poke my head in all the stores."

Alex was quite a good sport about it, Kristen thought. He came inside each store she wanted to check out. Not that she bought anything for herself. Still, she enjoyed the diversion as they made their way toward the lake.

They were getting along so well, she could hardly remember why they'd ever been at odds.

"THIS REMINDS ME of the view I had from my apartment balcony," Kristen said with a sigh. They had just finished dinner on an outside terrace of Geneva Lake Manor, a century-old

mansion that had been turned into a popular restaurant, and were coming down the stairs, facing
the lake on the other side of the street. "I used
to eat out there whenever possible. Of course,
my apartment was quite a bit higher up. Eigh-
teenth floor."

"I can understand why you would miss it,"
Alex said, though he thought this view was
pretty spectacular.

They were crossing the street not far from the
pier where the tour boats docked. Motorboats
cut through the bay and farther out, he spotted
several sailboats.

"I miss everything about Chicago," Kristen
said. "I wonder how long it'll take me to find
another job there."

Alex couldn't help wondering why Kristen
was so hung up on getting back to the big city.
He checked his watch. "How about a sunset boat
ride before heading back to Sparrow Lake—that
is, if you're up for that sort of thing."

"What? You mean drooling over all the fabulous lakeside estates from the water? Hmm. I
think I can handle that."

"Great."

The sun was low over the far end of the lake
as they approached the pier. Shards of gold and
red cut through the sky. A breeze skipped over

the water, ruffling her hair. Kristen lifted her face and Alex's chest tightened at the thought of just being with her. A sunset cruise would be the perfect way to end a perfect day.

Their timing was perfect, too. The boat was scheduled to leave the dock in five minutes, and since it was a weekday there were tickets left. Alex quickly bought them and escorted her onto the half-empty boat as the crew got set to shove off.

They found two seats near the prow, and when the boat started its tour of the bay, Kristen sighed. "It's like being in another world."

Alex continued their conversation. "I'm not from a small town, Kristen. I lived my whole life in Chicago until two years ago. That's when I moved to Wisconsin."

He could see that surprised her.

"Why did you choose Sparrow Lake?"

"My grandfather was from Sparrow Lake. Our family used to visit him for a couple of weeks each summer. I always loved the town, but I never thought about moving there until a few years ago. My immediate family—my brother and his wife and kids included—lives in Chicago, and ever since I was a teenager, I wanted to be a cop behind the wheel of a blue-and-white."

"What changed your mind?"

"Actually *being* on the job in the inner city. I worked in a gang unit, and I saw all those kids with wasted lives."

She nodded. "That had to be tough."

"More so than you can imagine. I wanted to make a difference, Kristen, and by the time we got to those kids, it was too late for them. They get on the wrong road young in gang territory. Nine. Ten."

"You must have seen some terrible things."

"Unfortunately. And when we caught the offenders, they'd crossed so many lines that it meant jailing them or worse rather than giving them a chance." He couldn't talk about the incident that had made him leave Chicago—it still made his gut clench and his heart pound every time he thought about that kid. "It became too much for me, and I started wondering what it would be like working in a smaller police department where I could actually make a difference."

The farther they got from the dock, the more elaborate the lakeside homes became. Some were modest in size and architecture, but many were multimillion-dollar mansions with incredible landscaping. They overshadowed the homes on Sparrow Lake, making even Margaret Becker's look humble in comparison.

"I thought about moving to Sparrow Lake

because a local cop steered me back onto the straight path one summer when I was a kid headed for trouble." And they hadn't just been playing innocent pranks, he remembered. "The police chief was a friend of Grandpa's. He took me in hand, straightened me out, made me want to be like him."

Kristen said, "Growing up, my brother never had a male figure to set an example for him. Brian was a little kid when our father abandoned us. He was always a good kid, though. Then Mom met her new husband and I guess Brian resented a stranger suddenly in his life, telling him what to do, trying to father him. That's why, after he graduated high school, Mom sent him back to Wisconsin to go to college. But if he really has gotten himself into trouble…"

Realizing Kristen was vulnerable where her family was concerned, Alex said, "Brian is lucky to have someone like you in his corner, but you need to be realistic about what is going on in town." He hoped she was ready for some straight talk. He didn't want to see Brian waste his life, and he didn't want to see the heartbreak on Kristen's face if her brother got into hot water. "If Brian is heading himself for trouble, then you may be the only one who can get him to straighten out."

Silent for a moment, she hesitantly said, "You can't ever let him know I did this, but…" She took a big breath and went on. "I got hold of his computer and looked at his BS page."

"He admitted to something in writing?"

Shaking her head, she said, "The conversation with his friends was vague, full of boasting and seemingly empty threats, but it was enough to make me uncomfortable. And concerned. I realized something weird was going on. So I waited up for him. He didn't come home until three. I asked him where he'd been, what he and his friends had been doing out so late." She sighed. "Of course he gave me nothing but vague answers. I told him that I was concerned, and that if he needed to talk, I would be there for him."

Alex was glad she'd finally believed him enough to pursue it. "Sometimes being there is all you can do. That and keeping an eye on Brian and his friends. You can always let me know if you suspect something might be wrong before the situation gets worse."

She thought about that for a moment before saying, "They've just been playing pranks, though, right?"

"So far. My fear is that they're going to cross the line, and because there are some truly bad people around, even in the small towns in this neck of the woods, I want to channel those negative energies into something positive before anyone gets into serious trouble."

"I'll do what I can. I just don't know what'll happen to my brother once I move back to Chicago. Heather already has too much responsibility. And it wouldn't be fair to heap this on Aunt Margaret's shoulders."

There it was again—Chicago—the thing that threatened to stand in the way of developing a real relationship with her. Alex would never return to the gang violence and misery he faced in the big city, but Kristen seemed determined to go back.

How could they ever have the relationship that he was just beginning to think was possible if she got a job that took her away from Sparrow Lake? Was it just her career or something else luring her back?

That idea threatened his good mood.

He couldn't let it happen, Alex thought. To his surprise, he realized he was developing feelings for her, and he thought they could have something good together.

He would just have to find a way to convince Kristen she didn't want to leave Sparrow Lake.

Or him.

WHEN THE BOAT circled the bay to run along the bluff on the opposite shore, Kristen moved to the railing for a better look at the estates. Alex joined her. The occasional fine spray of lake water felt great. So did Alex's arm casually draped across her back. Being in the shelter of his arm felt so right. Why had she been keeping him at a distance?

She gazed up into his eyes. "I want to thank you, Alex. This has been a beautiful day. The most relaxing that I've spent in a long time."

"No regrets?"

"What's to regret?"

He grinned at her. "Playing instead of working."

Kristen laughed. "I do occasionally take time off to play. I mean, I used to in Chicago."

"Alone?" When she gave him a puzzled look, he said, "I was just wondering if the reason you're so anxious to get back to Chicago is that you have someone special waiting for you."

A few weeks ago, that question might have bothered her. "Not anymore."

"Oh. Sorry. Sounds like it was serious."

"I thought it was. And I mistakenly believed Jason thought so. But someone who cares about you stands by you when you're in trouble. My worries about not finding a job, going through my savings and losing my condo were all too much for him."

"This Jason broke it off with you because you were in trouble? Not much of a man. You're well rid of him."

"Especially since he said it was for my own good, because I was simply too dependent on him."

"Wow. Nice guy. You, dependent? You're the most independent woman I've ever met."

"Thanks." She grinned at him. "I think. What about you?" She knew he wasn't married, but she had no idea if he was seeing someone else.

"Unfortunately, my wife divorced me over the job."

Kristen started at that. She searched Alex's face, but his expression remained neutral. To hide his feelings? Or because it didn't matter anymore?

"So you were married," she said, keeping her voice even. "Did you...do you have kids?" Is that why he'd been so natural with her nieces?

"No, Emma couldn't handle being a cop's wife. The marriage only lasted five months."

"I'm so sorry, Alex. That had to have been devastating."

"I've been over it for a long time. Over Emma. It was one of those whirlwind romances. We married too fast, before we really knew each other. I'm not interested in the past. I'm looking to my future."

And he was looking directly into her eyes.

Kristen's pulse began to thrum as his head inched closer and his features went all blurry. Her heart bumped against her ribs and her throat felt tight.

Why had she fought this? she wondered again, even as she wet her lips and parted them. She'd thought she couldn't get involved with someone who lived in Sparrow Lake when she was planning on leaving at the first great job opportunity. But why not?

Her thoughts got muddled when his mouth found hers.

Her breath stopped for a moment. Then she sighed and lifted her arms and wrapped them around his neck. She gave over to the moment and kissed Alex back. She indulged in a long, sweet, warm, tantalizing kiss.

What was the harm in dating a man she genuinely liked? She wasn't gone yet. She had time before she made another change. Why spend it alone?

Something that felt so good…so right…just couldn't be a mistake.

CHAPTER TWELVE

LATE ON WEDNESDAY night, Brian waited for his friends in a small park on the south side of town. He sat on one of the swings and toed his sneaker into the dirt, moving himself back and forth. He was still angry about the confrontation he'd had with Kristen a couple of nights ago and wondered if it had anything to do with that cop she'd been hanging out with. He'd seen Novak drop his sister off at the house yesterday. The police chief was probably filling her head with lies, just as his stepfather filled his mom's head with them. Just thinking about that had made him want to pull another prank as soon as he and his pals had a chance.

At a scuffling sound, he stiffened, then saw Matt's bulk slip out of the shadows followed by the skinnier form of Andy. "Hey, dudes."

"Hey, man," said Matt.

"Have any idea where we'll hit tonight?" asked Matt.

"I noticed that the Richardses don't even have a deadbolt on their diner. It's not far from here."

Off the main drag, too. Maybe the cops wouldn't be driving by so often.

"What are we going to do? Spray the place?" Andy asked.

"Nah, just move some things around." Brian always tried to limit the vandalism. Annoy and confound, not infuriate or scare. "Maybe help ourselves to a piece of pie."

"Let's go." Andy took off, keeping to the shadows.

They traveled the alleys, as usual, and the shady areas unlit by streetlights. Being on foot was better than driving a car. In a small town, late at night, it was far easier for the police to notice a car driving past than three young guys running or walking. Luckily, the cops of Sparrow Lake weren't too smart and were never going to catch them, Brian told himself. Besides, he and his posse were just having a little fun and showing everyone they could do what they wanted.

When they got to the diner, Brian used a plastic card on the back door. It took a couple of swipes to get it open.

"Whoo!" yelled Matt, dancing around when they got inside. "This place looks like *Happy Days* or something.

"A shabby version," Brian agreed. Paint peeled on one of the walls and some of the chrome chairs were patched in places. Even in the dim light, he could see permanent scuff marks on the linoleum floor. But the long lunch counter was clean and the dishes and menus and other items were all stacked neatly on shelves. "Richards and his wife are both old enough to retire. I heard they just keep this place open to have something to do." According to Aunt Margaret, anyway.

"I wish they had a jukebox," said Matt.

"Yeah, right, all we'd need is more noise," said Brian, disapproving of Matt scraping a chair around. "Settle down, will you?"

"So what shall we do? Break dishes?"

"No!" Matt could be a real bonehead. "Just take 'em and stack 'em somewhere else. Maybe let's set the tables. Something they don't expect. Move the glassware to the other side of the restaurant."

They got busy setting the tables.

Matt grabbed a ketchup bottle. "How about emptying some of this on a table?"

"Too much of a mess." They'd caused more trouble at the service station than he'd intended, and he didn't want things getting out of hand. He looked around. "Where's Andy?"

"I dunno. Andy?" Matt called.

"Shhh!" Brian cautioned him.

Matt lowered his voice to a hoarse whisper, "Andy? Where are you?"

Now Brian could hear the splatter of grease, like something was cooking. He took out his flashlight and moved around the counter, deeper into the kitchen. "Andy?"

A grunt answered him and his flashlight beam slid across the back of his pal standing at the grill. More grease spattered.

"What are you doing?"

"Cooking some burgers. Want one?"

"No, we don't have time to cook burgers." Sheesh, food always seemed to be the number one item on Andy's mind.

"They're almost done." Andy picked up a plate with an open bun. He used a spatula to flip the patties onto it. Then he picked up the burger and took a gigantic bite.

Matt came up behind Brian. "Food. All he's going to do is eat now." He asked Brian, "What else should we do?"

Brian watched Andy annihilate the burgers with a few more bites. As before, he was amazed anyone could eat so much, so fast. He whispered, "Is he starving or something?"

"Well..." Matt seemed reluctant to explain. "I don't think he gets enough to eat, ya know?

When he comes over to my house, he scarfs just about everything in the refrigerator."

Brian had noticed that when Andy was at his place. "He acts like he has a tapeworm."

Andy opened the refrigerator and rummaged around. He took out some potatoes, which he munched on, skins and all. Then he ducked into the refrigerator again.

Matt kept his voice low. "His family is homeless."

"Homeless?"

Shocked into silence, Brian remembered Andy's family lived in a small but adequate house. But he'd never visited the place since returning to town. He'd just assumed things were the same.

"Next thing to homeless anyway. His dad left Sparrow Lake looking for a job and his mom works part-time at the motel over by the highway," Matt explained. "They live in a room there, too."

"All five of them in a motel room?" Andy had two sisters and a younger brother, Brian remembered.

"He says they like it. They get all the old rolls and stuff after the motel breakfast is over. Hey, it's better than the car, especially in winter."

"Were they living out of a car?"

"For a while."

"Why didn't you mention this before?"

"He don't like to talk about it."

So the family was virtually homeless and living in a motel on part-time wages. No wonder Andy was always so hungry.

A pair of passing headlights suddenly flitted across the wall, making Brian jump. "The police?"

"I don't think so," grunted Matt.

The car disappeared down the street.

"Whatever. We should leave." He scooped up the menus and hid them under a big toaster in the kitchen. "Let's go."

"Mmmmp." Andy appeared, carrying a pie from which he'd spooned out a big mouthful. Chewing, he asked. "I thought we were all gonna have a piece."

"Bring the pie with you. We've got to get out of here." Brian moved toward the door. He opened and closed it carefully behind them. Then all three of them slid off into the night.

Brian hadn't intended for them to steal anything, but a pie and a couple of burgers surely wouldn't hurt anyone. Especially when a guy like Andy really needed something to eat. Or maybe he was going to take the pie to his family. Brian couldn't stand the thought of someone he knew going hungry. And not just Andy but his kid sisters and brother, too. Didn't small towns have food banks or something for starving, homeless people?

Not that it was any of his business, Brian decided.

Not that he could forget about it....

ON THURSDAY, A COUPLE of women from Gloria's quilting class came by the store to look at fabric for a special project they were creating. Kristen didn't ask for specifics because she wasn't a permanent member of the group. At least, that's what she told herself.

After examining the material, however, Laurie and Nellie started talking about the strange things that had happened at the Richardses' diner the night before. Kristen couldn't help but move close enough to listen in.

"The Richards are my neighbors," Laurie Jamison said. "Elsa Richards was extremely upset. She told me there was no evidence of a break-in, but about half the tables were set with plates. And a cherry pie was stolen."

"A cherry pie?" Gloria quirked her brows. "That's odd."

"I guess some other food was missing, too," Laurie went on. "I'm not sure. Elsa said she might not have noticed the pie but she had just baked it that morning."

Kristen listened carefully as she scrolled through some sewing goods sites on her laptop. She had a bad feeling. She only hoped the pranksters didn't include Brian, but she feared the worst. Up late, mulling over an email from a former colleague about a hot lead on a new job, she'd had trouble sleeping after going to bed and had gotten up to fix some chamomile tea. When she returned to her suite, she'd heard several thumps in the hallway. Brian must have sneaked in the lakeside door again.

"Why would someone set the tables?" asked Gloria. "That's weird."

"To try to spook people, make them nervous," said Laurie.

"Ha, don't feel spooked," growled Nellie Martin. "We aren't dealing with ghosts or anything strange. The culprits are flesh and blood just like me and you. I haven't talked much about it, but someone broke into my store, too."

"Really?" said Gloria.

"It was the same as the Richardses—no evidence of a break-in."

"What happened?" Laurie asked. "Was anything stolen?"

"No, thank goodness. But whoever did it

thought they were real funny. Dressed the mannequins in crazy colors and styles. One of them was wearing lingerie on the outside of her clothes."

"Lingerie?" Gloria's lips curved, then she seemed to repress the smile that had started. "Doesn't Madonna do that in real life?"

Nellie shook her head disapprovingly. "We're lucky if celebrities these days—and the kids that want to be like them—wear anything at all. But I certainly don't try to appeal to that kind of customer. I reported the incident to Chief Novak, but I don't know whether he believed me or not. He asked me about my eyesight and suggested I might have forgotten that I dressed the mannequins like that myself."

Despite herself, Kristen swallowed a nervous giggle. She could just hear Alex's dry, sarcastic tone in her imagination. Laurie turned to glance at her.

"You do wear large glasses, dear," Gloria told Nellie. "They magnify your eyes a bit, too. Are they strong?"

"Not that strong or I wouldn't be able to sew!" snapped Nellie.

Gloria stepped back, obviously surprised by the older woman's offended tone. "Well, of course not," she said in a soothing voice. "You stitch beautifully."

Emily Auerbach came in, looking a bit flustered, as usual.

"Alex Novak is a nice man overall, but he was wrong in that instance," said Nellie. "And I'm going to put in a deadbolt."

"Chief Novak?" Emily Auerbach pursed her lips nervously and grasped her purse tightly. "I wouldn't say the police chief is so nice. Why, I saw him arresting little children the other day."

All the women turned toward the mayor's wife and Kristen felt impelled to jump in. "Alex does not arrest children!"

Now the women turned to her. Kristen had been frazzled that day, but she remembered Mrs. Auerbach wandering by and had thought she'd been joking about the arresting children remark. It seemed that the eccentric woman had misinterpreted the incident.

"Alex didn't arrest my little nieces," she said emphatically. "He took them for a ride in the police car because they were upset, and he was trying to help." She rushed on, "I was the one who did something wrong that day. I was taking care of the twins and I let Addison walk out of FamilyMart with a couple of sweaters we didn't pay for. I didn't know she had them on."

Everyone remained silent. Mrs. Auerbach cleared her throat.

"Alex took us back to the store so Addison could apologize to the manager. She didn't know what she was doing." Kristen added, "And I certainly didn't know what I was doing, either. I'm not used to dealing with kids."

Gloria's hearty laugh relaxed everyone but Emily Auerbach. "Of course not. You have to watch children constantly. My Jackie is twelve now, thank goodness, but we had a few incidents ourselves when she was small." She shook her head and sighed. "When you look back at it years later, though, it's pretty funny."

"It's great that you try to help out your sister, Kristen," Laurie said.

"Thanks." Kristen looked directly at Mrs. Auerbach. "Anyway, Alex most definitely wouldn't arrest children."

"If you say so. I notice he's used his position to push you around, too, Ms. Lange."

Oops. Kristen didn't want to explain that she fully suspected Alex of enforcing some less than significant rules to get to know her better. "Well, uh, he just wanted to make sure I was aware of the laws in town."

Gloria gave her a knowing smile that Kristen wasn't sure she appreciated. Had the women been gossiping about her and Alex?

"He fixed the window that I broke," Kristen pointed out. She'd told the group about what happened the first week she met them. "He honestly cares about the safety of our citizens." He cared about many things, something she appreciated.

Nellie nodded. "At heart, he's a nice man."

"I agree," said Gloria. "He's a *very* nice man."

Kristen said nothing, focusing closely on her computer in hopes the conversation would change. It did, the women segueing back into a discussion of the project they were working on. She had been surprised at her own vehemence coming to Alex's defense when Mrs. Auerbach complained about him. She picked up her laptop and returned to the front desk, thinking about Alex. He could annoy her one minute and charm her the next. She found him quite intriguing in addition to being attractive, and he obviously felt the same.

So why didn't that make her happy? She guessed thinking about him so much made their relationship seem more intense than it was.

Kristen frowned, logging into her personal email. Yet again, she looked at the message about the job prospect she was considering. Her colleague urged her to contact the Chicago company and send them her résumé as soon as possible. She shouldn't be dragging her feet. As a young girl, after suffering through her family's problems—a dreamer of a father who couldn't be responsible and a mother burdened with meaningless, part-time jobs—Kristen had vowed she was going to be a big success. She was going to make lots of money in the big city. Coming back to Sparrow Lake made her feel like a failure.

Yet now that another opportunity had come up, after months of searching, she had mixed feelings about pursuing it.

The handsome police chief most certainly had something to do with that.

CHAPTER THIRTEEN

KRISTEN ROSE EARLY on Sunday morning to help her aunt bake several dozen rolls. The house smelled heavenly.

"You never go empty-handed to an event in a small town," Margaret told her. "But this will be enough for both of us."

While they packed the rolls into containers, Kristen thought about the résumé she'd finally sent out that morning. She'd also answered another email from a newspaper reporter who wanted to interview her about Sew Fine—a follow-up from publicity releases she'd sent out. She was happy about the latter but still more thoughtful than excited about the job opportunity.

"Alex should be here any minute, right?" asked Margaret. He had volunteered to pick up both of them.

"He's usually on time."

"You already know his habits, hmm?"

Margaret raised her brows meaningfully, making Kristen wonder who was setting up whom.

Supposedly, she was fixing her aunt up with John McClintock today. From the way her aunt was acting, though, Margaret thought Alex and her niece spending more time together was just peachy.

She *had* had a good time with Alex in Lake Geneva, Kristen thought, remembering their parting kiss. She shivered. However, she didn't think it was a good idea to have her head completely turned around when she was looking for a new job and trying to figure out what else to do with her life.

The doorbell rang and Margaret ran to answer it. "Alex! We're ready. Wow, is that our ride? Pretty snazzy." She obviously approved of the Jaguar convertible.

Kristen turned out the kitchen light and scooped up the large containers. She felt Alex's warm gaze sweep over her as they went out the door.

"Can I help you with those?" he asked.

"Sure, thank you."

The day was beautiful, bright and sunny but with a cool breeze. Light glinted off the lake as they drove toward downtown. Alex looked handsome in a dark blue T-shirt and jeans. Kristen had chosen to wear casual khakis, a matching summer-weight sweater and a casual pair of designer wedges.

"It looks like half the town is at this party," mused Aunt Margaret as they neared the fish and tackle store. Cars lined the nearby blocks and filled a vacant lot across the street.

"I can drop you off and find parking," offered Alex.

"Nonsense, walking will give us some exercise," said Aunt Margaret. "How about you, Kristen?"

"Sure, let's walk."

A few minutes later, Alex found a spot, parked, and helped the two women out. They strolled down the sidewalk, Kristen and Margaret carrying the bread containers, Alex bringing a case of soft drinks.

Not that there wasn't already plenty to eat. The concrete courtyard next to McClintock Bait and Tackle swarmed with townspeople, the women in colorful summer outfits, the men in short sleeves. Several large picnic tables had been set up in the center and were covered with plastic tablecloths. Platters of golden fried and grilled fish filets, corn on the cob, sliced fresh tomatoes and lemons, various salads, chips and dipping sauces sat under fly screens. As soon as the pile on one platter became low, someone put a full one in its place. Partygoers ate from paper plates and helped themselves to drinks from coolers and ice on one side of the space. Clumps of folding chairs and tables with shady umbrellas lined the courtyard, but many people stood.

"Hey, Alex!" John McClintock called out as he worked one of the grills at the edge of the party.

Alex waved.

Margaret admired the food tables. "Very generous," she murmured. "I like a generous host."

Kristen grabbed one of the rolls Aunt Margaret had brought, even as she placed the big container on the table. She couldn't wait to take a bite. She indicated one of the overflowing platters of filets. "Did John catch all this?"

"Hardly."

John had left his spot at the grill and joined them. "Hi, Alex. Oh, and this must be Kristen." He shook the hand that was roll-free. "Hope you're liking Sparrow Lake. I hear your family lived here a few years back."

"Some of her family still does live here." Alex indicated Aunt Margaret. "I'm sure you two already know each other."

"I've passed the bait and tackle store," agreed Margaret. "I think I've also seen you guys out fishing on the lake."

Kristen thought about the boat she'd noticed on the lake a few days ago. Had it been Alex?

"It's nice sitting out on the water in the early morning," said Alex.

John nodded. "Real peaceful. Extra special when you share those moments with friends." He gestured to the tables. "But back to the fish we're cooking up today—I bought local, so most of it is from Lake Michigan."

Alex laughed. "We'd have to fish for weeks to catch enough to feed this crowd. Besides, we usually let ours go. I think because John feels sorry for them."

"They're too small," John insisted. "You have to let them grow." He had a nice smile and looked dapper in a striped pullover and navy pants. He had a decent head of white hair and bright blue eyes. And from the way Aunt Margaret was furtively inspecting him, Kristen decided she just might be interested.

"Letting fish go sounds kindhearted to me," said Margaret.

"Eating them sounds tasty. Shall we help ourselves?" Alex grabbed some plates and handed one to Kristen. Then he found a couple of empty chairs at one of the tables with an umbrella to protect them from the sun.

Margaret swirled away, her draped summer

pants and loose blouse a bright magenta-and-orange print that made Kristen's eyes want to cross.

"Save me a place," her aunt called back to them. "John says he has something in his office he wants to show me." She winked knowingly. "Have fun."

Kristen again wondered what Margaret had in mind. Her aunt didn't need to work so hard, since Kristen had been spending time with Alex for more than a week. He pulled out a chair for her, then sat down himself.

After they'd eaten, he leaned back and asked, "How are things going at Sew Fine?"

"You mean the improvements I'm trying to make? The computer order system is great. It's going to make things a lot easier."

Now she just had to find someone to input the larger number of orders when they got them. Brian wouldn't be around once he started college at summer's end. And he'd been dragging his feet getting to work again after she'd caught him coming in so late.

"I contacted a newspaper in Milwaukee," Kristen went on. "They want to interview us."

"That's great."

"Yeah, it sure is."

If a news release worked that well and so fast,

what else might she be able to do? And who was going to keep up the momentum when she left?

Kristen thought about the résumé she'd sent out. The person to whom she'd emailed it was someone she knew, someone she thought respected her. If she got the job, though, how soon would it start? Hopefully not right away. She wanted to make sure the business was in good shape for her aunt.

Her thoughts were interrupted by Alex saying, "Maybe you'll make the store a famous attraction for this part of the state."

"Right. Really famous." She felt herself flush. Why? He always seemed to throw her off balance. She hedged, "I'm joking. I'm sure I can make some improvements, but I'm not a rockband promoter."

"You're not trying to compete with the cow parade, huh?"

Kristen quirked her brows. "The *what* parade?"

"Cows." Alex explained, "Wisconsin is the dairy state, remember. On the Fourth of July, some of the farmers around here dress up their best cows and run them down Main Street. After the floats and farm equipment roll by."

"Dress cows up in what?"

"Flowers, hats, beads."

Kristen couldn't help herself. She snickered.

Alex laughed. "Whoa, we're not talking complete costumes. It's not *that* elaborate. But everybody enjoys the fun. Well, except for the street cleaners who tidy up afterward." He added, "The cow parade is officially listed as a traditional summer event for this area, and it has been for several years, second only to the county fair."

"They must have started having the parade after I left town. But I have to admit that I can't wait to see it."

"Hey, some of those cows cut quite a figure."

Kristen grinned at Alex. She had to admit that she liked his combination of humor and sarcasm. She remembered not so long ago, she'd thought of him as snarky. Now she saw his sarcastic side as part of his charm.

"I heard you talking about the Fourth of July parade," Gloria said, as she pulled up a chair. "Mind if I join you?"

"Please," Kristen said.

Gloria slid into a seat next to her. "Hmm. We should decorate a car or small float from Sew Fine for the parade, you know. A couple of women from the quilting circle in my class used to help with that. So did I. That's a good old-fashioned local way to advertise."

"Why don't we talk about it in the next class?"

Kristen noted the mint-green ribbons scooping up Gloria's thick dark curls. They matched her sundress. "You look cool. And very festive."

"Thanks." Gloria gave her a brilliant smile. "How are you doing on your quilt?"

"You're making a quilt?" Alex asked.

"Well, hardly," Kristen said. "It's only big enough to be a place mat."

"Expand it a bit, and you'll have a nice light throw," said Gloria, always encouraging.

Alex seemed impressed. "Hmm, a quilt already. You've been here how long? Two weeks? You're taking the town by storm."

Two weeks? Right, it had been only two weeks. Kristen had to admit things were happening pretty fast in such a short time.

Gloria winked at Alex. "Kristen does make a nice addition to Sparrow Lake, don't you think, Chief Novak?"

"She sure does," he agreed with a big grin.

Though she was starting to get uncomfortable, Kristen forced a smile.

Gloria went on, "She's already made her mark on Sew Fine. Very impressive."

"I agree."

Kristen thought Alex's expression was a little too proprietary as he reached across and patted her arm.

"I need another drink." He nodded toward the coolers and buckets of ice. "Can I get you ladies something?"

Gloria said, "I'll take an iced tea."

"Kristen?"

"I'll have a diet soda. Thanks."

As soon as Alex left, Gloria leaned closer. "Nice catch, Kristen. The ladies have been eyeing that hunk for quite some time."

Growing seriously uncomfortable now, Kristen stirred in her seat. "I wouldn't say I've 'caught' him." And she didn't want to talk about it, either.

"Well, I've noticed the two of you hanging out around town together."

Kristen admitted drily, "I've had some run-ins with the law."

"Whatever it takes, girl."

It certainly wasn't as if Kristen had gotten arrested on purpose. About to say so, she stopped when a couple of older women approached the table. They seemed mildly familiar but she couldn't recall their names. However, they both knew Gloria and greeted her warmly. Obviously aware Kristen might need her memory nudged, Gloria made introductions all around.

"Welcome back to Sparrow Lake, Kristen,"

Mrs. Roberts said. "I love to see younger people returning to their roots."

"Well, I'm here for the summer anyway," Kristen told her. "Did I meet you one time in the past? Did you know my mom?"

"Sure did. We both worked at Unique Food Market with her," the other woman said. "I hear you're now running Sew Fine."

"And doing a great job of it, too," Gloria said.

"Actually, my sister, Heather, is the manager. She deserves most of the credit for the store's success."

"Well, of course we want everyone to have credit." But Mrs. Roberts gave her an odd look.

"Kristen is just being modest," Gloria said. "She's making improvements that will grow the business."

Kristen's neck warmed with her discomfort. She didn't know why, but suddenly everything seemed to be getting on her nerves. Her aunt had pushed her at Alex. Her sister had teased her about him, and Gloria had indicated that people already pegged her and Alex as an item. And now Gloria and Mrs. Roberts were acting as if they expected Kristen to stay in Sparrow Lake to run Sew Fine.

She'd only been here two weeks, as Alex had reminded her.

Suddenly things were moving way too fast for her.

It was as though everyone thought she was here to stay. In some ways, even she seemed to think so. It had taken her three whole days after getting her friend's email before she'd managed to send out a résumé.

Kristen gazed around the courtyard and thought it looked like a perfect scene from a movie about a happy small town: colorful, friendly, laid-back. Everyone seemed to know everyone else's business.

They all seemed to know what was best for her, pressuring her to make decisions she wasn't ready to make.

As if her doubts about returning to her childhood home suddenly manifested, she caught sight of a dark figure standing in the grill area. She stared, and Brian, dressed all in black, glared back for a moment before turning and sliding into the shady area behind the store. Andy Eccles, a paper plate loaded with food, followed. Neither young man bothered to return her wave. Maybe things had happened too fast for Brian, as well.

"Something the matter?" Alex was back with the drinks.

"Uh, no." She straightened and smiled. She

was being ridiculous, trying to find something wrong with a day that was absolutely right, something wrong in people who seemed nothing if not kind and encouraging. "Did you see Aunt Margaret? She said she would join us."

"She and John went inside. I think he's showing her something."

"His etchings?" she joked.

"I don't know if he has etchings, but I think he has art of some sort." Alex obviously hadn't heard the funny old story about a man who promised to show a woman his etchings just so he could get her alone.

"I'm sure they have plenty to talk about, even without art. They're both interesting," he pointed out.

"Well, Aunt Margaret is plenty interesting. I don't know John all that well."

"He's a good guy."

"I'm sure he is."

He gazed at her closely. "I assure you, his intentions are honorable."

"Aunt Margaret can make her own decisions about what she wants to do and who she wants to do it with."

Again, he asked, "Is there anything wrong? You seem a little tense."

"It's just that we can't force things to happen for other people. We need to give people space."

"Well, sure…" Alex leaned back in his chair, a thoughtful look on his face. To her relief, he changed the subject. "When I went to get the drinks, I saw them whipping up some home-made ice cream for dessert. It's made from local cream."

Trying to relax, Kristen took a deep breath. "I don't think I've ever had homemade ice cream."

"Well, then, it's time you tried some." Alex rose and held out his hand. "Come on, let's go get dessert."

Realizing she'd been panicking over nothing worse than good intentions, Kristen hesitated only a second before taking his hand and getting to her feet.

A soft rock song started up. Someone had brought a portable stereo. Kristen recognized the song, one of her favorites, and let the melody flow through her.

Relax, already.

What in the world had gotten her so uptight? No one could force her to do anything, and she didn't want to spoil the day. She was determined to decompress and not think about jobs or futures or anything. That could all wait.

She would just enjoy the present.

MARGARET WAS IMPRESSED with the watercolor John had hanging in his office. "Ed Williams. I know him. He was a visiting artist at the university for a semester." Her finger near the glass covering the painting, she traced a curving line. "Even though it's abstract, you get the feeling of movement and sky and water."

"That's what I love," said John. "Anything with sky and water and sailing gets to me every time."

She could see that. He'd decorated his office with a nautical theme. Sea colors. A ship's rail and wheel. He definitely had a creative side, which appealed to the artist in her.

He said, "I'd have Turners if I could afford them."

"Good taste," remarked Margaret. "I'll have to look at the other pieces you've collected." He'd already invited her over to his house for coffee some afternoon, and she was thinking she would take him up on it. "Do you sail?"

John laughed. "At the moment, I just motor—I have a small bass boat. When I lived in Chicago, we had a twenty-two-foot day sailer."

"We?"

"My late wife and I." He suddenly looked a little sad.

Margaret nodded. She knew that sadness well.

"You must miss…your sailboat." She didn't want to make him uncomfortable by getting personal too quickly.

"Yep, I sold it. I plan to get another one someday, though."

And another woman? Margaret wondered. Maybe he hadn't only called her to make sure Kristen came to the fish fry.

"Do you know how to sail?" he asked.

"Oh, I used to know a little about it. It's been years."

"If you got on a boat, it'd probably come back to you."

"Maybe. I'm sure not as strong as I used to be, though. The body kind of goes downhill as it gets more miles on it."

He glanced at her appreciatively. "Maybe you're stronger than you think. You've held up pretty well."

They laughed together. Margaret liked John's compliments, and she also appreciated his sense of humor.

"Besides, you can get yachts now with all kinds of automatic thingamajigs," said John.

"That would definitely help."

Was he just making conversation, or was he suggesting they sail together sometime? Margaret wondered. Intriguing thought. She'd always loved a bit of adventure.

John walked to a window and checked on the party outside. "How are Alex and your niece getting on?"

"Actually, they were getting along just fine before tonight. They went out to dinner in Lake Geneva earlier this week."

"Great. Shall we go see how they're doing?" He added, "But first I have to check on the food, make sure it's holding up."

"I'll help."

They headed back outside and cut through the crowd to the food tables.

Margaret had to admit John was the most intriguing man she'd met in a while. He was warm and had a sense of humor. Even better, he had a hidden creative side. Who would have guessed that he collected art? Exactly the kind of man she would like to get to know better.

AS MUSIC WAFTED through the balmy afternoon air, Alex was happy to see that Kristen seemed more relaxed. She'd definitely been a little on edge today and he hadn't even arrested her for anything. On the one hand, she hadn't seemed averse to fixing up her aunt up with John McClintock.

On the other hand, Alex had gotten the strong sense that Kristen might not be totally comfortable with the way he'd been pursuing her. Okay. So they had only known each other two weeks. And just because he felt they could easily develop something more meaningful didn't mean that she was in the same place.

Yet.

He wasn't ready to give up on the possibility.

They watched as a group of young guys moved the food tables to clear a small dance floor. People drifted out into the space with partners or even alone, every age group represented from two-and-a-half to eighty.

"Are the twins coming today?" Alex asked.

"I don't know. Heather said something about dropping by, but it may be later. She has a busy schedule."

Alex nodded. "A lot for a single mother." He nodded toward the dancers. "Want to take a spin?"

"Sure."

They did a kind of modified two-step to the soft rock, Alex's arm around Kristen's waist. He wanted to draw her closer but decided he would respect her desire for space on all levels until she learned to completely relax with him. She sure felt good in his arms, though.

Margaret and John also made use of the dance floor. Over Margaret's shoulder, John flashed him a thumbs-up.

Alex merely smiled and was glad that Kristen hadn't seen the gesture. Maybe having everyone in town take an interest was too much pressure on a new relationship.

WHEN ALEX DROPPED Kristen and Margaret off at the house later on, Kristen was in a much better mood. Dancing had been fun. She had enjoyed the music and the freedom of moving around the concrete slab of a dance floor. She had to admit she'd enjoyed sliding in and out of Alex's arms even more.

Of course, dancing had taken its toll. Her feet hurt. As she took the wedges off and tossed them near the bed in her suite, she heard laughter from a television show coming from Brian's side of the house. Recalling the somber black figure at the party, Kristen padded down the hallway to see what her brother was doing. The door stood ajar and Brian lay stretched across the bed on his stomach. Kristen took a deep breath and knocked.

He didn't turn around or look up. "Yeah?"

"I want to talk to you. I know you've had a lot to deal with—"

"I don't have much to say."

She didn't like his belligerent tone or the way he'd cut her off. "You *should* have something to say. You were late for work every day this week." She'd been busy on the phone or at the computer when he came in and, later, hadn't wanted to talk to him when others could hear. Then he'd apparently slept all day Saturday so this was the first chance she'd gotten to have a talk. She said, "We depend on you to process the orders," hoping he still liked that sort of approach.

"I won't be there forever. I'm going to college in the fall."

She swallowed her annoyance. "Yes, but you're supposed to be helping out this summer."

He glanced over his shoulder. "So are you. Does that include hanging out with cops?"

So that was what had prompted his sour expression earlier. "I've gone out with Alex in my free time."

"Yeah, you two are having some big romance. I saw you sucking face with him at the fish fry."

They had never kissed at the fish fry, but she ignored the sarcastic remark. "It's not some big romance," she said, wondering if it could be. Ignoring the sudden rush of her pulse, she asked, "What were you doing this week, say, on Wednesday night?"

He swung his feet across the bed and sat up, but his back was still to her. "Is this another interrogation?"

"Brian, I really am wondering what you're doing when you're out...alone or with friends. Some truly strange things are going on in town."

"People *are* strange." He snickered.

"It isn't funny, Brian. Breaking and entering isn't amusing...and neither is stealing pies. You told me before that you weren't involved with stealing."

Now he stood up to face her, an expression of mock horror on his face. "Someone stole a pie? Wow, big crime!"

She was beginning to get angry. But she tried again to sound understanding, "We all have changes to deal with."

"Changes? So what?"

"What is the matter with you?"

"Nothing's wrong with me. It's you who's got your pantyhose in a wad." He started for the door but stopped short, since he was going to have to go around her. "Why don't you call your cop boyfriend and talk to him? Ask him about the stolen pie. Maybe he ate it himself when he ran out of doughnuts."

"You're being facetious."

"Ooh, big word. Did you learn it in college?"

"That's it!" she snapped. "I don't appreciate your tone, Brian. I'm trying to deal with a bad situation—"

With one step, he brushed past her. "Deal all you want."

"Brian!" She turned to watch him stride down the hall. "I don't want us to be like this! Don't you care about your family? We care about *you.*"

He didn't answer. Heading toward the lakeside door, he stopped for one last comment. "Call Mom and talk to her if you want. Talk to her stupid husband, too. I'm sure he'll have plenty to say about me."

"Acting out won't make things better."

He slammed the door on her final words, though it was already past ten o'clock. What could she do? Run after him and tackle him? Upset, Kristen stalked back to her bedroom. For a moment she just stood there, considering whether or not she should indeed call their mother. Her mother would no doubt share concerns with their stepfather, and she worried that getting Mike involved would make things worse.

Alex would be a better person to talk to. He would understand where a rebellious teenager was coming from. Their conversation in Lake Geneva had struck a good note with her. She glanced at the clock, halfway tempted to call him, even this late. But there was no reason to get someone else involved with family problems, she soon decided, especially not when she was upset.

Resolving to sleep on it, Kristen only hoped that tonight Brian would not go out and do something worse than stealing pies.

CHAPTER FOURTEEN

KRISTEN FOUND HERSELF agreeing to twin-sit again on Monday. Heather had called with another emergency—the regular babysitter had the flu. Planning to redeem herself, Kristen readily agreed. Her sister had been nice about the FamilyMart fiasco, but she wanted to show Heather she could handle anything that came up. As the oldest in the family, Kristen had always been ultraresponsible, so she wanted to make up for getting so frazzled the other day.

When Heather opened the cottage door, however, the twins weren't in sight. "Where are they?" she asked, noting her sister looked tired.

"Playing in their bedroom," said Heather. "Having a major sort-out with dolls and horses."

"Are you feeling okay?"

"I was up late. We have an exam tonight."

Kristen shook her head. "I don't know how you do it all."

"Come on, you've gone to college. You've worked. You know how it is."

"Yeah, I kind of do. I don't have two children, though."

Heather went on, "You've always been busy. You were never home when I called in Chicago. Probably working overtime. I know you're some kind of incredible workhorse."

"You tried to call me? And I wasn't there?" Apparently, Heather hadn't wanted to leave messages, and Kristen hadn't noticed the number coming in to her caller ID.

"Now don't start feeling guilty, Kristen. I know you loved your job. And I love studying landscape design and maintenance. I love my kids, too. I'll get through this."

Noticing Heather didn't say she loved her job managing Sew Fine, Kristen promised, "*We'll* get through it." She didn't want Heather to think she was totally on her own. "And we all love Addison and Taylor. They're bright spots for the future of the family. I look forward to spending more time with them."

"Let's see what those 'bright spots' are up to." Heather laughed and motioned Kristen down the hall toward the bedrooms.

The twins had twin beds, a dresser and a couple of toy chests in their room. At the moment, the rest of the floor space was filled with an army of fashion dolls, mostly naked, some flat on their backs, others stacked in piles, the majority with wild long hair. Horses of various materials and sizes lay here and there among them, hooves in the air. Various pieces of doll clothing were scattered about. Kristen was reminded of a movie scene depicting the end of a battle back in the days when there was cavalry. Addison and Taylor sat in the center of it all, moving people and animals around.

Addison glanced up to see her and jumped to her feet. "Aunt Kristen!" she yelled, grabbing Kristen's legs.

"Hi, sweetie." She hugged and kissed her little niece, thinking it was getting easier to tell the two apart—Addison's face was rounder and her blond hair a little shorter than her sister's.

"Aunt Kristen!" shouted Taylor, following suit. "What are you doing here?"

"I'm going to stay with you tonight. We'll have fun."

"Fun!" yelled Addison. Then she seemed to realize she had a redheaded doll in her hand. The doll was wearing only a pair of shoes and a crown. "This is Scarlet, the princess."

"Scarlet isn't a princess. Throw her back in the box," declared Taylor.

"Is too a princess! And I want to play with her!"

"You got plenty of dolls for your side already."

Sides? Sheesh, maybe they *were* playing war, Kristen thought.

Taylor flopped back down on the rug. "I have the most horses."

"I have the most dolls," Addison came back.

"You've both got a lot," agreed Kristen, trying to mediate before the war between the twins became real.

"Mostly gifts from the host of loving relatives who thought they needed all this stuff. Now, girls, you don't have to make it a contest," Heather told the twins. "Play together peacefully. And that also means doing what your aunt tells you tonight. Play nice and then go to bed."

"Bed? Not now," said Addison, pouting. "It's too early! And the dolls need a bath."

"The horses need a bath, too." Taylor showed her mom and aunt a palomino with a long, sparkly tail.

"Ugh, those horses have cooties!" Addison made a face.

"Do not!" answered Taylor, pushing Addison. "Your dolls have cooties."

Addison pushed back. "Do not!"

"Stop it, girls!" Heather said firmly. "Nobody has cooties." Aside, she whispered to Kristen, "I'm sorry I ever brought up the term with them."

She ran her hand through Addison's hair. "Hmm, a little greasy. It looks like some humans could use a bath here."

"They need a bath?" Kristen asked.

Heather sighed. "Well, I didn't get around to it. We just had supper." She narrowed her eyes, looking the twins over. "They get sweaty and dusty at camp."

"I can give them a bath."

"Would you mind?"

"What can be so hard about bathing five-year-olds?" They weren't babies. "They'll get in the water by themselves, right?"

Heather laughed. "They certainly will, and you don't have to stand there and shower them or anything. Just supervise and adjust the temperature." She cautioned, "You'll have to help them wash their hair, to make sure they get all the soap out. We have 'no tears' shampoo, of course."

The bathroom of the cottage had both a large built-in soaker tub and a separate shower. "Do they like showers or baths?"

"Either."

Addison piped up. "I want a bubble bath."

Taylor agreed. "Bubbles."

"Okay, bubbles it is. And I'll read them to sleep," Kristen assured her sister.

"If they get too hyper or act up, give them a timeout."

"I'm not going to be bad," asserted Taylor.

"Me, either," chirped Addison.

"Good girls," Heather said. "But you're tired... and dirty. Now do what Aunt Kristen says, okay, sweethearts?" She leaned down to hug and kiss both twins.

Kristen followed her sister out to the living room where her book bag and purse lay on the couch. "Don't worry about anything."

"I won't. Thanks again." Heather hugged her. "See you around nine-thirty."

Kristen returned to the bedroom to watch the twins play.

"See this lady?" Addison held up a blonde fashion doll with a long ponytail. "This is you! And this is that nice policeman." She grabbed a boy doll and put the two dolls' faces together to make kissy noises. "Ooh, I love you, Aunt Kristen, I love you!"

Oh, for goodness sakes! Was everyone on the romance bandwagon? Kristen sat down on the tallest bed and picked up Scarlet, who was lying at her feet. "This princess has a crown, but she doesn't have a dress." She looked around but only spotted a pair of tiny shorts and a cape of some sort. "Doesn't she have a nice princess gown? Doesn't anyone have clothes to wear?"

"We. Can't. Find. Them," Taylor told her, enunciating each word separately as if Kristen might not understand. "Besides, everybody's gettin' ready for a bath."

Right, the bath. The twins wanted bubbles. Kristen left for the bathroom. The tub was a nice big one, set in a tiled enclosure that formed at least a two inch rim on three sides. She turned on the water until it got warm enough, then set the stopper.

As she went back to the twins' room, her cell phone rang. She felt a little thrill, thinking it might be Alex, and answered without glancing at the caller ID. But it was no one she knew and the man chattered away in Spanish. "Wrong number," she told him. *"Numero incorrecto."*

Addison glanced up. "Can you teach us Spanish, Aunt Kristen?"

"I don't know enough Spanish to teach it, but I'm impressed you recognize some words."

"We're learning counting in Spanish at camp," said Taylor. *"Uno, dos, tres..."* She made a horse gallop over the rug. *"Uno* horsies, *dos* horsies, *tres..."*

Addison grasped Kristen's hand to look at her phone. "Can I see it?"

"Okay, but don't call anyone."

"I know how to work it," said the little girl, and hit Menu. "Here are the phone numbers." Her small fingers seemed pretty adept.

"You're good. Are they teaching you about phones at camp?"

"No, but Mommy lets us use her phone sometimes."

"She lets us call Gramma," put in Taylor. "And Aunt Mar-grit."

It was unbelievable how the young took to technology, Kristen thought. Most kids knew far more about it than adults. She slipped the phone into her pocket. "Let's put that away for now and get ready for our bath."

"I'm not done playing." Taylor frowned.

"You can play after your bath," said Kristen. "Then you can put all your horsies to bed."

"Or the horses can take a bath, too," Addison said. "They're stinky."

"You better wash your dolls," Taylor told her. "They're wa-ay stinkier."

Addison stiffened, probably spoiling for a fight, but Kristen interrupted, "Don't you have a dolly bathtub when they get ready to bathe? They'd like that better." She gestured to the door. "Now be good girls and go in the bathroom and get undressed. I'll add the bubble bath."

"Bubbles, yay!" squealed Addison, obviously forgetting any tension.

There was a box of bubble bath right by the tub. Kristen poured about half a cup under the stream from the faucet. Bubbles frothed and spread around the tub.

"Yay!" Addison squealed again, taking off her bright green T-shirt. She threw it up in the air, followed by her shorts and underwear. Two of the garments landed half-in and half-out of the tub.

"Oops, we're making a mess," said Kristen, taking out the wet garments and placing them in the sink. "Where's Taylor?"

"I dunno. Back in the bedroom, I guess." Addison plopped herself in the tub, accidentally but thoroughly splashing Kristen. "Ooh, nice and warm!"

Kristen went into the hall. "Taylor? Your bath is ready."

In her bedroom, the little girl was gathering up her horses.

"Leave them on the floor, honey," Kristen told her. "You can pick them up later."

"Yay!" came Addison's squeal, followed by more splashing.

Taylor told Kristen, "You can pick up the dolls. I'll do the horses." She guessed that would be all right and leaned over to pile the dolls up. "Okay."

Taylor took off, running by her. Returning to the bathroom, Kristen met Addison running out, soaking wet. They collided.

"Oof! Where are you going? I haven't washed your hair."

"I'll be back," the little girl said, leaving sopping footprints behind her.

Meanwhile, Kristen saw that Taylor had shed her clothes and left them on the wet floor. She and all the horses she'd been carrying were in the bathtub. Whether she liked it or not, the toys were getting a bath, too.

"Yay!" Addison shrieked, back with an armload of dolls. She threw them in the bathtub with multiple splashes that made Taylor screech and duck, then climbed in herself.

Water sloshed over the edge. If the clothes on the floor weren't wet before, they were soaked now. So were the bath mat and a couple of the towels, not to mention Kristen. She figured she was going to have to do at least one load of laundry. Suddenly remembering her cell phone, not wanting to expose it to any more dampness than she could help, she took it out of her pocket to set it on a shelf several feet from the bathtub. The twins splashed and shrieked and sang.

"Well, I'm glad you're enjoying yourselves."

She reached over to turn off the water. They already had plenty.

Taylor splashed Addison in the face and Addison splashed back.

"Hey, let's settle down." Kristen was looking for the shampoo.

Taylor pulled a bedraggled doll up from the water by its dripping long red hair. Then she dunked it. "Oh, oh, I'm drowning!"

"No, you can't drowned Scarlet! Stop it!" cried Addison.

"Taylor!" Kristen frowned at the little girl.

Taylor assumed an innocent expression. "It's just a doll."

"But Addison cares about her," said Kristen.

Taylor brought the palomino with the sparkly tail, long and wet now, up and over the water. "Okay, here comes Rainbow, the flying horse, to save her. Whee!"

More water splashed and bubbles spilled out onto the floor. Kristen could hear water pouring down the overflow drain. "It's still too full. We should let a little water out." How could half a cup of bubble bath produce so many bubbles? They seemed to be a foot high. From the corner of her eye, she saw the box of bubble bath… which was empty. Somebody's little hands had been busy. "You used *all* of the bubble bath?"

"We need lots and lots of bubbles!" yelled Addison.

Well, there was nothing to do now. Parting the sea of bubbles, she found the shampoo. "Let's get your hair clean." Kristen reached for the nearest twin. She squirted a generous amount of shampoo into her hand and rubbed it into Taylor's wet head. The little girl wriggled, still playing with horses.

Suddenly, Taylor stiffened, then screamed. "Owww, it hurts!"

Kristen jumped, scared. "What hurts?"

"Ow, ow, my eyes!" Taylor screamed louder, thrashing.

Addison pointed at the bottle in Kristen's hand. "You used Mommy's shampoo."

Oh, no, she hadn't paid enough attention and snatched up Heather's shampoo! Before Kristen could say or do anything else, Taylor clambered out of the bath, still shrieking.

"Taylor, stop!"

"Eeeeek! It hurts." The little girl sped out of the room. Outside, there was the sound of something falling. And more shrieking, even louder.

Kristen stumbled to her feet and grabbed a big towel from the linen shelves. "Come back, I'll wash it out, Taylor!"

She was horrified when Taylor ran away from her, still screeching. "You hurt me!"

A lamp tumbled to the floor with the sound of glass breaking.

"I didn't mean to! Taylor!" Kristen pleaded, just about in tears herself. "Please come back here! I'll make it better!"

With another shriek, Taylor ran into her bedroom and slammed the door.

Kristen pounded. "Taylor, let me in!" There was no lock, so Kristen pushed inside.

"No!" Taylor shouted as Kristen tried to wrap the big towel around her niece. But the little girl jerked away to run out into the hall.

"Taylor!" yelled Kristen, in fast pursuit. They circled the living room several times before she finally caught the child. "Hold on, honey." She swabbed at Taylor's eyes.

"No, no!"

"Taylor, please!" With subliminal awareness, she heard a thudding sound.

"Hurts!"

The thudding sound got louder and Kristen suddenly realized that someone was pounding on the front door of the cottage.

"Police! Open up!"

Police? What on earth?

OUTSIDE THE COTTAGE, nothing had seemed to be
wrong when Alex drove up and parked. He knew
the place belonged to Heather Clarke. He had
checked when the County Emergency Operator
told him where the 911 call originated. Inside,
he heard more high-pitched shrieking.

"Open up! Police!" he shouted again, pounding on the thick wood.

This time the door gaped inward and, to his
surprise, a bedraggled Kristen stood there with
a screaming child bundled in a towel. Kristen's
hair was plastered around her face, her eye
makeup smeared, her clothing soaked, and her
expression desperate. She didn't say a word.

Instinct told Alex not to laugh. Besides, he
still didn't know if anyone was hurt. "What's
going on?"

"Soap," croaked Kristen, nodding at the
shrieking Taylor. Or Addison. Alex couldn't be
sure. "In her eyes."

"Soap in the eyes, huh?" Alex quickly gathered up the twin, pulling the towel tight around
her. He strode inside, heading for the kitchen.
"Come on."

Holding the child between them, Alex turned
on the sink and put the little head beneath the
stream of water. He rinsed her hair and her face
thoroughly. The shrieks turned into sobs. She

merely whimpered when they set her down and dried her hair and face with a kitchen towel.

"Better?"

Her eyes were red but he didn't know if that was from soap or crying. "It hurts."

"But not so bad, right, sweetheart? It'll get better. A little soap won't kill you." He rubbed her back soothingly and glanced at Kristen. "Is this Taylor or Addison?"

"Taylor." She explained, "I was trying to wash her hair and I picked up the wrong shampoo." She leaned over to check Taylor's eyes. "I'm so sorry, sweetie."

"Mkay," murmured Taylor.

"We'll put some soothing drops in your eyes." Then she glanced around, searching. "Addison? Are you still in the bathroom?

"Auntie Kristen!" came a little sing-song cry from down the hall. "Washing the dolls! Washing the horsies!"

Kristen sighed, obviously relieved. "Thank goodness she's not drowned. That would be about par for the course tonight."

"Bathing twins can definitely be a two-person job." He added, "Though you didn't really need to call 911 for help. We take that seriously."

"Nine-one-one?"

He smiled. "Next time just call the station and ask for me personally."

KRISTEN RECOGNIZED THAT snarky expression Alex didn't even try to hide. "This isn't funny." And she couldn't believe he thought so.

The smile disappeared. "Dialing 911 isn't funny. I agree."

"I did *not* dial 911." And she was outraged that he would think she did so just to get his attention.

"Well, somebody called. From this location."

"I wouldn't call 911 for a nonemergency."

"How about one of the twins?"

Kristen looked at Taylor.

The little girl shook her head. "Not me."

"Addison?" called Kristen, heading toward the bathroom. Her niece was happily playing with bubbles, dolls, still singing. The floor was wet, the rug soaked, and damp towels lay about. "Addison, honey, did you dial 911?"

Addison quieted, looking up. "It was a 'mergency. Taylor was hurt." Her eyes grew big as she looked at Alex. "You said to call 911 if someone needs help."

Kristen remembered the conversation at the ice cream shop. "You did."

"I did," Alex admitted somberly. "I guess I didn't explain well enough what an emergency entails. Is this your cell?" He picked up the phone from the floor. "It's a little wet, too."

"Covered with little fingerprints, I'm sure." But the phone wasn't ruined, Kristen noted, glancing at its screen. She turned back to Addison. "You used Aunt Kristen's cell phone."

Addison looked upset. "Don't be mad!"

"We're not mad," Alex told the little girl. "We just wanted to know how this happened."

"Finish your bath," Kristen told Addison calmly, though she felt thoroughly embarrassed. "I had no idea," she muttered while walking with Alex back to the living room.

He explained, "Out here, 911 calls go to a county operator. That person notifies the local law. At county they heard a lot of shrieking and couldn't understand much except the word *help*. They called me."

"Unbelievable." She once again felt near tears. She tried to get angry to fight against them. "I'm sure you charge someone for a bogus 911 call, right?"

"We charge pranksters, yes."

"Well, then, lock me up," she said, holding out her wrists. "Or whatever. I'm responsible, since I'm supposed to be watching these children."

Alex looked surprised. "I'm not going to lock you up."

Taylor rushed to grab her legs. "No, no! My eyes are okay. Aunt Kristen didn't mean to!"

Alex clasped Kristen's outstretched hands, but his expression was comforting. "Calm down. Nobody's getting arrested."

If he embraced her, she knew she would break down.

She slid her hands away to pat Taylor's wet head. "We weren't trying to pull a prank."

He shrugged. "Children can be a little too helpful sometimes."

"I feel awful about it. Embarrassed."

"Well…stuff happens." Alex glanced around. "This place is certainly a disaster." Stepping back out into the hallway, he cautioned, "Watch your bare feet, Taylor. Don't step on the broken lamp." Then he smiled at Kristen. "How about I help you clean up?"

She took some deep breaths, pulling herself together. "I have to wash Addison's hair. With no-tears shampoo." While giving her a talk, though nothing threatening, about making 911 calls.

"And I'll put some drops in Taylor's eyes," Alex said, looking down at the child. "Why don't you go put your jammies on first?"

Between the two of them, they made fairly short work of cleaning up the broken lamp, mopping up stray puddles, gathering soaked towels and clothing, cleaning out the bubble-choked bathtub, drying hair, and putting two five-year-olds, twenty-one fashion dolls and at least ten horses to bed.

Addison and Taylor were so tired that they barely stayed awake for two pages from the bedtime book that Alex read to them. Alex could definitely handle kids, Kristen realized. The twins had requested that he read to them and seemed very taken with him. He'd be a natural dad. Whereas she'd have to work hard at being a decent mom. She had to admit she was a little jealous.

When they came out of the twins' bedroom, Kristen quickly checked herself in the hallway mirror. She'd wiped off the runny eye-makeup—which had made her resemble a bedraggled raccoon—and had tried to fluff up her hair.

He followed her into the kitchen where she opened the laundry closet, took the clothes from the washer and put them in the dryer. "So what's your secret, Officer Friendly?"

"Secret?"

"I bet there wouldn't have been a flooded bathroom or a bogus 911 call if you'd been on babysitting duty tonight."

"Two people are probably better than one with

five-year-old twins. Plus I think I told you I had younger siblings growing up."

She vaguely remembered something he'd said about that. "I had younger siblings to take care of, too, but if I had any special knowledge about how to deal with them, I seem to have lost it." Along with any influence over Brian.

"Don't give yourself such a hard time. Everything isn't always perfect, especially when it comes to kids," he pointed out. "And it probably wasn't perfect in the past, either."

When she'd taken care of Brian as a child, he'd seemed easy to deal with. Maybe he'd saved up his misbehavior through the years and it was coming out now. Or maybe he'd only acted like a good little boy. She wasn't sure.

"Would you like a cup of tea or coffee before you go back to work?" she asked.

"I'll take some coffee. I'm on the night shift."

She carefully measured grounds into Heather's automatic coffeemaker and put a kettle on for her tea. Then she got cups out and set them on the table.

"You can really be Ms. Perfectionist, you know," Alex said.

She wondered if that bothered him. "Is that a bad thing?"

"Not for a career, but it can be a recipe for failure when it comes to human beings. You can't expect kids to follow a particular plan all the time."

"Are you saying that I wouldn't have this mess if I hadn't expected the twins to follow my plan? I didn't have a plan."

"I'm just saying that you expected everything to go smoothly. Life only does that sometimes. And I'm in a profession to know, believe me."

"Well, thank you for the advice." The coffee was done, so she poured him a cup. She also put out a plate of cookies, the rest of a package Heather had hidden high on a shelf, out of the reach of little hands. She fixed her tea and sat down.

He sat, as well. "You're sounding a little sarcastic."

"Well, I'm not the sort who likes to be rescued every other day."

"Helping is different than rescuing."

She sipped her tea, some of it going down the wrong way, which made her cough. She held up her hand. "Don't worry, you won't have to perform the Heimlich maneuver on top of everything else."

His eyes softened. "No mouth-to-mouth, huh? Now, that would look good on the 911 call report."

She had to smile and felt warmth course through her. "Maybe later."

"Great." He looked ready to perform mouth-to-mouth right now.

"You seriously don't think I'm one of the worst aunts in the world? I let my nieces steal sweaters and then I tried to put their eyes out with soap." She went on. "They were out of control all evening, used a whole box of bubble bath, just about flooded the cottage, and nearly came to blows over horsies and dollies. And they weren't even being bad. I'm sure Heather could have dealt with everything."

"But your sister is used to kiddie chaos. She's had a few years of experience that you haven't."

"I bet you wouldn't have had trouble babysitting Taylor and Addison."

"Don't bet too much. I could have gotten shampoo in their eyes, too. And who knows what other kinds of trouble we would have gotten into? One time, I babysat my brother's little girl and helped her bake cookies. We blew up my sister-in-law's oven."

"Really?" She grinned. "I would've liked to have seen that."

"We had to peel cookies off the kitchen walls for days."

Kristen laughed.

"You are absolutely beautiful when you laugh."

"Even with stringy hair and smeared makeup?"

"Especially with messed-up hair and makeup." He leaned closer and tucked a strand of hair behind her ear. "Now about that mouth-to-mouth resuscitation you need, ma'am..."

Thrilled by his caring touch, Kristen couldn't resist, learning forward herself. The kiss was soft and firm at the same time. Exhilarating. The embarrassment of the evening burned away.

He pulled back a second to ask, "Better, ma'am?"

She felt a little breathless. "I'm not sure. I might need more." And not only of his kisses. She wanted to be with this man who had such easy charm, and not just for his prowess at dealing with emergencies.

Alex covered her mouth again, sliding one warm hand behind the nape of her neck. Kristen lost herself in the embrace, felt as if it went on forever. Felt as if she were melting...

"Ahem."

The spell of the kiss was broken when Kristen's eyes popped open, registering that Heather was standing in the kitchen. She must have let herself in the back door.

"Sorry to interrupt."

Kristen sat back as Alex released her. "Uh,

235

that's okay. The twins are bathed and asleep. I did a load of laundry and it's still drying."

"I noticed." Heather gave her a curious look. "Is there more tea? I'll join you."

"Help yourself."

"When I saw the police cruiser out front, I was afraid the twins had been robbing the town's merchants again."

"They're good little kids," said Alex. "You don't have to worry."

Kristen noted that he shared nothing about the 911 call, the true reason for his visit. She didn't want to bring it up, either. She hated to tell her sister about the latest mess she'd gotten into.

Alex said, "I wanted to talk to Kristen, just to see how she's doing."

Kristen appreciated that he didn't mention the big mess they'd cleaned up, though she had no idea of what the twins would say about the evening. Or how she would explain the broken lamp.

"I'm sure she'll be doing fine after you get through with her." Heather sat down with a cup of tea. "She's always needed some police intervention."

They all laughed and chatted about college studies and kids for a half hour before Kristen announced they should leave so her sister could wind down for the evening.

Alex walked Kristen to her car. "Would you like to do something this coming weekend?"

"Sure. Do you have something specific in mind?"

"I just might," he said. "I have something specific in mind right now."

Alex brushed her lips with his but made no move to leave. Kristen's pulse began to thrum. The way he was looking at her made her flush in response. She waited breathlessly to see what he would do. He smoothed away the hair from the side of her face and slipped his hand to the back of her neck.

When he kissed her again, he took his time. She swayed into him, and he caught her by the waist and held her possessively. It had only been a few days, but she'd missed Alex intensely. Her heart began to pound and her breath caught in her throat, and just when she started to lose herself in the kiss, he pulled away.

With a big grin softening his face, Alex brushed her lips again before walking to his cruiser.

Kristen was left a little breathless and definitely wanting more.

CHAPTER FIFTEEN

THE REPORTER FROM Milwaukee showed up midway through the next week to interview Kristen at Sew Fine. She turned out to be a pleasant, middle-aged woman named Sharon Brinkley, who already knew quite a bit about needle crafts—as a matter of fact, her jacket was a piece of wearable art.

They sat near the front desk for the interview.

"I've never done quilting, but I'm good at needlepoint and embroidery," Sharon told Kristen, looking over the brochures Kristen had given her. "Are there quilting classes for beginners, as well as advanced seamstresses?"

"We have two that cater to beginners, but most classes mix students of different levels. The instructor works with each student individually... and students who are advanced enough can help the beginners, as well."

"Collaborative learning, hmm? Well, I'm a fan of that," said Sharon, scribbling in her notebook. "Do you ever have a real quilting circle, where everyone works on the same quilt?"

"Some are working on group quilts now, either here in class or on their own time."

Sharon indicated a couple of Aunt Margaret's stunning quilts hanging on the wall. "Well, those certainly are beautiful."

"They're art quilts involving appliqué and hand-painting, quite a bit more difficult than your average design," Kristen explained. She motioned toward the back of the store. "There's a small strip quilt hanging on that column in the rear. You can buy the materials in a packet and finish it in a day." She laughed. "Well, experienced quilters can finish it in a day. I'll be doing well if I get through the placemat I've started."

"Oh, so you're at a beginner level yourself." Sharon looked pleased. "That's a good angle for readers who have little or no sewing experience."

"I had no sewing experience until I started working here with my Aunt Margaret, who owns the store, and my sister, Heather, who runs it." Kristen nodded toward Heather as she scooted by to ring up a sale.

"Sew Fine is a family affair. That's sweet," said Sharon.

The reporter asked several more questions, and Kristen took her for a short tour of the store. Heather was counting some bills up by the front desk when Sharon stuffed her notebook back into her shoulder bag.

"I know someone who runs bus tours of interesting places in rural Wisconsin," Sharon said. "They visit dairy farms, cheese factories, historical sites. They're thinking of offering a craft tour. Sew Fine would be a perfect addition for that. You'd probably get some sales, as well as some students. Women who don't live too far away will be able to take classes."

"That would be wonderful!" enthused Kristen, thinking her aunt would be pleased.

"Do you have a website where people can order online?"

"I just set it up and I'm working on making additional products available. We're already getting more orders."

Behind them, Kristen heard Heather cough.

"That would definitely be a bonus for interested customers. Can I mention the website in the article?"

"Please do."

"I think covering sewing machines—costs and types—would be good for the website. You could also discuss fabrics suitable for quilting and offer some very nice kits."

"So it would be educational, as well as geared for business." Kristen had considered the same elements. Out of the corner of her eye, she saw Heather slam the cash register shut. Was something wrong? "I was already thinking about uploading a gallery of quilts created by Aunt Margaret and other women associated with Sew Fine. The possibilities are endless."

"In this day and age, websites can offer a substantial boost in sales," Sharon said. "I think this article I'm writing should help. We're going to put it in the Sunday supplement."

"Thanks so much." Kristen saw the reporter to the door. Her smile felt as if it stretched ear-to-ear when she came back to discuss the interview with Heather and Gloria.

"Wow!" said Gloria, clapping her hands. "Maybe I'll be working more than part-time."

"Will you be able to do that?" Kristen asked.

"I can rearrange my schedule," Gloria promised. She turned when a customer entered the store. "May I help you?"

"So what do you think?" Kristen asked Heather.

"Sounds like you're doing a great job with the marketing."

"But?" Thinking about the slammed register, she said, "You don't look happy."

Heather sighed. "I asked you before who is going to do the extra work. Brian is leaving for college. Not that he's been in much lately, any-

way. I haven't seen him since Monday afternoon."

"We'll hire people. Gloria will work more
hours."

"And who will train the new people? I'm the
current so-called manager. I want to take a full
course load starting in the fall, and I'll have to
do an internship next summer."

So-called? What did that mean? Did Heather
think she was trying to steal her job or something? She was just trying to find ways to improve business, the way Aunt Margaret asked
her to. Now Heather was upset, sounding both
like her job was being taken from her and also
like she feared the work Kristen was creating.

Kristen thought she could get some work off
Heather's back. "I can come back on weekends
to help you."

"Come back on weekends?" Heather's eyebrows shot up in alarm. "Have you got another
job already?"

Oops. "Not yet."

But Kristen had heard back from the company to which she'd sent her résumé in less than
twenty-four hours. They'd set up an interview in
Chicago for next week. The vice president had
already done a preliminary phone interview with

her, and they'd spoken for a whole hour. It really sounded like they might want to hire her.

Tears pooled in her sister's eyes, nearly breaking Kristen's heart.

"I can't deal with all this stuff," Heather said. "You won't come back on weekends. And weekends aren't enough anyway. I love my family. I care about this store. But I also love landscape design, and it looks like I'm never going to get a chance to pursue it. Maybe I should just quit school and be done with it!"

That was the last thing in the world Kristen wanted to have happen. She tried to reassure Heather. "You're not going to have to do that. We'll find a way to work things out. You have my word on it."

She didn't have to leave Sparrow Lake that soon, she told herself. Should she get the new job, she could tell her bosses that she'd start in September, which would give her time to find solutions to the problems. She only hoped the company would be okay with that.

"But you *are* going, one way or the other. And you can't be sure that everything will work out." Heather grabbed her purse from beneath the counter.

"Heather?"

"I'm sorry. I hate hearing myself whine!" Her

sister headed for the door but stopped for one last word. "Both of us have our own interests and our own obligations. I guess sometimes they're just at odds!"

"Heather, wait a minute!"

The door slammed and Kristen stood there, immobile. Now both her siblings had walked out on her.

After Heather left, Kristen felt distracted. She tried to take care of a customer who wanted two yards of cloth and ended up measuring incorrectly. Gloria stepped in. Then Kristen found herself at the cash register looking at the same receipts over and over, not knowing what she was supposed to be doing with them. It would help if there were more than two people to take care of the store. Although Wednesday was not usually a busy day, there had been one phone call after another and a steady stream of customers coming in. Kristen hadn't even had time to check Sew Fine's email.

Where on earth was Brian?

Heather said she hadn't seen Brian since Monday. Kristen had argued with him on Sunday evening and he hadn't spoken to her since. In fact, she hadn't seen him or heard him moving around in his room.

"Was Brian here yesterday?" Kristen asked Gloria.

"No, he wasn't. Is he sick?"

"Probably."

Kristen wasn't so sure of that. When Brian was sick, he usually moped about and wanted everyone to wait on him and feel his forehead for fever. He didn't keep to himself. Was he just avoiding her or was he getting himself into more trouble with his buddies? Irritated and wanting to focus on something concrete, Kristen called her brother's cell. It surely would help if Brian would do his part, whether or not he was only filling in for the summer.

No answer.

She sighed. Maybe he was asleep. Thinking she wasn't about to promote any more laziness or peevishness, whichever it was, she reluctantly called her aunt. However, Margaret had not seen Brian and couldn't find him, though she checked his room.

"Are you worried about something, Kristen?" Margaret asked.

"No," Kristen lied, since she had begun to feel uneasy. "Did you see him yesterday?" She had the car herself, so he wasn't driving around.

"I haven't seen Brian at all. I know he keeps late hours. Are you sure you're not worried?"

"Everything's okay, Aunt Margaret. He's probably just hanging out with his friends. What are those two guys' names again?"

"Andy Eccles and Matt Stapleton. Do you want me to look up their phone numbers?"

"I can do that myself. I have a phone book right here."

Thanking her aunt, she hung up. The phone book for Sparrow Lake was combined with a couple of other towns in the area. Kristen could find no listing for anyone named Eccles but she located a couple of Stapletons and called both residences. An elderly man answered the first call and said he was not related to Matt. The second call went to voice mail, so Kristen left a message. Now what?

"I can see you've got something distracting going on," Gloria said, having finished with a customer. "If you need to leave, I can handle this place."

"Will you? I hate to leave you alone. It's been kind of busy today."

"The phone calls and emails can wait. I know most of the people who come in here and they can wait, too. Go on and do what you have to do."

Thank goodness, Gloria didn't seem to want to pry. "You're wonderful." Kristen hugged the other woman warmly. "If we can hustle up more business, I'm going to get you a raise."

Kristen left and drove off, wondering where she was going. She decided to drive by the second Stapleton address, not that it was going to help her if no one was home. Which proved to be the case, she found out ten minutes later. She had a bad feeling.

Should she call Alex for help? He had indicated he was willing and, though the teenager had only been gone for perhaps twenty-four hours, she thought Brian could be classified as "missing." Yet, she remained reluctant and drove on, turning into the convenience store where she'd once seen Brian hanging out with his pals. She also stopped by FamilyMart to check their small food court. She didn't see any teenagers at all.

Getting back into the car, Kristen sped out onto the highway bordering the town. Where to go? She glanced at the gas station and fast food restaurants she passed, but saw no sign of Brian or his friends. This was crazy. How could she expect to find anyone just by driving around?

Suddenly, up ahead, she spotted the familiar black-and-white police car. Alex? She took off after it.

As soon as Kristen got close enough, she recognized Alex in the driver's seat. She flashed her lights until he pulled over then parked behind him.

"Yes?" Alex stepped out, looking handsome in his black uniform and sunglasses. "Was I speeding?"

She'd like to say yes, that she was making a citizen's arrest but this was no time for joking.

He put his hands on the roof and leaned in to look her in the eye through her open driver's window.

"Brian is missing," she blurted out.

"Brian? Hmm."

"I don't know if he ran away or headed back to California…or what. We haven't seen him for at least twenty-four hours."

Alex looked thoughtful, then said, "See that lot with the farm equipment over there? Park there and get into the cruiser with me. I may know where he is."

"Really?" She wanted to sigh in relief, but Alex hadn't said whether or not Brian was safe.

Kristen started up and waited for traffic to pass before turning into the lot Alex had indicated. She locked up and jumped into the cruiser's passenger seat.

She was still upset but feeling better now that she wasn't searching alone. "I've been beside myself. There hasn't been an accident, has there?"

"Not exactly."

"What do you mean by 'not exactly'?" she asked, her worry increasing.

"We got a call. A farmer named Anderson discovered some teenage boys bothering his cows in the wee hours this morning. He thought they had gone, but just now he saw them hiding out on his property."

A farm? "Brian doesn't have a car."

"Matt Stapleton does. An old beater. Anderson says it's stalled out on a country road." He looked at her. "Don't worry. He's physically safe. The farmer didn't shoot him."

"Shoot him?" That didn't help her nerves any. "Are there guns involved?"

"Anderson says he fired a couple of shotgun blasts to scare them off. In the air, not at the boys." Alex went on, "They must be plenty scared and uncomfortable by now. They've been there for hours."

"Well, at least they're in one piece."

"I agree that's a plus. Did you just notice that Brian was gone?"

"He doesn't check in with us, especially not with me since we had a talk about the break-in at the diner. And his bedroom is in a different wing of the house."

"You had another talk, huh?"

"I had a strong feeling that he and his friends were involved. But he just got defensive again and even more sarcastic. He said you must have stolen that pie when you ran out of doughnuts."

Alex laughed softly. "What a mouth. I guess wisecracking runs in the family."

They drove on, Alex turning off the highway onto a gravel road.

"He was always a good kid, at least when I lived at home," Kristen told him. She had been ten years older, however, and left for college when he was still pretty small. "I don't understand what's happened to him. Resenting a stepfather is one thing but acting like a twelve-year-old is another." She shook her head sadly. "He's smart, too. He took accelerated classes and graduated from high school a year early."

"Maybe he was less mature emotionally than his classmates, though."

"I'm beginning to think so. But no matter the reasons, this has got to stop."

"I agree. We'll see what we can do."

She only hoped things would turn out all right.

TIRED, SORE AND hungry, Brian sat on a tree stump and scowled at his friends. "This sucks!"

"Anderson is still around," Matt said, sounding defeated. "I saw him drive down the road in his pickup a few minutes ago and stare over here. He knows where we are."

"I told you this was a stupid idea." When Brian had argued against the plan last night, both Matt and Andy had countered that he never did anything *they* wanted. "We're going to be arrested for vandalism and trespassing. All because you thought it would be fun to spray-paint some cows."

Neither of the other young men responded. Matt hung his head, his hands in his pockets. Andy just sat on the ground and picked at a string in the tattered jeans he wore.

"And we can't even get away," Brian went on. His cell phone had run out of juice. Not that there was anyone he wanted to call for help.

Fearful of the farmer's shotgun blasts, they'd run to the car through the semidarkness of dawn, crawling over fences and tripping over rocks. When Matt's car had proven to be dead, they'd ended up taking cover in a wooded area of pasture.

"The cops are going to arrive any minute, I bet," said Brian.

Matt nodded glumly.

"We're sitting ducks." Brian slapped the tree stump and was rewarded with a splinter in his hand. "Oww!"

Andy spoke up, "We could try traveling across country. Circle around back to town."

"Why bother?" said Brian. "They'll know who did it when they identify Matt's car."

"Think we'll go to jail?" asked Matt.

"I don't know. What age is considered juvenile in Wisconsin?" Brian had never thought much about it before, since he never intended to be caught.

"You're a juvenile if you're under eighteen," said Andy, rising from the ground. He glanced around. "You two can do what you want. I'm taking off."

Brian felt concerned. "Hey, don't make it worse, Andy. They'll just track you down."

"Maybe. Maybe not."

"If they take us into custody, they'll have to give us food," Brian said, hoping that might influence Andy.

But the boy had started walking away. "I can live off the land."

"What about your family?" said Brian.

"They'll be better off without me," Andy muttered, sounding defeated. "Less to share."

ONE HOLSTEIN COW had three crude-looking purple stars decorating her black-and-white hide. Another cow displayed splats of fuchsia. The animals didn't seem upset, though their owner said the ordeal was sure to affect their milk production.

A short white-haired man, Ralph Anderson wore striped overalls and sounded tired and putout. "Who knows how long it will take to clean this mess off? You can't use turpentine on animals."

Alex examined the cow with the stars, running his finger over the purple lines. "Maybe there's some other kind of product. I'll ask around."

"Where are the boys?" asked Kristen, no doubt still worried about her brother.

"They're over in that patch of timber in the west pasture," Anderson said, pointing.

"One of them is my little brother," Kristen told Anderson. "I'm so sorry. We're going to make sure he doesn't do it again. He'll make it up to you somehow."

Alex liked her sense of responsibility. "Can I take the cruiser over there?"

"Go down the dirt road."

Alex nodded. "I'll take the boys back to town, and you can meet us there to press charges."

"What kind of charges? I don't want to send

kids to jail," Anderson said. "They just need to be taught a lesson."

"We'll work something out," said Alex, heading back to his car. Kristen followed.

As they pulled out of the farmyard, Alex told her, "I'm glad you came along. I think Anderson was impressed that one of the teenagers has family looking for him. You didn't offer to pay off Anderson, either. Some families try that or deny that their precious loved ones have done anything wrong."

"That wouldn't be right. Brian has to face the consequences of his actions."

"Good for you. Tough love."

They passed the old car parked on the dirt road and pulled over near the fence bordering the woods. Alex hoped he wouldn't have to climb over the fence and drag the kids out.

"Hey, Brian! Matt! Andy!" he yelled. "Come out. You're busted!"

Kristen stood beside him. "Brian, come out here!"

Rustling noises could be heard from the brush as two young men made their way out to the road through the trees. Matt looked scared but Brian's expression was sullen. However, he climbed over the fence and Matt followed.

"Where's Andy?" asked Alex.

Brian kept his gaze aloof, not looking at Alex or Kristen. "There's just the two of us."

"There were three of you guys last night," Alex told him, wondering why he was trying to protect the third kid. "Ralph Anderson saw you."

"Arrest us already," said Brian. "That's what you're here for."

"I'm not leaving until I have everybody."

Matt put in, "Andy left. Honest, there's nobody but me and Brian."

"Andy left how?"

"He took off on foot," Matt said. "We don't know where he went."

Alex stared at Brian, who finally nodded. "Yeah, he's gone. Maybe you should form a posse and ride out to look for him."

"If I were you, I would tone down the smart remarks," Alex told him, "and come up with the truth."

"Yes, please tell the truth, Brian."

Kristen sounded sad, not angry, but Alex noted that her brother gave her a wide berth when he walked past her toward the cruiser saying nothing.

Alex put the two boys in the back of the police car and closed the doors.

On the drive back to Sparrow Lake, Kristen noticed that her brother's hand was bleeding.

She stuck a Kleenex through the steel mesh and Brian actually took it from her.

"It's just a splinter," he said.

"But it could get infected," Kristen told him. "You should put something on it when we get back to town."

"Do you really care?" Brian asked. "I'm a criminal."

"I still care about you no matter what. You're my brother."

Her tone was warm but she didn't say anything else. Instead, she turned back to look at the road ahead. Alex thought the gesture was just about right. No doubt upset, despite his bravado, Brian might get even more defensive and angry if Kristen scolded him now.

Matt asked worriedly, "Are we going to jail?"

"I don't know," said Alex, though he was pretty sure he wasn't going to have to lock them up. "We'll see what Mr. Anderson wants to do."

"The farmer?" Matt asked. "We didn't hurt those cows."

"No, but you probably scared them. And they're someone else's property, expensive property. You can't just waltz onto private land and do whatever you want. You were trespassing."

Matt slid down in the seat. "I'll have to call my parents."

"Yeah, you will."

Remaining cool and impassive, Brian just stared out the window. As the cruiser headed for town, neither kid said anything else.

Hoping to relieve Kristen's worries, Alex lowered his voice. "They'll probably get off with community service and some counseling."

"Do you think so?"

"Neither of these guys has a record and Anderson didn't sound like he wants throw the book at them."

She looked relieved. "I just hope Brian will straighten out."

He hoped so, too. Dealing with her wayward brother may have helped get him together with Kristen in the first place, but it could just as easily put an obstacle between them. Not to mention he would hate to see problems with the law mess up another young kid's future.

CHAPTER SIXTEEN

ALEX KNEW KRISTEN was still concerned about her brother, but he hoped an outing on Saturday might take her mind off things. He'd promised her a dinner at an establishment so exclusive you couldn't even make reservations unless you knew the chef. He'd also told her he was going to take her to a show that was more fabulous than anything offered in Hollywood or New York.

The weather turned out to be beautiful on Saturday, if a little cooler than average for June. As he'd planned, Alex left the Jaguar's top down when he picked up Kristen in the early evening.

He admired the length of leg she flashed when she got into the car. "You look gorgeous."

"Thanks," she said, smiling.

She wore a blue-printed dress with fluttery sleeves and strappy high-heeled red sandals. The soles of the shoes were red, too, so they were probably the fancy, pricey type she favored. Alex had read about red soles somewhere.

Brian was out on the lawn watering some flowers with a hose as they pulled away. The teenager's back was as straight as a steel pole, and he didn't look in their direction.

Kristen sighed. "I'm not sure how Brian's feeling on the inside. Outside, he's polite and is doing everything he's supposed to. He's minimal in communicating with me but I heard him telling Aunt Margaret he was sorry for causing problems." She paused. "At least there's that."

"You'll need to give him time to come around as far as you're concerned. You were there when we caught him. He's embarrassed."

After Anderson had come in and said he wasn't going to press serious charges, Alex had put Matt and Brian to work at Sparrow Lake Community House. Both young men had also made appointments at the local counseling center. On Monday, Owen was driving them out to the Anderson farm for cow clean-up.

"Has Andy shown up yet?" Kristen asked.

"No sign of him. The police department notified state troopers to keep an eye out for the kid, but we didn't issue an official arrest warrant. The crimes the boys committed, after all, were minor."

"I hope he'll be okay."

"We talked to his mother at the motel." One of the few things Brian said at the police station was that Andy was next to homeless. "She hasn't heard from Andy and is worried. I also told her that her whole family is now on the meal schedule from the Soup Kitchen. They might not be elderly, but they sure can use some food."

"Brian actually seems concerned. I'm glad he has a good heart, at least."

"The family could have gotten some help before now. Maybe they didn't know it was available." Stopping at a light before entering the highway bordering the town, he switched subjects. "But enough about problems. Are you ready for the best meal of your life?"

"Where are we going?"

He chuckled. "I told you it's a place that's extremely exclusive. It's a surprise."

He wondered what she was going to think.

A couple of miles down, when he turned off the highway onto a street leading into town again, she did a double take. "Are you trying to get me turned around?"

"I'm trying to turn your head."

"This place must be local."

"Very local. You'll see."

Slowing on a shady street, he pulled into the driveway of a small two-bedroom house with a neat lawn and minimal landscaping.

"Who lives here?"

"Me. And Spike. He guards the place."

"You're fixing me dinner?"

He parked, got out and opened her door with a flourish. "Welcome to Chez Alex, mademoiselle."

"How delightful." She beamed.

He took her hand to help her out, enjoying the warmth and texture of her skin. Grinning at her, he said, "I'm hoping that the way to your heart is through your stomach."

KRISTEN TOOK IN the details as they entered Alex's house. The front door had a transom in which hung the stained glass they'd picked up in Lake Geneva. A small entryway led into a living room with a bay window, where another piece of stained glass was displayed. A matching brown tweed couch and chair, along with a leather recliner, faced each other. On a stand sat a large black flat-screen television, a single man's favorite possession, Kristen had heard. The house was orderly and clean, meaning Alex either was a good housekeeper or he hired someone to straighten up.

They crossed a short hallway to the kitchen, which featured an adjoining sun porch facing the shady backyard. All the windows on the porch were open, and in the center of the room was a small table covered with a white tablecloth, folded napkins, two place settings, a candle and a vase holding a bouquet of fresh flowers.

"Lovely," said Kristen, meaning it. He had obviously gone to a lot of trouble.

Alex plucked a yellow rose from the vase and handed it to her. "For you, mademoiselle."

"Merci, monsieur." She held the flower beneath her nose to inhale its delicate scent.

He pulled out a chair for her. "Please sit. Would you like some champagne?" He pulled a bottle from a bucket of ice.

"Of course. Wow, you've gone all-out."

He popped the cork and poured the champagne into graceful flutes. Handing her one, he offered a toast. "To the future."

"I'll drink to that."

"Things are looking pretty good."

She hoped so, but couldn't help thinking of Brian. "If only my little brother will straighten out. Do you think being the youngest in our family might have influenced his misbehavior?"

"There are a variety of reasons for teenage angst," said Alex, sitting down. "Take Matt Stapleton. When we talked to his parents, his father really got on his case. I think Matt believes he's a failure because of his dad. Stapleton actually asked the kid if he thought becoming a criminal would make up for not being a first-string athlete. This, right in front of Owen and me. I felt sorry for Matt. He's not the only one who needs counseling."

"That's terrible," Kristen agreed, frowning. "I hope we haven't made Brian feel that he's a failure."

"I don't think so. He excelled in school, right? And I haven't heard you putting him down."

"His new stepfather and he have had disagreements, but I think it's been more about personality differences. At least, according to my mother."

"Yeah, remarriage and stepparents can be stressful."

"Plus moving to a new state." Kristen sighed. "And I've come to realize I may not have been there for my brother when he needed someone. I left home for my last two years of college and…"

"You've been working."

"I guess my work has taken its toll on everyone."

"Come on. It's your choice. You have a right to a good career."

"I thought so." Though Kristen was starting to wonder. Her sister had complained about her too-diligent work habits. Had she been selfish? she mused. Then she realized they'd gotten onto worrisome topics again.

"I'm sorry, enough of that. What are we having for dinner?"

"Well, the first course is salad." Alex put his drink down to light the candle. "I know the French eat salad last, but I prefer my greens the American way."

"Salad sounds good to me. What's the main course?"

"Grilled lobster."

"Double wow." And fancy. She joked, "Did you catch it in Sparrow Lake?"

"I had them shipped in from a fish place John recommended."

He took a big salad bowl from the refrigerator and placed it on the table, along with some French bread. Then he placed a serving for each of them in smaller bowls and took a seat.

"I'm going to have to be getting up and down for a while here," he told her. "When I put the lobster on, it'll cook fast."

Kristen sampled her salad. "Delicious." And admirable. Jason had never taken this much time to impress her. If they ate at his apartment, they'd ordered out.

"So, do you do a lot of cooking?"

"A fair bit."

"I'm impressed. Did your mom teach you?"

He shook his head. "I learned on my own. I

like to eat, and while the Busy Corner is good for a quick breakfast or lunch, it has its limitations."

They made small talk until Alex rose to place the lobster and asparagus on the grill. At the same time, he stirred something into a pot of rice on the kitchen stove.

"Need some help?" she asked.

"Please sit. I want to wait on you."

As expected, the lobster and asparagus cooked quickly. Alex put the latter into a serving bowl and topped it with butter, then finished the lobsters in a sauté pan on the stove. When they were done, he slid each lobster onto a large dinner plate.

Kristen smelled something burning. "I think you may be overcooking the rice."

Alex grabbed the pan from the burner. "Oh, no!" He took off the lid and peered inside. "So much for the rice pilaf."

"We'll have plenty to eat anyway," Kristen assured him as he dumped the contents of the pan into the garbage. "Besides, it makes me feel better to see that you can't do every single thing perfectly. You have flaws."

Alex brought the dinner plates to the table. "You thought I didn't have flaws? That's a compliment coming from a woman like you."

"I guess we both do have high standards as far

as work is concerned." Kristen hadn't thought about that before now.

"I like people with high standards and a work ethic, people who are responsible."

He sat down and they dug into the perfectly cooked lobster.

"Yum." Kristen wiped a dribble of butter from her chin with her napkin. "I don't think I've ever eaten lobster grilled, but this is fabulous."

"Glad you like it. How's the asparagus?"

"Also yummy." She helped herself to another forkful, musing about work ethics and standards. "I wonder why some people work hard and others don't?" For herself, she'd always wanted to do the very best she could so she'd never be like her father. "I've always been ultraresponsible."

He looked thoughtful. "Then again, there are different ways to be responsible."

"What do you mean?"

"How about emotional responsibility?"

Kristin quirked her brows.

"Some of us believe we're our brother's keeper," said Alex. "I thought about how important it was to keep the peace when I became a cop."

She nodded. "You're serving and protecting society."

"Makes me feel useful to help others. I have a social conscience."

Social conscience? She considered that claim. His concern with the community was one of the things she liked about Alex. "I don't know that I can exactly say the same. I try to have a conscience for the members of my family, I guess. And I feel of use, too. Even if I'm working for a company, I'm helping them provide services to others."

"And helping them make money."

"Making money isn't a bad thing," she insisted, "as long as you don't trample others to get it."

"I agree. It must feel a little different when you're helping someone you love make a living, though. Running Sew Fine is more personal than working at some corporation, don't you think?"

She hesitated. "I haven't seen it that way, exactly."

"You just said you try to have a conscience for your family. You obviously like helping them or you wouldn't go looking for your brother or babysit for your sister…or come back here when your aunt asked you to."

"How do you know she asked me?"

"Oh, we were talking one time," he said.

"I also came back here for myself." She felt

it necessary to admit the whole truth. "I needed to regroup, recharge." Plus, she'd had few other places to go.

Alex's warm gray eyes met hers across the table. "But now that you're here, you've made a big difference, to your aunt, your sister…even Brian, though he won't admit it yet. Doesn't that make you feel good?"

"Well, yes…" She pondered the job interview she'd set up for next week.

"You sound ambivalent."

"I just never thought about the helping people angle. As you know, I've had to get some help myself recently."

He laughed. "Whether you wanted it or not. Those twins can definitely put you through the wringer. Speaking of the twins, did their mom find out what went down that night of ten thousand bubbles and a pack of dolls?"

"I don't think so. She hasn't said anything," Kristen admitted, "Of course, we're not talking all that much lately."

"Too busy?"

Kristen thought about the way her sister had been acting lately. About her threat to quit school. Now that worried her.

"I think Heather's frustrated with her schedule. She has too many things on her plate."

"She must have appreciated your being willing to babysit."

"Well, yes. But she normally would have had a babysitter anyway. It's my marketing plans that are getting on her nerves." She put down her fork, feeling comfortably full. "I've been drumming up more business. I told you about that reporter from Milwaukee who interviewed me—it seems she knows about a bus tour that's interested in putting Sew Fine on their itinerary."

"That sounds great."

"And I'm setting up a web page with links to an online ordering system."

"Also great. What's Heather's problem?"

Kristen sighed. "She's a mother, a college student *and* the manager of the store at the moment. She doesn't think she can handle more business."

"With your help, she can. Just ask if she'd rather you take on the duties of manager. From the sounds of the situation, your sister will be all for it."

Manager of Sew Fine? Kristen felt uncomfortable. She wasn't staying on in Sparrow Lake, and surely Alex wasn't expecting her to do so. Something told her not to get into that subject with him.

Instead, she insisted, "It will work out. It just

has to be organized well, and we need more employees."

"Sure. If business is picking up, I say go with it." He looked at her plate and the chunk of lobster remaining on it. "You aren't finished, are you?"

"I don't think I can eat another bite."

"I can wrap it up for you to take home, I guess, but I can't make one of those fancy foil take-home things." His own plate was clean. "Want some sorbet?"

"Not right now, thanks."

He picked up both dinner plates and took them to the kitchen. "You like what you're doing, right?"

"What do you mean? Do I like doing the marketing for Sew Fine?"

"Right. Rebuilding an existing business, one in which you have a personal stake."

She had to admit she'd been excited by all the improvements she could make. "I've truly enjoyed it."

"I get the idea you're even beginning to like quilting."

"I like the preciseness of it, sewing all the strips or blocks together to make a pattern." Though she couldn't say she was all that creative.

"See? Managing Sew Fine is a perfect fit for you."

If it were only that simple, she thought, telling herself not to be annoyed with Alex trying to find a solution that would fit them all.

Hearing some movement from the opposite side of kitchen, she glanced that way and caught a blur of movement. "Was that Spike, or do you have him locked up somewhere?"

"Nah, he goes where he pleases. That was him sneaking around the corner. He was probably hiding under the bed until he made sure you weren't dangerous."

"You have a shy guard dog?" she asked, surprised that he hadn't barked at a stranger.

Alex laughed. "Wait right here, it's time you met tough old Spike."

He disappeared into the living room, saying, "There you are." After some scrabbling noises, he appeared again, a big, fluffy, cream-colored cat in his arms. "Meet Spike."

Kristen had to laugh. There was something incongruous, if adorable, about a tall, strong man holding a cute, fuzzy cat.

"What's so funny?" Alex grinned at her.

"And here I thought you had a German shepherd!"

"Hey, don't insult Spike. He looks unassuming, but he works undercover."

"Under covers is more like it, I bet."

"That, too." He moved closer. "You aren't allergic, are you?"

"No." Kristen reached out to take the cat, who struggled a little but allowed himself to be held. She stroked his soft head and admired his big, blue eyes. "Hi, Spike. You're very handsome." She told Alex, "I always thought about getting a cat myself. I just wasn't home enough for any kind of pet."

"Well, I didn't 'get' this cat. He started hanging around and I fed him. I put up notices, but nobody claimed him. I took him to a vet but he doesn't have a chip. What could I do? He moved in, and I didn't have the heart to kick him back out to the street."

Another thing to like about Alex—his soft side.

"This guy looks like he might be a purebred, maybe Himalayan," she said. "They're expensive. It's odd that he'd be a stray. Maybe he got outside and wandered away."

"If he belongs to anyone in town, they should have said something."

"Because you're not giving him up now?"

"He's weeks into training. He's a valuable addition to the police force."

"I'm sure." Kristen laughed again. "You ought to buy him a black leather collar with spikes so he looks tougher."

She put the cat down and picked up the salad bowls and stray silverware, taking them to the kitchen to be loaded into the dishwasher.

"You shouldn't be doing this," he told her. "Customers don't work at classy restaurants."

"Well, this is a more homey, classy type of restaurant."

"Since you insist."

Between them, they made short work of clearing the rest of the table.

"I truly loved the meal," she told him. She also thoroughly enjoyed his company. Alex was not only good-looking but intelligent and intriguing. With his dry sense of humor and unusual ideas, he always managed to surprise her. Now she realized he was also something of a homebody, a trait that attracted her, as well. He would be the perfect man to settle down with...for someone.

The evening was darkening as they sat on the enclosed porch. The candle on the table between them flickered and the wind murmured through the backyard trees. Although there must be lights in the windows of some nearby houses, trees and bushes obscured them so that Kristen could feel as if she and Alex were alone. A very nice feeling, indeed.

"That must be east over there," she said, motioning. "That glow. The moon is rising."

"Oops, I almost forgot. We don't want to be late for the show." He got up and held out his hand. "Come on, we're taking a drive."

Outside, Alex helped Kristen into the car and took off. Soon they found themselves on the road that circled the lake. The June air was fragrant but cool and Kristen shivered, wishing she'd brought a sweater.

She barely noticed the dark and twisty path leading off the main road until Alex turned the car onto it. Nosing upward, their headlights searched the opaque darkness and gravel crunched beneath the tires. The car bounced over ruts as it climbed. Tree branches hung so low and thick that they seemed to be driving through a leafy tunnel.

"Where on earth are we going?"

"To get the best seat."

Whatever that meant.

A little farther on, they exited the tunnel of foliage and came out onto a rise overlooking the lake. The gravel road widened into an area a little bigger than a turnaround. On one side was a sheer drop, offering a sprawling view. Alex pulled up to the small barrier near the edge, parked and turned off the engine.

"The show," he said, with an expansive gesture. "Much bigger than anything Hollywood has ever produced."

Taking in the scene before her, Kristen had to agree. A vast canopy of stars twinkled overhead, as well as below, where the starlight became liquid pinpoints in the water. More gentle lights flickered from houses near the lake on the other side.

"Fantastic," she breathed.

"You won't see this in a city. Not all these stars."

"The city lights blot them out," she agreed.

To the east, the dark horizon smoldered.

"And here she comes," said Alex. "We're just in time."

As they watched, the moon suddenly slid up into the sky, a silvery orb above the dark shapes of hills and trees.

"She? What happened to the man in the moon?"

"I see the moon as a beautiful woman." He turned toward her and, though she couldn't make out details in the moonlight, she knew his eyes were intense and warm. "Like you."

She shivered, partly from the power of his gaze, partly from the beauty of the night and partly because she was cold.

"Hmm, you didn't bring a sweater, did you?" he murmured. "Guess I'll just have to help you out." He slid a warm arm around her shoulders.

She leaned back against him. "Feels good." The whole night felt good, better than any in recent memory.

"Now listen," he told her. "We have a concert, too."

Both remained silent, letting the sound of night insects and birds permeate the air. The wind moved the branches of trees, making leaves whisper. There was a light splat of water below the rise where the car was parked—probably a frog or a night bird.

Feeling at peace and warmed all the way through by Alex, Kristen took a deep breath, inhaling the fresh scents of water and growing things.

"Smells good, doesn't it?" He leaned closer to nuzzle her neck, his lips gentle but seeking. "But not as good as you."

Tracing a path from her throat to her mouth, he covered her lips with his own. Contrasted with the hardness of his chest, they were unbearably soft. She wrapped her arms around his neck and closed her eyes, losing herself to sensation. His breath tasted of lemon and champagne. His skin was smooth with a little rough stubble on the lower part of his face. He was the warmth at the center of darkness, night sounds and circling breezes. The embrace went on and on, and she had no desire to cut it short. He held her against him so that she could feel the rapid beat of his heart. Surely her heart was pounding just as quickly.

Slowly, she became aware of other noises in the background, crunching sounds. Like tires on gravel? Accompanying the crunching was a low growl. A car engine?

Alex must have heard it, too, because he broke their kiss to glance over his shoulder. A car emerged from the shadows, its lights off. It pulled up to park beside them. A startled young face gazed out the window at them. Alex waved.

The person in the car window waved back halfheartedly, as if he or she were timid. Then, just as quietly, the car backed up, turned around and left.

"They didn't like sharing this view with us, huh?" said Kristen.

"Actually, they probably got nervous seeing the police chief in the Sparrow Lake make-out spot."

"Make-out spot?"

"This is considered the best place for stealing a kiss from your girlfriend."

"You brought me to a make-out spot?" she said in mock outrage. She made a show of pushing against his chest to put a few inches between them.

"Now, now." In the same teasing tone, Alex pulled her back to him.

"And you plied me with food and drink," she complained. "All with ulterior motives!"

"I wanted my girl to see the moon tonight."

His girl? Again, he sounded proprietary, but she had to admit she liked it. She wanted to belong with this gorgeous man. She wrapped her arms around his neck again and offered him her lips.

CHAPTER SEVENTEEN

SINCE GETTING TOGETHER with John McClintock at the fish fry Margaret had been having a fine time. They'd gone for walks, out for coffee and caught a movie. Next weekend, they planned to attend a concert in Lake Geneva.

Now, if only the rest of her life were as much fun.

Margaret had been quite upset when she heard about Brian's escapades. Teenage boys will be boys, but Brian was getting a little too old to be acting out. She worried that more serious issues were at the heart of the matter, and she didn't want Brian ending up like his father, her own spoiled younger brother.

At least Brian had apologized for causing problems after she'd been kind enough to offer him a place to stay for the summer. That was a good sign.

Margaret hated to broach the subject again, but she found herself doing so as her nephew hung around in the kitchen while she was straightening up after a light supper. "I'm so happy you were honest about your actions the past few weeks, Brian," she began. "That was mature of you."

He made a sound like a snort. "Ri-gh-t, I'm so mature." He added sarcastically, "We got caught."

"You handled it much better than you could have. According to some people, they're never to blame. Everything happens because of someone else." She took a deep breath. "Your father was like that, you know. Samuel never took responsibility if he could help it."

"Is that why he left us?"

The poignant note in Brian's voice got to Margaret. She knew at least part of his acting out stemmed from insecurity over being abandoned by his father.

"I think irresponsibility was the major reason he took off. He just couldn't handle a family and a job, all the ordinary problems that life dishes out." She stacked plates, noticing that Brian had stayed put. "I felt very bad about it, you know. I thought it reflected on our family. Sam was always funny and sweet, but we spoiled him, since he was the youngest. We just gave him too much room to make excuses."

"And you want to make sure I don't turn out like him?"

The question was blunt, surprising her. "Well, everyone is different but…"

"I gave you a lot of excuses."

"Not exactly," she said. "But you deceived me these past weeks and sneaked around with those other two boys."

"Yeah." He looked down, examining his fingers. "I guess it's because they acted like they respected me."

She digested that. "You mean they treated you like a leader?"

He nodded. "I had ideas that I thought were fun without hurting anyone…and they did what I said. Most of the time, anyway."

"Well, I'm sure you're smarter than either of them, Brian. Look at you—you graduated from high school a whole year early." His age was likely another reason he wasn't as responsible as they thought he should be.

"Uh-huh."

"Aren't you looking forward to going to college?"

"Kind of."

Margaret sat down at the table opposite him to look him in the eye. "You don't sound very enthusiastic."

He shrugged. "I'll be in a new place, doing something new…."

"And making friends and learning subjects that will help you prepare for your future." She noticed that idea didn't perk him up. He actually looked sad. "Don't you find that exciting?"

He sighed. "To be honest, I kind of wish this summer would last longer. I don't want it to end. I've moved around enough and had plenty of new experiences since Mom met Mike. I'd just like it to stop for a while."

"Like what to stop?"

"All the moving around and being with new people and doing new things. I miss the old things."

"Such as…"

"Living in Sparrow Lake. I went to school here most of my life, had friends. Then we up and moved to California where I was an outsider."

She nodded, thinking she could see how he resented his stepfather for making all those waves in his life.

"I liked hanging out with people from my old life again," Brian said. "It was fun being with kids I knew growing up, even if we were doing stupid things."

"I see what you mean." And an idea was growing in her mind. She frowned and tapped her fingers on the table. "You know, nobody is forcing you to go off to the University of Wisconsin in

September." Where he planned to live in a dorm, which meant meeting all new people again.

"We already paid the admissions fee."

"You can still drop out before entering in September."

He looked shocked. "You're saying I should drop out of college?"

"Not at all. But, as a professor, I've advised a lot of students in my time." She asked, "Do you even know what you want to do?"

"Well...not exactly."

"And no wonder, you're just turning eighteen in September." She thought about the classes Heather was taking. "Have you ever considered going to a community college for a year or two, just to acclimate yourself, to think things over?"

"Community college?" He frowned.

"You could take your basic courses and it would be a lot cheaper," Margaret said.

"Which community college?" His frown deepened and his voice took on an unpleasant note. "You mean go back to California?"

Margaret hadn't meant to upset him. "Why not here in Wisconsin? That way, you can stay in Sparrow Lake and continue living right here with me, if you want to."

He was quiet for a moment. "You'd trust me to stay after all the stuff I've done?"

"I give people second chances." She cautioned, "Though there will be rules. No more silly shenanigans. And you have to maintain a certain grade average, maybe get a part-time job elsewhere if you don't want to work at Sew Fine."

"Hmm."

"You don't have to make a decision right now. Think it over."

"I guess I could check when the last date is to withdraw from the university."

"Think about your options." Maybe it was too soon for him to be going off to college, Margaret thought. He was younger than average, after all. Plus, she thought he'd lost some part of his identity when his mother had remarried. She felt he could find his sense of purpose again with some encouragement. "You have a family here, people who love you and will celebrate your victories and help you with problems." She was certain he could use a family in close proximity, at least for another year or two while he got his act together.

"*Some* family, anyway."

"Well, I know your mom is in California, but you'll have Heather and the twins. And Kristen—"

"Kristen is going back to the city."

Margaret frowned. "Not necessarily. She's met a nice man."

"Yeah, a cop."

"That cop is a decent guy. You think Alex is your enemy, but he doesn't hate you."

"He probably said bad things to Kristen about me."

"He probably told the truth about what he knew you were doing. He wants the best for you, Brian. He doesn't want to see a good kid waste his life. And Kristen doesn't hate you, either. She loves you. Surely you've always known that."

"She left home when I was seven or eight."

"Oh, come on, that was a long time ago. And she took care of you when you were a child."

Brian shrugged. "She's got her own concerns. That cop won't stop her from leaving, either."

"And you know this how?"

"There's gossip at the store. Sometimes I listen in," Brian admitted. "Word has it that Kristen's been offered a job in Chicago."

Margaret felt her heart drop. "When did *this* happen?"

"Last week. Kristen and Heather were going at it because Heather doesn't think she can handle any more business as the manager of the store. And Kristen is drumming up business, messing up Heather's life. And then she's taking off."

"Are you sure about this?"

"I'm just reporting what I heard."

"Well…" As much as she would hate to see her niece leave, Margaret knew it was Kristen's decision. She thought it sounded as if Brian didn't want Kristen to leave, either. "Adults have the right to do as they want, but…well, would you rather she stayed?"

"I don't have anything to say about it, Aunt Margaret. If Kristen goes back to Chicago, we'll hardly ever see her. I went there and stayed with her for a weekend when I was thirteen. Just once. I mainly hung around her apartment and watched movies."

"While she was there?"

"Sometimes she was home. Other times, she had to go to her office." He asked, "How often did she come out here and visit you through the years?"

"Not often," Margaret mused, "Perhaps that girl is a workaholic."

"She seems to love her work more than anything."

Thinking of the importance of art and teaching for herself, Margaret admitted, "Work can be important and very fulfilling."

"But don't you think you should make time for other things? I wouldn't want to work 24/7 for the rest of my life."

"You should try to balance relationships and work, I agree."

"Mom worked all the time when we were growing up, too," Brian went on. "But she had to."

"Maybe Kristen is following her precedent."

"Doing what she thinks she has to?"

"Maybe. And perhaps also proving to herself she's nothing like her father. She said something to that effect one time."

"Dad kind of made a mess of things, didn't he?"

"His actions had all kinds of repercussions. But we don't want to blame everything on him, just as he blamed everyone else. It's important to remember we're responsible for our own actions." Margaret sighed and pushed back her chair. "I need some tea and a few cookies. How about you?"

"I'll take the cookies."

They talked a while longer about this and that, Margaret secretly concerned about the news of Kristen's leaving. It could indeed be that family had no say in the matter. Kristen wasn't a child or still balancing on the cusp of adulthood like Brian. Maybe Kristen felt her degree in marketing would be wasted if she didn't hold down a high-profile job. Margaret only wished Kristen would realize the potential she had for making a difference in her own hometown, and that she would recognize how much people cared about her.

People here also needed Kristen. Heather was overworked. Brian needed a feeling of family. And she, herself, well…among other things, she could use the extra money that better business would bring in.

Speaking about needing and caring, she wondered what was going on with Kristen and Alex.

KRISTEN HAD NO idea whether she should tell Alex about her job interview or not. It was an awkward situation. What if he decided that Chicago was too far away for them to date? She soothed her worries by reasoning that surely he would be willing to adjust. Maybe, despite what he'd said so far, he'd even be willing to move back to the city someday.

Still, she wasn't certain about how to bring up the subject. The chance came on Monday after she and Alex had coffee at the Busy Corner.

"How about getting together another day or evening this week?" he asked, opening the door for her.

Pausing on the sidewalk, she realized this was the perfect opportunity to tell him about the potential job. "I have to make a trip into Chicago on Wednesday, and I have quilting class on Tuesday night. Any other time would be great."

"You're going to Chicago?"

"I have some business I need to take care of." Part of her wanted to tell him. The other part was stalling.

"Well, I suppose we could go to dinner somewhere nice and enjoy some city sights."

Kristen started. "You mean you want to go to Chicago with me?"

"Sure. I can drive. I know the city at least as well as you do. Unless you don't want me to go, of course."

"I would appreciate a ride, Alex. Thanks." Now, to get to the reason. . . .

Before she could think of a way, he asked, "Any place you want to eat, maybe take a walk afterward?"

"I like just about any kind of food, but I hope we can stay near the downtown area." Again, she tried to broach the subject. "That's where I have my appointment."

"Good. That gives us lots of choices. Navy Pier is beautiful at this time of year." The large pier jutting out into Lake Michigan had shops, restaurants, art galleries and attractions such as its huge Ferris wheel. He asked, "So what prompted this sudden need for you to go back to Chicago?"

Kristen swallowed. No more stalling—it was time to fess up. "I have a job interview. A hot lead."

His expression went neutral. "I thought you were considering being the new manager of Sew Fine."

"Some people have me pegged to take the job, but it belongs to my sister." To be fair, though, she knew Heather would gladly give it up to pursue her own dream. If her sister could afford to do so before finishing her degree. Kristen tried not to sound defensive when she said, "I'm keeping my options open until I can decide what I really want to do."

"Of course."

Alex's tone might be as neutral as his expression, but Kristen had the distinct feeling that he was holding back what he truly wanted to say.

Looking around the street at passing pedestrians, she realized several people had glanced at them with interest. Warmth crept up her neck, but when a familiar woman—a customer of Sew Fine—waved, Kristen returned the wave.

Turning her attention back to Alex, she tried to remain relaxed when she said, "If I move back to the city, it doesn't mean that I can't come here on weekends."

He digested that before asking, "So you did that in the past?"

"Well, probably not as much as I intended, but things can change. I have to make sure Heather isn't overwhelmed by her work schedule. And Brian... I need to see how he's doing."

"Uh-huh."

"And, of course, there's you. I want to see you. You can also come to see me in Chicago," she told him. "I won't be moving to the other end of the country or anything."

"Sure."

Alex sounded even more removed. Kristen wasn't certain what he was thinking, but she gave herself points for being honest and up-front. She had every reason to feel a little edgy.

They may have been dating for only a couple of weeks, but she believed Alex was someone special, and she didn't want to lose him.

ALEX GUESSED IT was a good sign that Kristen wanted him to drive her into Chicago. On the other hand, she was keeping an appointment that could change their future. He wasn't happy about the thought of her leaving Sparrow Lake, but he forced himself to remain hopeful. Surely she would realize that what was most important wasn't a job away from her home.

When he picked her up she looked good, as usual, though more formal in a soft gray suit, cream blouse, and a pair of fancy pumps. He had the Jaguar's top up, figuring she wouldn't want her hair to be ruined before a job interview.

Before he drove away, he raked his eyes over her. "You love nice clothes, don't you?" Maybe that's why she had to have a job that brought in the bucks.

"I admit that I have a fondness for designer clothing and footwear. I've always bought them on sale, though, sometimes at consignment shops."

"Why? Do you think it's too frivolous to buy such stuff at full price?"

"I'd have to be a CEO or have a trust fund to afford full price."

"Some people would just charge away, get themselves into debt. At least you're practical."

"*At least?* Meaning I have problems other than my choice of clothing?"

She sounded like she was only half-kidding.

So he deliberately teased her. "I've heard you're wanted for multiple misdemeanors in Wisconsin."

"I suppose the jay-walking is on my permanent record."

"Along with 'flaunting dangerous curves.'"

That made her smile. "I didn't know about that one."

"We're very strict in Sparrow Lake." Once he got onto the highway, he changed the subject. "Actually, buying expensive things that are used or on sale is a good idea. I got this car for a little more than half the price of a new one. We all need small luxuries."

As they sped toward the Illinois border, they discussed what they could and could not get along without in life. Kristen sounded reasonably practical. Alex didn't think they were likely to get into arguments about money. Not that he should be worrying about that, he told himself. At the moment, he was most concerned about whether or not she'd even be living where he would get to see her.

Once in the city, an hour later, they took the outer drive downtown, Alex enjoying the view of Lake Michigan on one side and the tall buildings on the other. It wasn't long before he let Kristen off at a building on Wacker Drive.

"Call me when you're ready," he told her. "I'm going to park the car and make some calls. For one thing, I have to check on our reservations for tonight."

He knew he should wish Kristen good luck but he just couldn't find it in himself to do so.

A COUPLE OF hours later, Kristen waited for Alex to pick her up. The interview had gone so well, she should be thrilled out of her mind. Instead, she felt conflicted and flustered. To her surprise, she didn't know what to do. The company wanted her to fill out personnel forms and get ready to start the following week…at a salary higher than any she'd ever received before.

She hadn't been ready for a job offer. She didn't even know if she wanted to accept.

In reality, she hadn't done so. The vice president who'd interviewed her had simply assumed that she would jump at the opportunity.

So, why hadn't she?

It had taken all her charm and persuasiveness to get her prospective employer to give her time to straighten things out in Sparrow Lake. She'd estimated a month; he'd countered with the standard two weeks. In the end, she'd neither accepted nor declined the position, but had promised a definitive answer by the following Monday.

Soon, the sleek Jaguar appeared, gliding in

and out of traffic. A little thrill ran through Kristen, but she wasn't certain whether it was because she was going to see Alex or because he would ask her about the job. He pulled the car over to the curb and opened the door. She got in, greeting him with a wan smile.

"So?" he asked.

"So *what?*"

He was having none of her evasions. "Come on. Do you think you'll get the job or not?"

"Um, maybe."

"Maybe?"

Feeling doubly pressured, Kristen said, "Let's discuss it when we get to Navy Pier." Which is where they'd decided to go that evening.

"All right." But Alex didn't look all right. He hid his scowl quickly, though, and took off.

As always, downtown Chicago was crowded, the streets bumper to bumper. The complete opposite of Sparrow Lake. Unable to help making comparisons between the two places she could live, Kristen had to admit that it was nice not having to face the crush of traffic every day. One for Sparrow Lake.

Alex had chosen Toscana, a restaurant on the Pier known for fine Italian cuisine. In contrast, Sparrow Lake had places like the Busy Corner. Not that her decision would be made because of the quality of restaurants or the amount of traffic she would have to endure.

She had to admit Alex looked just as at ease in either environment. Tonight he wore a dark shirt and tie with his crisp sport coat and slacks, making him as well-dressed as any of the other restaurant patrons.

She was happy he didn't bring up the job interview until after they'd left the restaurant and were walking down the broad concrete expanse of the pier. A historic structure built in 1916 to dock freighters as well as passenger ships, the pier was also designed as a cool place for public events before air conditioning was invented. Now the place housed a lively mix of shops and restaurants, plus a large conference space. Boats still docked there, as well, though they were meant to give visitors tours of the lakefront or serve as places to book private parties.

They were admiring a modern metal-hulled version of a four-master when Alex said, "You were in that interview for hours. Must have had plenty to talk about."

She turned the conversation back to him. "I hope you weren't bored waiting around."

"I called my brother and an old colleague."

"One of your police contacts?"

"Uh-huh. Jimmy Rodriguez. We worked in the same unit. Good man."

"The gang unit?" When Alex nodded, she asked, "You don't miss anything about being a cop in Chicago?"

"I miss some of the people. Not the work."

"You just decided one day it was too depressing and quit?"

"There was a lot of stuff going down. I was taken off the street and put at a desk for a while."

"You didn't mention that before."

"I don't like to think about it."

Alex had obviously gotten into trouble and had painful memories, Kristen thought as they paused to gaze out over the lake. The summer sun was sinking and the water looked dark blue-gray. On the horizon, lights from the urban skyline sparkled.

"You might as well know what happened. I shot a kid and he was critically wounded...."

She hadn't expected anything quite so dire. "Oh, how terrible!" She quickly added, "But you must have had a good reason."

"Sure. He was armed, and he was firing at us." Alex took a deep breath. "But he wasn't even sixteen years old."

"I can't imagine you shooting anyone. You're such a caring person."

"But I'm also a law enforcer." For once, he was blunt. "We do what we have to do, and sometimes that isn't easy or pretty."

She merely nodded and reached over to touch his hand. He grasped her fingers and held them.

"Anyway, the upshot is I resigned and headed for tamer places. I wanted to go somewhere I could make a difference and actually see the results."

"You *do* make a difference in Sparrow Lake." A man like Alex would make a difference wherever he went, though she could totally understand why he'd left the city. Not that bad things couldn't happen anywhere.

They walked on in silence, hand in hand. After a few more minutes, Alex said, "But let's get back to your job interview. Now that we're out here and fed and relaxed, who's giving the 'maybe' for this job? Is the company deciding for sure if they want you?"

"They actually appreciate my experience and background."

"But they have other applicants?"

"I'm sure."

A muscle in Alex's cheek worked as he stared at her. "You're not giving me straight answers, Kristen. Be honest, here, would you? What exactly went down?"

Though Kristen would have liked to evade the question for the evening, she knew he wasn't going to let her. "They offered me the job."

Alex gazed at her intently. "You're not celebrating. Does that mean you didn't accept? Why not? I thought that's what you wanted."

She looked into his eyes and felt more torn than ever. "I thought so, too, but now that I have the offer, my decision just isn't as clear-cut as I thought it would be."

"You're having mixed feelings?"

"Yes." Absolutely true, Kristen thought. Mostly because of him.

"Good."

Something about the way he said that word irritated her. "It's not a negative thing to work for an up-and-coming company in a big city. It's not dangerous like your job was, either."

"I didn't say that it was negative."

"But you implied it."

"I don't think I did. I'm just happy you're questioning whether or not marketing for a big urban company is what you want to do."

Her pulse picked up a beat. "Because you believe I should be satisfied managing a place like Sew Fine?"

"What's wrong with Sew Fine? It's a family business."

"Maybe I can better help my family by making more money. I could pay part of Brian's tuition." She'd already thought about that. "Or I could invest in Aunt Margaret's business."

"You could," he agreed. "But maybe your family would appreciate having *you* more than they would your money."

"It's *my* decision."

"True. But there are a lot of other people who will be affected by it."

Including Alex himself, and he was obviously feeling insecure. Kristen didn't want to think her moving to Chicago meant she would never see him again. The thought put a knot in her stomach.

"We can still see each other, date, even if I don't live and work in Sparrow Lake," Kristen told him.

"Maybe."

"What do you mean, maybe?" she asked, her voice going tight.

"I've heard that you like to work on weekends."

Who had been talking about that? It was the second time he'd mentioned it. She countered, "I don't like to work weekends but if you're a professional, you sometimes don't have a choice."

They had reached the barrier at the end of

the pier. An elderly couple walked toward them, the woman grasping the arm of her companion. They looked as though they had been a couple for a very long time. Kristen couldn't help wondering if she and Alex would ever be able to grow old together. Then she shook her head—where had that thought come from?

"Is something the matter?" Alex asked.

She hated to ask, but she felt compelled to do so. "Would you not want to date me if I lived in Chicago?"

"I want to date you no matter where you are."

She felt happier with that remark, but she still couldn't relax. She watched as the elderly couple came abreast of them and moved on. The woman of the pair exchanged a smile with her. She was a sweet-faced lady, wearing a flowered hat and carrying a large white purse.

"It's just that it would be easier if you lived closer, considering I would like to spend more time with you," Alex explained.

"Not night and day, surely, 24/7?"

"I didn't say that…."

But he sounded as if he meant that.

He went on. "You're a woman who likes to work and, well, that's fine with me. I just think you need someone to distract you once in a while and he has to live in close proximity."

"You're not just a distraction to me," she told him, thinking perhaps he didn't realize how much she wanted to be with him, as well.

"I'm glad to hear that." He gazed at her intently. "I don't know how it's been for you, Kristen, but I have to tell you that I'm developing feelings for you."

Was he talking about love? She swallowed hard. "You are?"

"Feelings that could easily become serious."

The thought stunned her. She'd avoided analyzing exactly how she felt about him. They hadn't even known each other a month. Things were continuing to go too fast for her.

Alex sighed. "I'm getting the idea you want your space again."

"I didn't say that."

Awash with powerful feelings, Kristen looked out at the broad expanse of the lake, which was restless as usual. Waves undulated against the shore. She didn't know how to respond. Her throat felt constricted. But Alex had just laid his heart on the table. She had to say something.

"I'm in a transitional phase of my life, Alex. It's…it's too soon. It's only been weeks. I have so many decisions to make. About work… family…and what I want to do with my professional life…"

A loud cry interrupted her. She and Alex both jerked around to look behind them. To Kristen's horror, she saw a youth grappling for the elderly lady's white purse. The old man tried to intervene and the thief struck him so hard, he fell to his knees.

"Hey!" shouted Alex, taking off.

"Help!" cried the woman, whose companion had now toppled to the sidewalk.

The thief ran and Alex ran after him. Kristen hurried toward the couple. The old man was already trying to get up again.

"Maybe you should stay down," Kristen told him. "We'll call an ambulance."

"Ah, I'm not hurt," muttered the fallen man. "Just my dignity." But he accepted Kristen's help in getting to his feet. "I'm shook up, is all."

A crowd was gathering, and a cop had appeared on a Segway, a motorized two-wheel scooter. As she watched, Alex helped the policeman grab the young thief, throw him down on the sidewalk, and fasten his wrists with handcuffs. In another minute, the place was ablaze with blue flashing lights as several police cars drove up onto the promenade of the pier.

As soon as the suspect was headed for the nearest police station, along with the couple to give their statements, Alex rejoined Kristen. "I'm ready to go home. You?"

"Sure."

They headed for the parking lot on the other side of the pier, crossing the mall that housed shops and restaurants.

"That was shocking," said Kristen.

"Yeah."

"Just a kid?"

Alex nodded, his expression stormy. "Probably all of fourteen and already headed for a life in prison. Or worse."

"Worse?"

"He could be dead in a few years. That can happen when they get involved in crime, then pick up with other criminals. Gangs."

"How terrible."

Alex didn't answer, steering her toward the other side of the pier and the parking lot. "I'm never moving back to Chicago, Kristen."

Maybe even visiting the place made him uncomfortable. Would he want to maintain a relationship with a woman who lived here? Kristen didn't know what to say.

THEY WERE SILENT much of the way back to Sparrow Lake.

Finally, Kristen said, "I guess it's more dangerous to live in the city than a small town."

Alex didn't want her making a decision based on fear. He tried to be reassuring. "Bad things can happen anyplace."

"Uh-huh. I lived in the city for years and I never saw a crime happening."

"Today was your turn." Alex wanted to lighten up the conversation, lessen the tension radiating through the car. He changed the subject, "So, how're things with your aunt?"

"Excellent, it seems. She's been seeing John. They're getting along very well."

At the moment, though he cared about his friends, Alex wasn't interested in hearing about other relationships. Before the purse snatching, Kristen had indicated she didn't feel the same about him as he felt about her. It had been one bust of an evening.

Still, he managed to mutter, "That's great."

"You wouldn't think a man like John would be interested in art. He's pretty conservative."

"Conservative-looking, anyway."

"In comparison to Aunt Margaret." Kristen's soft laugh sounded a little tense. "John doesn't stand his hair on end or wear clashing colors."

"Margaret must have a good time figuring out what to wear every day."

"She has her closet organized like a color wheel."

They sped along the freeway north to Wisconsin, along with a smattering of other cars. Trying to make conversation to avoid more dead silence, Alex said, "Not too much traffic tonight."

"I'm glad we decided to have dinner. Otherwise, we would have been caught in rush hour."

"That's something I've never understood. There wouldn't be a rush hour if everybody didn't want to go to work and come home at the same time," Alex said. "Why don't they space it out? I've never understood people's reasoning."

"Your hours have never been nine to five, right?"

"I guess not. I kind of like it that way."

"Most people want to be with their families in the evening and on weekends. School and jobs have to coincide for that to happen."

"I suppose so."

He only wished she wanted to line up her life more in sync with his. To give them a chance to work. But, having calmed down, he told himself that at least she hadn't completely rejected him.

Kristen peered out the window. "I can almost see the stars again, now that we're farther out from Chicago."

Which reminded Alex of the night they'd sat above Sparrow Lake and watched the moon come up. The kisses they'd shared had been just as beautiful.

"But I like the blaze of lights from the tall buildings, too," Kristen mused.

"Uh-huh."

What else could Alex say? He knew what he preferred, where he wanted to live. And Kristen wasn't sure. Perhaps the discrepancy in how they felt about each other had to do with his knowing exactly what he wanted, while she was at, as she'd said, a transitional point in her life. The fact was, she might be too transitional to want to develop something serious with him. He had to accept that possibility, and he had to take care of himself. Maybe he should back off.

In another few minutes, he turned off the freeway onto the local highway toward town. There was only one other car visible far ahead, its red taillights winking in the darkness.

"It's amazing how things change when you get off the more-traveled routes," murmured Kristen.

Which, for more than half of the country's population, would be living in a city, Alex thought. "It's like a different world," he said.

One in which he couldn't be sure that Kristen wanted to live, even with him. "I'm sorry if the evening kind of brought you down."

"It's not your fault that some kid decided to steal a purse."

THOUGH IT *WAS* his fault that he'd laid his heart bare right before the incident and then been disappointed when she hadn't responded as he'd desired. Trying not to let that get him down, he drove her to her house, parked and got out to walk her to the door.

"That's okay. I'll be all right," she told him when he came around the car to accompany her.

Was she already intent on doing without him? he wondered. "I want to say good-night properly."

In case it was also goodbye.

For all he knew, this could be the last time he would see her alone. Maybe she'd pack up and head back to Chicago, the place he'd bid a permanent farewell to.

The thought tore him up, but there was nothing he could do to change the way she felt. He'd already tried his best.

They walked along silently, Alex aware of the gentle sound of the wind in the trees and the less gentle beat of his heart. At the door, he reached for Kristen and enfolded her in his arms. Then he kissed her, savoring the sweetness of her lips and the subtle, clean smell of her skin. She felt perfect against him, perfectly partnering him.

Why couldn't she recognize that?

When Kristen wound her arms around his

neck, he wanted to squeeze her tighter, but he merely kissed her again, then drew back to trace the outline of her beautiful nose with one finger.

"Well, good night," he said reluctantly, his heart full to the breaking point.

"Good night," she whispered.

Then he walked away, wondering if he was going to have to learn to live without her.

CHAPTER EIGHTEEN

THE DAY AFTER her interview in Chicago, Kristen woke up tired. She'd tossed and turned all night, unable to get Alex off her mind. Still, she made it to work on time, entering through the back door of Sew Fine, going straight to her desk and turning on her computer.

Heather was already there, straightening a display. "How's Brian doing?"

Kristen hadn't thought much about her younger brother since she'd started worrying over the possibility of leaving Sparrow Lake and her relatives and friends. And especially Alex. "Fine, I think. You haven't heard about any more pranks, have you?"

"No, thank goodness. Facing up to their actions seems to have gotten those boys back on the straight path. We're lucky to have a man like Alex in charge around here."

"I agree."

Alex was a fine man for all kinds of reasons. The best man she had ever dated. The only one who had ever made her heart pound crazily.

The only one who had ever made her question her decisions.

"He's good with kids of all ages," Heather said with enthusiasm. "Addison and Taylor loved having him read them a story before they went to sleep."

"I know." Her sister's expectant look made Kristen shift uncomfortably. She supposed she could talk to Heather about her feelings, but the thought made her downright edgy.

"It was nice to have a positive male role model for them," Heather went on. "Considering they're missing a father. Bring him over anytime."

"Okay." Though Kristen wasn't certain when she'd be seeing Alex again. And thinking about all his good qualities somehow made her feel worse.

"Are you all right?" Heather gazed closely at her sister. "You look a little peaked."

No wonder, considering the decisions she had to make. "I'm fine."

"Well, as I've been telling you, I'm back on track. I was just a little tired last week. We all get that way."

"I know. I don't hold it against you. You have a lot of responsibility." And she meant to take her sister's situation into consideration when changing anything about the business, including her plans for improvement.

Gloria arrived with a sunny smile. After storing her purse behind the counter, she went to work opening some boxes of new fabrics that had been delivered the day before.

Kristen drew a tall stool up to the counter to make to-do lists on a notepad, her normal procedure. Without even thinking, she realized she had created one list for things to do if she took the job in Chicago and another list for if she kept working in Sparrow Lake. This was nuts! She tore off the pages, crumpled them and threw them away.

She'd started a whole other list of things to do—for this day alone, since it was as far ahead as she could think—when Shara came in carrying a big bag.

Trying to be perky and positive, Kristen said, "Hi! Run out of fabric?"

"No." Shara appeared rather glum. "I'm glad you're still here."

"You mean today?"

"I mean anytime. I heard you were leaving."

Beyond Shara, Kristen noticed Gloria shaking her head vigorously at the other woman while mouthing "no."

"You heard that from whom?" Kristen asked,

a little miffed that people were gossiping about her again.

"I'm sure everyone witnessed our public spat the other day," Heather put in. "They couldn't help it."

Kristen guessed that was a fair observation.

"When are you going?" Shara asked, laying her bag on the counter.

"I don't know. I haven't even decided yet if I want the job or not."

"You mean there's still a chance?" Shara brightened. "Is there anything we can do to get you to stay?"

Gloria was watching closely, as was Heather, Kristen noted.

"I just need time to think about it. Myself." She made haste to change the subject. "What have you got in the bag?" She pulled up an edge to peek at what seemed to be a quilt in blues, soft grays and creams. "Wow, it looks beautiful."

"I'm glad you like it," said Shara.

"May I take it out and examine it more closely?" Kristen asked.

"No!" Gloria's response was so emphatic that it made Kristen flinch.

"It's best not to look." Shara glanced anxiously at Gloria. "I'm sorry, I'm making a mess of things here."

"Let's go to the back of the store," Gloria said.

Now Kristen was really curious. "Wait a minute. What's going on?"

Shara said, "We might as well tell her."

Gloria sighed. "Okay, I guess."

"This is...*was* for you," Shara explained. "A gift from the quilting group on Tuesday night."

"We're still working on it, though," Gloria added. "It's not done."

A gift? Why? Kristen wondered. They surely couldn't have put something together so fast as a going-away present.

"The theme is true blue." Shara ran her hand over the quilt. "A true blue, true love quilt, that is. For you and Chief Novak."

"Oh." Kristen felt her face grow warm. "That... that's sweet..." She didn't even know if there would be a her and Alex. "A true love quilt?"

"That's what the pattern's called," said Gloria.

"What's going to happen with you two when... if...you leave?" asked Shara.

"I'm hoping we can still see each other on weekends." Though she wasn't confident that Alex was on board with that. Since he wanted nothing more to do with the city—for good reason—he might not even choose to date a woman who lived there.

"Well, you two look so cute together," Shara

said. "Sometimes you can just tell that a couple are perfect for each other."

Gloria nodded, and Heather just smiled.

"The quilt is really special. Thank you. But I don't know if I deserve it. I mean, I don't know what is going to happen with Alex and me. Right now I'm not sure about anything."

"Okay, enough." Gloria motioned to Shara. "Kristen's obviously got a lot on her mind. Come on back and let's talk fabric."

As they moved off, Shara said, "We love you, Kristen, no matter what you do."

Kristen was left staring at her list, unable to make sense of the words. Someone she had known for so little time said they loved her. None of her friends in Chicago—people she'd known for years—had said that when she'd told them she was going back to Sparrow Lake. She remembered one of her longtime friends saying, *Hope we'll see you again when you come to your senses.*

Furthermore, she was stunned—she couldn't believe the Tuesday group had actually started a "true love" quilt for her and Alex.

People thought they looked perfect together.

Truthfully, when she was relaxed and not worrying about her future, she felt time spent with Alex *was* perfect.

If she did leave Sparrow Lake, she was going to miss a lot of people, but most of all, she would miss him.

KRISTEN STAYED AT Sew Fine until midafternoon. When she left, she drove to FamilyMart, which featured a full grocery store in addition to its other merchandise. She did a little shopping, picking up fresh fruit along with the usual bread and milk. Afterward, she drove around rather aimlessly, just thinking.

Alex had as much as said he loved her after they'd had dinner in Chicago. In response, she'd told him that, for her, declarations were too soon. She certainly cared about him, couldn't imagine not seeing him.

It was just that… It was just that what? Again, she became aware of a flicker of fear. Was she afraid of falling in love, afraid a man would leave her like her father had left her mother, like Jason had so easily quit seeing her? She'd never consciously thought about that before, but perhaps her father's betrayal of his wife and family had affected her more than she'd thought.

Arriving home, she put the groceries away, then went to her bedroom to lie down. She stared at the ceiling, watching the fan go round and round. Her eyes drifted shut.

She awoke later to smell toast and cinnamon in the air. Heading for the kitchen, she found Brian working the toaster and slicing up a banana. He nodded, though he didn't smile. She helped herself to a glass of iced tea from a pitcher in the refrigerator and sat down at the table.

"Whatever you're making smells good."

"Hungry?" he asked.

"Hmm." She hadn't even eaten lunch. "What are you fixing?"

"Extra-crunchy peanut butter and banana sandwiches on cinnamon swirl toast. Want one?"

"Actually, that sounds pretty good." Comforting. "Remember when Mom made us peanut butter and banana sandwiches late at night?"

"Yeah, after her last work shift." He told her, "One PB and B coming up."

At least he was acting fairly friendly.

And he made a good sandwich, she found out when he served her a few minutes later. She bit into it, savoring the salty peanut flavor mixed with the sweetness of banana and the crunchy cinnamon of the toast. "Very tasty, Brian."

"Want some milk to go with it?"

She had the tea but milk sounded better. "Yes, please."

He poured her a glass, then sat down with his

own sandwich and milk. After he took a bite, he asked, "So how're things going?"

"What things? Work?" Surely he didn't mean Alex.

"Are you moving back to Chicago?"

She sighed. "Not you, too."

"Other people have been asking you about that, I guess."

And she told him what she'd told everyone else. "I haven't decided yet. The job is a great opportunity."

"Then why haven't you taken it? I assume you'd make a lot of money, get an apartment with a view of Lake Michigan again."

"I would hope so." But somehow those things didn't seem as important as they had a month ago.

"Bet your cop boyfriend doesn't like the thought of you leaving."

She gave him an annoyed look. Though she couldn't imagine Brian telling her how perfect she and Alex would be together. She was pretty sure her brother didn't like the police chief.

To her surprise, Brian said, "I kind of know how you must feel, thinking about leaving him behind. I was dating someone in California."

"You were?" He hadn't talked about it before.

"We broke up when I said I was coming back to Wisconsin."

"That's too bad." And probably another reason for him to be unhappy.

"Nah, it's all right. We weren't serious."

Not as serious as she and Alex, Kristen thought.

"I don't think I'm ready for a long-term relationship," said Brian. "That would be plenty hard to do."

"It didn't work out for our parents."

"And Aunt Margaret's been married three times."

"She does say that the first two marriages were mistakes." Kristen mused, "But how do you know when you're making a mistake?"

"You got me."

"You're pretty young," Kristen acknowledged. "Though Heather was about your age when she started dating Scott."

"You should probably talk to her, then." He took a last bite of his sandwich.

"I remember her saying she just had this feeling about him from the first time she met him." She'd had a definite feeling about Alex from the first, but it was more irritation than attraction. "Do you recall her talking about it?"

"No. But I was only twelve or thirteen." He

looked at her quizzically. "You're not asking me for advice or something, are you?"

Kristen laughed. "Why not? In love, it seems to be the blind leading the blind."

He laughed, too.

"It's great to see a smile on your face," she told him.

"Are you in love with that cop?"

Her laughter dissipated. *Was she?* Just thinking about having to come up with a definitive answer made her stomach knot.

"You probably didn't like getting arrested all those times," Brian said.

"Alex couldn't find any other way to get my attention."

"He did it on purpose?"

"I pretty much think so. Come on, jaywalking?"

"And breaking and entering." Brian sobered, adding, "When some of us were doing that for real."

Kristen said nothing, not wanting to rub in his past mistakes. Laughing and joking with Brian was such a relief that she didn't want to spoil things between them. "I wasn't that mad at Alex. He can be funny and charming."

"I guess he's not too bad...for a cop." Brian

cautioned, "You should make your own decisions, though."

"You mean about the job in Chicago?"

"Yeah, if you want it, take it." He gulped down the rest of his milk. "And work, work, work all you want. As long as you're not doing it just because of dad."

"What do you mean by that?"

"None of us wants to be like the guy who went off and left his family because it was too much responsibility. Maybe you think you have to be like Mom, just make more money."

She gazed at him closely. "Maybe Dad's walking out on our family affected all of us in ways that we didn't realize."

As if he thought that was aimed at him, Brian said, "I don't want to be irresponsible. I'm not usually."

"You were unhappy." Kristen reached over and put her hand on his and was glad that Brian didn't pull away.

"I had some kind of rebellion thing going on. I was just messing around, I guess."

She realized he was attempting to make peace with her. "I'm glad you've thought about it."

"I know, uh…I know people care about me."

"We do," she said warmly, wondering if he would complain if she hugged him.

He set the glass down. "Because of that, I kind of need to ask your opinion about something."

This was new. Wondering what he could want, she said, "Sure, fire away."

"Promise me you won't tell Novak."

"Is it about something illegal?" she asked, suddenly concerned.

"Not exactly, not about me anyway. I promised a friend I wouldn't tell anyone and here I'm telling you."

She nodded. "Okay, I can keep a secret. What is it?"

"I know where Andy is." He watched her expression. "Approximately, that is. He phoned me today from some place out in the country."

She was happy she didn't know the exact location because then, if questioned, she wouldn't have to lie. "Is he okay?"

"So far."

"Meaning he won't be okay in the future?"

Brian shrugged, but his expression showed his worry. "I think he's hanging with some really bad dudes. Andy says one guy has been in and out of prison."

"That sounds dangerous." And like the scenario Alex had described about wayward youth being influenced by older criminals.

322 HOME TO SPARROW LAKE

"I tried to talk him into coming back to Sparrow Lake, but he doesn't seem to want to listen."

"Did you tell him his family misses him?"

"Yeah, and I also said the community service he would have to do wasn't that bad. He says he plans to stay with these guys and make money."

"Make money?" Andy was just a teenager, still in high school. What did *these guys* want him to do? "That sounds like it could be something very dangerous."

"That's what I think." He gave a big sigh. "And I'm afraid I may be responsible for his taking off."

"How could you be responsible?"

"I led him into doing all those stupid stunts."

"He wouldn't have done them on his own? Or something similar?"

"Well, maybe," he agreed, his expression earnest. "But still. I'm afraid he's going to ruin his life. What can I do?"

She thought about her own worry when she'd realized Brian was messing around. She also remembered Alex's advice to her.

"Just tell him you're on his side and want what's best for him…if you get the chance."

"If I get the chance is right. He may never call me again." Brian shook his head. "Thanks for listening."

"Anytime."

Since the conversation seemed to be over, Kristen rose to rinse her dishes. Brian came up behind her and placed his plate and glass in the sink. She was so proud of her little brother for being concerned about someone else. It was a side of him she hadn't seen in a long time, one she appreciated. Feeling better than she had all day, she turned and gave Brian a quick hug. He hugged her back.

"I'm glad you confided in me," she told him. "Don't worry, I won't tell anyone else."

He left the kitchen to go watch TV. Kristen wandered out onto the brick patio facing Sparrow Lake. She stretched out in a lawn chair and enjoyed the breeze. It was still daylight, though the shadows were starting to lengthen. Everything was peaceful without the low background roar of traffic that was ever present in the city.

She'd lived here for almost twenty years and had liked Sparrow Lake just fine. She'd also liked Chicago, however, and had found its constant activity exciting. When she'd had a good job and a nice place, she'd regarded herself as successful. Somehow she'd thought of her return to her hometown, unemployed and homeless so to speak, as a failure. She'd felt as if she'd lost her identity.

But what defined failure and success? Her professional efforts had certainly been putting Sew Fine on the map. And, as far as relationships went, she'd had friends in Chicago, still had one or two, but she again thought about the comparison. No one had paid so much attention to her personal life that they made a quilt in celebration of her dating someone.

Today had been a very good day, she thought, with warm wishes from both friends and family, exactly when she'd needed the support. Maybe living in Sparrow Lake would give her things she couldn't get in Chicago.

She certainly couldn't ask Alex to spend a lot of time in the city. His confession of what had driven him to Sparrow Lake made her heart ache. What a horrible thing to have happen to a wonderful man.

She gazed up at the sky where a few brash stars already glimmered. They brought back memories of the night she and Alex had parked at the make-out spot. His kisses had been exciting, exhilarating. What was he doing tonight? she wondered, wishing he would call.

ALEX STOOD AT the front desk talking with Janet, the good-natured nightshift clerk, and Owen, who was getting ready to go home. He wanted to call Kristen in the worst way, but he feared talking to her would backfire on him. Telling her how he felt hadn't gone as he'd hoped, and he was still a little raw from that evening in Chicago.

"No more pranks going on," Janet was saying. "Right?"

"Nope. Everything's back to normal," Owen agreed with a laugh. "Some guy over on the east side of town complained about his backyard being ruined by a neighbor's weed spray. That's all the excitement for today."

"Did you check on it?" Alex asked.

"Yeah, I warned the neighbor to keep the spray in his own yard and I told the other guy his actually looked better without the jungle he'd had growing back there. Whatever, I think he's settled down."

Janet read a note on her desk. "Jergens, one of the state troopers, reported that he sighted a skinny redheaded kid walking around Lake Geneva."

They were still looking for Andy Eccles, but Alex said, "There are a lot of redheaded kids."

"He was hanging out with someone suspicious," Janet added.

"Hmm, maybe I should talk to Jergens," said Alex, though he was pretty sure he could wait and do that tomorrow. Jergens might not be on duty—the note was from the day shift.

Owen took out his own cell to read a text, then grinned. "I'd better head home."

Alex only wished the woman he wanted would urge him to hurry to her side that evening. Or anytime. He was trying to give Kristen the space she needed so that he didn't chase her straight back to Chicago.

He might not be ready to throw in the towel, but he knew he had to maintain a little distance until she made one of those lists she was so fond of, until she decided what was important in her life.

He only hoped he would be at the top of her reasons to stay.

CHAPTER NINETEEN

KRISTEN HAD STILL not heard from Alex by Saturday. Though she'd planned to stay home and clear her head to make some important decisions, she realized she'd forgotten her most current list of things to do and would have to go to Sew Fine to find it. Around noon, she made a trip to the store. Driving down the street, she glanced at the family restaurant on the other side and spotted two men in black uniforms sitting in the front booth near the window.

Alex?

Her heart beating faster, Kristen slowed, and seeing only one car coming from the opposite direction, did an abrupt U-turn. She passed the restaurant again and recognized Alex and Owen inside. She braked hard, accidentally making the tires squeal, and Alex looked up. She waved, ignoring the beep of the other car, which had come up behind her quicker than she'd expected. Looking puzzled, Alex waved back but didn't move from the booth. Kristen drove on, slowly.

Unbelievable! Surely he saw that she was trying to get his attention. Why didn't he come outside and ask her what she wanted?

And what would she say if he did?

She drove on, nosing into the restaurant's tiny parking lot where the police cruiser sat. Turning her car around again, she came back out into the street. His back to her, Alex wasn't even looking around to see where she had gone.

She felt a chill. Had Alex already written her off because he thought she was leaving Sparrow Lake? Surely not.

Parking the car in front of Sew Fine, Kristen started for the front door, then halted. If she wanted see Alex, she would simply go talk to him. She started back for the restaurant, not even thinking about the fact that she was crossing in the middle of the block. Another passing car beeped at her, making her jump.

She gave herself a mental talk. Maybe she was being impatient. Maybe she should wait to talk to Alex.

Then again, why couldn't she just follow her instincts for once and face him?

She turned around, then turned the opposite way again, finding herself pacing back and forth in the center of the street. And someone was watching her, she realized, wanly returning the wave of the friendly motorist who'd politely stopped a few yards away, probably wondering what direction this crazy woman would eventually choose.

How embarrassing!

Her face hot, forgetting about Alex for the moment, she nearly ran back to her car.

ANDY ECCLES WAS staying in an old farmhouse that looked abandoned from the road. Up close, Brian saw there were newspapers taped over the windows from the inside, though an air conditioner droned away in one of them, and the front door was shut tight. A couple of unsavory-looking dudes lounged on the wide, sagging back porch. They glared when he got out of the car.

"Thanks, man," Brian told the driver, an acquaintance of Andy's who had given him a ride from town. "Can you wait for a few minutes?" Until he rounded up his friend.

But he'd barely closed the door before the car backed up and took off, leaving him standing there between a pickup and a beat-up sedan. He looked around, feeling exposed and uncomfortable. Then Andy ambled out from the shadows of a small shed, one of the decrepit outbuildings in the farmyard. There were several, including a skeletal barn leaning so badly to one side that the next storm might topple it.

As skinny as usual, Andy appeared the same as when he'd run off, except his hair was a little longer and his clothes looked as if they needed to be washed.

"Hey," he said to Brian, pounding him once on the shoulder. "Wasn't sure you'd come." He motioned to the nearest outbuilding. "Let's get out of the sun." He led them over to a pile of boards. "We can sit here."

"It feels real tense around here." Brian indicated the two guys on the porch. "Who are those losers?" He wondered what sort of illegal activity was going on. At the least, drinking and partying. At the worst, serious crime of some sort.

"I don't know anything, not even their names."

"They aren't the guys you've been hanging with?"

"No, Jerry and Leon are in the house."

"Are you ready to come back to Sparrow Lake?" asked Brian, who'd been hopeful when a seemingly unhappy Andy had called him earlier.

"I don't know what I'm gonna do." Andy was acting nervous and jumpy.

"Your mom misses you, you know."

"Yeah." Andy sounded sad. "I miss her, too. You didn't tell her I called, did you?"

Brian didn't answer the question. "Your family's getting food from the community kitchen now. They still have a place to live." Even if it was a motel room. "You need to come back, man. You've got your last year of high school to finish."

"Graduating from high school don't mean I'll get a job."

"Not graduating will ensure you don't get one."

Andy merely grunted.

"And if you keep hanging around with these guys—" Brian nodded to the men on the porch "—you may end up in jail. Or worse."

"Thought about that," Andy admitted.

"Then why don't you just come back to town with me?"

"How? Our ride left." Andy was obviously referring to the driver who'd delivered Brian. "I had to just about beg for the favor of bringing you out here anyway."

"We can call someone else to come get us."

Andy shook his head. "Jerry said I wasn't goin' anywhere. He has plans for me."

Some bozo had told Andy he couldn't leave? Now that concerned Brian even more. "Well, I'm leaving after I talk to you...one way or the other." He'd walk back to town if he had to.

"You can go. But be careful about it. Maybe

wait till it starts gettin' dark," Andy advised him. "Then they won't notice."

Obviously Andy had gotten himself mixed up in something pretty bad. And hearing he'd have to sneak away after dark made Brian uneasy about his own safety. There were no neighboring farms in sight. The closest was a place he'd seen about two miles down the road.

As they sat there, another pickup arrived driven by a big guy with long matted hair and more tattoos than Brian could count. The man had a woman with him who also sported multiple tattoos. They approached the farmhouse porch where one of the sentries greeted them and took them inside.

Brian pulled out his cell phone. "So are you with me or not?"

"You don't understand. I don't have a choice."

"You always have a choice. And I think you know that or you wouldn't have called me."

At that moment, the front door of the farmhouse opened and a wiry, bow-legged man strode out. Despite the heat, he was wearing a leather jacket. He looked directly at Brian and yelled to Andy, "Who's that?"

"A friend of mine," Andy shouted in return.

Brian slipped his phone back into his pocket.

"Come on over here. I wanna talk to both of you."

Andy said, "He's just visiting, Jerry."

"Come here," the man said sternly.

Now what? Hand on the pocket with his cell phone, Brian wondered if they were going to be able to escape.

KRISTEN FELT HUMILIATED over having a local motorist witness her pacing crazily up and down in the middle of the street. And Alex probably hadn't even noticed. After grabbing the list she'd gone after, she'd hurried out of Sew Fine and headed home. She was nearly there when her phone rang. She answered as she was parking in the driveway.

"Kristen?" said Brian, sounding tense and out of breath.

"Is something the matter?" Kristen asked.

"I need some help here."

"Help? What's wrong?" Her mind started spinning, imagining all kinds of things.

"I need someone to come pick me up…and Andy."

At least he wasn't hurt. "Where are you?"

"I'm not sure…but you need to take the second turn off the highway on the west side of town, then turn onto the gravel road off the blacktop. The farm looks deserted, but it's not."

"Are you in danger?" She recalled what Brian had said about the company Andy had been keeping.

"Uh…maybe. I had to sneak away to make this call."

Kristen reached for her keys. "I'll be there as soon as I can."

"No, not you, Kristen."

"What do you mean, not me?" she asked indignantly.

"There's some bad people. I don't want you getting mixed up in this. Find Alex."

"Did you call the police station?"

"He's off shift." There was some noise in the background. "Get him, will you? I have to hang up—"

Then he was gone. Kristen just sat there with the cell phone in her hand for a moment before she reacted.

Brian was in trouble. Her pulse began to race. If he wanted Alex to come get him, it must be serious. Brian had said that at least one of Andy's new "friends" had been in prison. She started up the car again and pulled out, intending to find Alex in person and fast.

One good thing about small towns…he didn't live far away.

ALEX SAT AT the kitchen table, thinking. He was tired after finishing the night shift and then going out for breakfast with Owen. He'd been surprised to see Kristen, though he supposed he shouldn't have been, considering Sew Fine was right across the street from the restaurant. What was even more startling was the way she'd acted, driving recklessly up and down the street, then walking out into the middle of the road until cars beeped at her.

Why hadn't she just come into the restaurant and talked to him? he wondered. He could have gone out and arrested her for jaywalking—something she might have been tempting him to do, he guessed—but he was reluctant, still avoiding the break-up he feared might be coming. He didn't want to play games anymore. Since taking Kristen home on Wednesday night, he'd been mulling over the possibility that the woman he loved just might not love him back. Might never love him. Otherwise, she wouldn't be seriously considering moving away. Yes, they'd only known each other a short time, but they had something wonderful. If she didn't realize it, she might not be the woman for him.

The doorbell shrilled suddenly, making Alex jump. Spike, who'd been eating out of a bowl on the floor, bolted out of the kitchen, heading for the safety of the bedroom.

The bell rang again.

"Coming!" Alex yelled, thinking it must be the postman.

He strode to the door and opened it to see Kristen, her face flushed and eyes wide. Part of his brain asked hopefully if she had come to tell him she couldn't live without him, but then he realized she was panicked and trying to hold it in. "What's wrong?"

"It's Brian. Come right away. He's in danger!"

"Brian?" His tired brain wasn't functioning at its best.

"My brother."

He frowned. "I know who he is. What happened?"

Her words spilled out in a gush. "He's with Andy Eccles. Out in the country. It sounds like there are some dangerous people involved."

"And you're asking me to go get him?"

"Brian called and told me to find you, Alex. He must be desperate."

That was true. The kid definitely wasn't his biggest fan. "All right." Alex motioned for her to wait while he grabbed his gear. Adrenaline coursed through his veins, waking him up.

Outside, the cruiser was parked in the driveway. Alex unlocked the door for Kristen, then climbed in himself. Backing out, he asked, "Where are we going?"

"He said they're on some farm." She gave him Brian's directions and he thought he knew the roads she was talking about.

A few minutes beyond the town limits, he slowed down and turned onto a county blacktop.

"Do you think you might have to arrest someone?" she asked anxiously.

"Actually, illegal activity outside the city limits isn't the responsibility of Sparrow Lake," he told her. "It's county. Or possibly even state or federal."

"What about the spray-painted cows?"

"I dealt with that because the boys were from town and I knew the farmer."

"So this isn't your responsibility."

"I'm making it my responsibility, no matter what." He explained, "We'll say that I'm just picking up some minors who've been messing around in town. I don't have any beef with anyone else."

He glanced over at Kristen. Concern and fear made her appear more vulnerable than he'd ever seen her. He wanted to take her in his arms. He would, if he wasn't driving, no matter the state of their relationship.

"Don't worry," he told her, attempting to be comforting. "This police car will be a red flag to lowlifes. They won't expect us to drive right in the gate. Hopefully, they'll freeze. I'll tell them I'm not interested in anyone but the boys. We'll pick up Brian and Andy and get out of there. And if the guys they're staying with are doing something illegal…" Which probably they were. "…I'll call it in."

They passed farms from time to time with big red barns and silos. Cows dotted the pastures, along with sheep or horses, and, sometimes, pigs. Finally, Alex turned onto a rough gravel road bordered closely by empty fields with sagging fences and ragged foliage.

"Brian said the farm looks deserted."

"There are several places like that around here. Old houses and buildings that look like they're ready to fall down. Perfect hideouts for squatters up to no good."

Driving along, looking on both sides of the road, Alex gave her directions. "You'll wait in the car." He flicked on the police radio. "If anything happens, push this button to alert dispatch."

"Should we tell them we're out here?" she asked.

"If we do, they might tell me to back off or send for backup. We don't want to wait if the boys are in trouble."

"That makes sense." She added, "But I'm not staying in the car. Brian is my brother."

He gave her a disapproving look. "You need to keep out of it." He wouldn't even have brought her along except that he knew she'd follow him anyway.

"And what if someone gives you trouble? I can't just sit there and watch someone hurt you."

Alex's chest tightened at her caring tone. "So what do you think you can do? Take your heels off and pound them on the head?" He'd noticed she was wearing some kind of spike-heeled platforms with her jeans.

She hardened her lovely jaw. "That wouldn't be a bad idea. These heels are made of steel."

He would laugh if the circumstances weren't so serious. He had to give it to the woman. She had guts.

Another reason he loved her.

KRISTEN REMAINED QUIET as they drove a few miles down a length of country road. White dust rose behind them. She tried not to worry, but she couldn't help imagining her brother in trouble just when things had been looking up. What if they were too late?

Finally, Alex spotted the farm he'd been seeking. "Here we go."

As Brian had said, the place seemed deserted, the house gray, its white paint peeling. The outbuildings were skeletal and close to falling down. As they turned into the farmyard, they could see several people sitting or standing on the large porch outside. All faces turned in the police car's direction, clearly registering surprise.

"There's Brian," Kristen said, spying her brother and his friend on the porch.

As the cruiser rolled to a stop, a man and a woman broke from the group and climbed into a pickup. They took off, leaving dust in the air.

"Great," said Alex. "The fewer to deal with, the better." Again, he tried to tell Kristen what to do. "Stay in the car."

He should have known better.

Kristen opened the passenger door. "I'm coming with you."

"Then stay in back of me, at least. I don't want anyone grabbing you."

Grabbing her for what purpose? Kristen wondered. As a hostage? These people already had Brian here against his will.

Despite her bravado, she was happy to let Alex take the lead. He strode past a broken gate into the yard and stopped at the bottom of some steps leading up to the porch. He placed his hands on his hips, staring right back at the group glaring at him.

A particularly mean-looking guy in a black leather jacket seemed to be in charge. "What do you want?" he asked.

Not a very respectful way to address a policeman, Kristen thought.

"I'm here to pick up some minors from Sparrow Lake."

"No minors here that I know of."

"Let me be more specific," Alex said, his voice calm, authoritative, not wavering. In no way did he appear alarmed or afraid. "I'm here to get Brian Lange and Andy Eccles." He looked directly at the boys before turning his gaze back at the leader.

The man in the jacket definitely wanted to seem threatening. He stood on the edge of the porch so he could tower over Alex. "What if they don't wanna go?"

Brian didn't speak up, though he was watching everything closely. He glanced at Kristen where she stood, his expression apprehensive. She felt a thrill of fear herself, since the people occupying the farmhouse didn't seem inclined to back down easily.

Alex stated, "They're coming whether they want to or not."

Mr. Leather Jacket wasn't impressed. "Who gave you the right to come and arrest guests on my property? Got a warrant?"

"This lady can identify the boys as trouble-makers who vandalized some property," said Alex.

"Yes," Kristen spoke up, as the man's attention swung her way, his gaze insolent. Glad Alex could make use of her presence, she pointed at Brian and Andy standing on one side of the porch. "Those are the kids."

Alex told the boys, "Get a move on. We're getting in the car."

"Yes, sir," said Brian. Instead of taking the steps, he jumped off the low porch, Andy following.

The man in the jacket wasn't about to shut up. "I don't like this."

Alex didn't bother responding, just turned to walk away casually, flanking the boys.

Kristen stayed where she was for a moment, wondering if the group on the porch would pull something. She had no idea if they had weapons or not. As Alex neared her, he reached over and took her arm. She turned to accompany him.

Unbelievably enough, some creep in back of them made a kissy sound and said, "Hey, Momma."

She ignored the remark, relieved Alex had Brian and Andy. Alex opened the cruiser's back doors and the boys got in. She made haste to climb into the vehicle herself, and Alex slid into the driver's seat. He backed up the cruiser and headed out onto the gravel road.

They were at least a mile away before Kristen let out her breath. "Whew!"

She looked back at Brian, and his expression suggested he felt the same way.

"That guy was unpleasant," she told Alex.

"He's pushing his luck," Alex said. "I think I heard about somebody like him and his group being wanted by the state police. Maybe they've even got a sting set up."

"They seemed up to no good," Kristen agreed.

Alex glanced in the rearview mirror at Andy, who was sitting quietly in the backseat. "Know much about that guy?"

"Only that his name is Jerry," Andy said. "They're selling small electronics out of that house. Don't know any specifics about how they got the stuff. They didn't talk in front of me. But it was a truckload."

"When I get back to the station, I'll put a call in, see if someone doesn't want to clear out that viper's nest."

Brian looked directly at Alex via the mirror and said, "Whatever. Thanks, man."

Alex half smiled, but he didn't press for more.

Kristen realized he would have to deal with Andy and the problems the kid had gotten into when they returned to town.

The farther they traveled, the more relief Kristen felt. The police car was a refuge, an area of safety provided by Alex. He had come to her rescue, to her brother's rescue, without a moment's pause. No matter how he felt about her, or whether or not he was still interested in pursuing a relationship with her, he had taken responsibility for a situation that was above and beyond his job.

She couldn't help but be moved.

CHAPTER TWENTY

BACK IN SPARROW LAKE, Alex took Andy and Brian to the police station, where he and Owen went with them into a private office for a talk. Kristen waited in the small seating area outside. Cars and pedestrians passed by. She tried to read a magazine but finally tossed it aside.

In about a half hour, Brian emerged from the office alone. He walked over to Kristen and gave her a hug. "Thanks, sis."

She was also pleased that he'd thanked Alex in the car. "I'm happy you're all right. And that your friend is all right. Is Alex questioning him?"

"He's doing paperwork, signing Andy up for community service. Andy also needs a place to stay, other than with his family. Just in case that guy Jerry decides to come to town looking for him. He probably needs to keep off the streets for a while."

"Should you be careful, too?"

"I'll watch out, though I wasn't really hanging with that bunch," he explained. "Jerry demanded that we do some errands for him today. What, I don't know. He told us we'd be sorry if we didn't do what he said. That's why I called you."

"I'm so proud of you," she said. He seemed to be growing up in just days. She hoped it was the family's influence, but she knew it was also Alex.

Brian seemed a bit embarrassed by the attention she was giving him. When she reached out to hug him again, he said, "Let's not get too sticky about it. I'm almost a college freshman, after all." But he smiled. "You know that I'm going to be attending the same community college as Heather, right?"

"You are? When did this happen?"

"Aunt Margaret said I could stay in Sparrow Lake if I wanted to. I think I'd like to have a more familiar place to begin with."

So Aunt Margaret had been talking to him, too. "That sounds great, Brian."

"It'll be good to have some family around." He looked at her. "I know I told you if you want to go to Chicago, you should…but, well, if you want my vote on it, I hope you stay here."

"Thanks for your input." In the past couple of hours she'd made a decision herself, but she wanted to talk to Alex first.

Brian and Kristen turned to look when a small redheaded woman in glasses came in the front door. She was sniffling as if she had been crying. "Is Andy Eccles here?"

Janet, at the front desk, told her, "He's talking to Chief Novak, Mrs. Eccles. Just have a seat. He should be out soon."

Probably noticing that she'd arrived, Andy came out of Alex's office to hug his mother. Kristen thought about introducing herself but decided to give the pair some room. They had personal issues to work through.

Alex and Owen also emerged from the office. Alex stretched, looking tired. No wonder. Kristen had learned on the ride back to town that he'd gotten off the night shift just before she'd come to find him. "Can you give me a lift back to my car?" she asked Alex.

"Sure."

"I'll walk home," said Brian. When the police chief frowned at him, he pointed out, "It's broad daylight."

"I think you should be escorted home," Alex told him.

"I'll take him," Owen offered, perhaps to give Alex and Kristen some time to talk privately.

Because Kristen certainly intended to talk. She had so much to say, the air seemed filled with tension. She only hoped it wasn't a bad sort of tension.

The first thing out of her mouth when they climbed into the cruiser was "I truly appreciate your courage."

"It's part of my job."

She'd known he would say that, so she insisted, "You didn't have to do what you did. As you said, that deserted farm isn't even in your territory." Just as coming to the aid of the elderly couple in Chicago hadn't been his responsibility.

"It's still my job." He looked stern as he drove toward his house, passing shady streets and green lawns. Quite a few people were out mowing today. "Though it wasn't your job, Kristen. You shouldn't have been out there when I picked up the boys. You wouldn't even stay in the car. But then, you've been skirting danger all day."

She wasn't surprised by the lecture. "What do you mean, skirting danger?"

"I saw you doing wheelies in the street in front of Sew Fine this morning."

She snorted. "I wasn't doing wheelies. Though I guess I did make an illegal U-turn."

"I heard that car beep at you. You were being reckless. Then you jaywalked all over the place, could have gotten yourself run over. What got into you?"

"I'm not sure." She shrugged, giving a mock

sigh. "But being a lawman and all, you should know I'm rotten to the core."

"Your safety isn't a joke."

"I just was trying to figure out whether or not I should talk to you."

"You didn't have to act crazy. If you needed to talk, you could have come into the restaurant and faced me."

"My, you're prickly." And he wasn't making it easy for her.

"I'm tired." He looked it, the tiny lines at the corners of his eyes appearing deeper and more numerous. They reached his home and he turned the cruiser into the driveway, which was shaded by a big elm. Her car waited in front. "And I don't want to play games anymore."

"Well, neither do I. Though games can sometimes be fun," she teased.

He slid his arm across the back of the seat. "You didn't act like it was that much fun when I had to arrest you."

She was happy he didn't seem eager to get out of the car. "Right, I definitely needed to be arrested."

"According to the law—"

She broke in, "Oh, come on. I know you had ulterior motives. Well, maybe not for the shoplifting incident or the 911 call." She admitted,

"But I like your sense of humor, Alex. I always have."

He seemed to be suppressing a smile. "Sometimes we need to be serious."

"At the moment, I think you're just trying to be grouchy."

"I told you I'm tired. I haven't even slept in... well, a long time."

"That makes it even more impressive that you threw everything aside when I needed your help." From the corner of her eye, Kristen noticed a neighbor working on a flower bed and watching them.

"Oh?"

"I could trust you to do whatever was necessary. You take responsibility."

"We've talked about this before. I'm a responsible type of person."

"Which others are sometimes not. Responsible, that is." She told him the truth, "I've been thinking about my father a lot these past few days. He ran off and left us, you know." She might have mentioned it before. She couldn't remember.

"I heard something about that, but I don't know the particulars."

"Having a family to support was too much for my dad."

"That's terrible," he said, disgust in his tone. "I would never desert my family."

"I know." She had realized that even more profoundly in the past few hours. "Dad just took off when my brother was still little. My mom had to work several jobs to keep us afloat. She was always working. She came home late at night a lot."

"And so you took care of the younger ones."

"To the best of my ability, which you've seen is limited."

"I don't think so. They turned out pretty good. Even Brian—he's going to be okay now."

She hurried on, wanting to get everything out in the open. "When I was a teenager, I swore that what happened to my mom was never going to happen to me. I was going to earn a degree that would make me independent and enable me to get a good job."

"Which you had."

"Until the recession. But I was able to find another." She added, "More than one. I have choices. I always wanted to make a lot of money."

"Which you can."

Alex still made no move to get out. Neither did Kristen.

She admitted, "I thought money and a fancy condo were my goals."

"*Thought?* As in past tense?" He looked very interested. At least she hoped he was still interested.

"I've changed my mind, Alex. I would be even more of a stubborn, crazy person than I already am if I wasn't able to recognize my opportunities." And recognize who she wanted to be with.

He just watched her. Waiting.

"Why not stay here and manage my aunt's business?" she went on. "And get to know my siblings all over again?"

"You know I've always thought that was a good idea."

"It doesn't matter if I live here or in the city." She went on quickly. "I like both equally. What I really have to consider is the people I care about."

His expression shifted, became expectant.

"You're one of a kind, Alex. I know I won't find you anywhere else."

His smile broadened.

"I hope your offer is still open."

"Which one?"

"Dating a lot. Maybe 24/7." She touched his face and met his warm gaze. "I want you to know I have serious feelings for you. I—I love you, Alex."

He let out his breath slowly, his eyes speaking

volumes. "Wow. Something I never thought to hear. You continue to surprise me."

"Is there an ordinance against public affection?" she asked, noting that the curious neighbor at the flower bed was still watching them.

"I'm not sure. Why?"

"Because I want to sit here and make out in your driveway."

They might as well fuel more gossip, she thought, as his lips covered her own.

EPILOGUE

ON THE FOURTH OF JULY, Kristen picked up her sister and the twins to take them to the Sparrow Lake parade, along with a couple of lawn chairs for the adults and a blanket for the children. She smiled as she passed some stock trailers lined up in an empty lot, transportation for the cows that would be trotting down Main Street later on.

"There really are cows," she muttered, half to herself.

"Yes, and there will be cheese, too," said Heather. "People on the floats throw little wrapped wheels of cheese, along with candy, to the kids as they pass by." Then Heather indicated a crosswalk. "Turn here. Let's head for the corner near the ice cream shop where there'll be shade."

"Ice cream?" piped up Addison hopefully from the back of the car.

"No ice cream today, honey," Heather told her. "You're going to collect candy and stuff when the floats go by." She held up a large pink shopping bag. "You can put it in this."

"Candy. Yum," said Addison, with Taylor chiming in.

Kristen raised her brows at the size of the bag. "That much?"

"As many pieces as their little hands can scrabble up. I don't let them eat it all, though, at least not today. They'd get sick."

As Kristen slowed and pulled into a parking spot, Heather asked, "Are you meeting Alex afterward?" Her tone was mischievous, ripe with meaning.

Kristen grinned at her. "Of course."

At the moment, Alex was busy overseeing the parade and clearing its route down Main Street. He'd asked her if she wanted to accompany him, but they'd decided she ought to view the parade from a spectator's viewpoint, at least the first time.

Soon they trooped out of the car carrying the chairs, blanket and a cooler with drinks. Taylor and Addison ran ahead, shrieking when they saw some of their playmates from camp.

As they set up the chairs in a shady area, more spectators arrived. The sounds of the high school band tuning up could be heard from a few streets away.

"I'm so glad you're here," Heather told Kristen after they'd sat down and settled Taylor and Addison on the blanket in front of them.

Kristen knew her sister meant "here" as in Sparrow Lake, not just for the parade. How many more parades would she be seeing? Kristen wondered happily. She looked forward to them, along with the change of seasons and other minutiae of small-town life…as long as Alex completed the pictures in her mind.

"I'm glad to be here, too." She decided to broach the topic she'd been thinking about for a few days. "You know, we're getting quite a few orders online now."

"We sure are." Though this time Heather didn't sound tense about it.

"I think the online business will continue to increase. The craft bus tour is set to stop at Sew Fine in August. They'll be back once a month through December."

"Uh-huh."

Then Kristen put forth her idea. "I think we could use an online manager *and* an on-site manager."

"Oh?"

"The online manager can work at her own home, set her own hours…."

"If you're talking about me, I'll be happy to

do the online stuff, but I don't have to be called a manager."

"Well, I don't want to usurp your role," Kristen said, not wanting to push her sister aside.

"Usurp all you want," Heather told her. "I don't even care if I cut back my hours. I'll be happy to have some time for classes. There's a great internship I heard about that'll be available next summer."

Heather went on about what she'd be doing, quickly explaining the basics of something called sustainable landscaping. Kristen didn't understand all of it but realized how enthusiastic her sister was. Heather hadn't sounded this happy since Kristen moved back to Sparrow Lake.

"But enough about all that." Heather reached over and patted her arm. "Thanks for being so thoughtful."

With a trill of trumpets and the thud of bass drums, the high school band marched around the corner up the street.

"The parade is beginning," said Heather, grabbing Addison and Taylor who'd jumped to their feet. "Sit down, girls. Let them come to us."

Led by the parade marshal in a convertible, the band came down the street to a chorus of cheers. Following were floats, mostly simple and created by those who were affiliated with the stores and clubs and organizations that had entered them. Among the group was the Sparrow Lake Community House. The float featured crepe-paper streamers, posters and some of the community house staff waving to the crowd. A couple of teenagers—Brian and Andy—walked alongside the vehicle and threw wrapped candy to the crowd.

"Yay, Brian!" yelled Heather.

He responded by smiling, then throwing some candy nearly at the twins' feet. Heather let the girls jump up, screaming and grabbing.

"Here, Mommy," said Taylor, returning to throw a fistful of candy into the pink bag.

"More!" said Addison, adding several pieces.

Kristen enjoyed the scene, though she was waiting anxiously to see what the Sew Fine float looked like. She'd had to leave the night before while the crew had been putting on the final touches.

"Nice," said Heather when their store's trailer came into view.

The float was beautiful, decked out with a bright patchwork of crepe paper in different colors. Painted wooden letters glittering with sequins spelled out the name of the store. A rainbow of quilts were draped over wooden supports in the center. One of them was the blue-themed true love quilt, which was now finished. Kristen loved it and the idea that the quilting circle had made it for her and Alex. Gloria and Shara sat near the quilts, waving and throwing out candy in little packets. They had all done a terrific job and could be proud of themselves.

"How come you're not on there?" Heather asked.

"I wanted to observe. I'll participate another time."

More floats from local businesses came by. Candy flew through the air and the twins caught more than their share. They filled the pink bag with lollipops and bubble gum and other types of candy.

Next came the farm equipment—brand-new tractors and combines so large they towered over some of the buildings. A group of local stock-car racers dressed as clowns brought up the rear, weaving back and forth across the street and joking with the crowd.

Then the cows trotted down the street, a sea of black and white because most were Holsteins. The animals wore brightly colored halters and some sported beads and bells and even hats. One large cow was decked out in a feathery red boa. All had caretakers leading or accompanying them, while other people walked amid the herd carrying baskets from which they scooped tiny wrapped wheels of cheese to throw to the crowd. Kristen grinned when she saw the cow with the boa being led by Matt Stapleton. Alex said the boy had taken a shine to the animal he'd sprayed with purple stars. He'd gotten to know the cow pretty well after washing her multiple times to get rid of the markings. Matt waved to her.

Finally, as the last of the cows passed by, a street-cleaning crew made its way at the end of the parade. At the same time, a police cruiser appeared in the nearby side street.

Excited at seeing Alex, Kristen got to her feet.

"Go ahead," Heather told her. "I'll get Brian to help me with these chairs and stuff."

Kristen needed no more urging. "See you later."

Then she ran to join Alex.

He stopped the cruiser and opened the passenger door. She'd hardly had time to climb inside before he reached over and pulled her closer for a quick kiss.

"What did you think?"

Kristen grinned at him. "That Sparrow Lake has some really wonderful things Chicago just can't beat."

Starting with Police Chief Alex Novak.

SITTING WITH JOHN across the street from her beautiful nieces, Margaret smiled with pleasure. She was so proud of her family. And so happy that Kristen had decided to stay in Sparrow Lake.

"Things worked out well, didn't they?" said John as they saw Kristen get into the cruiser to drive off with Alex.

Margaret had a feeling he meant their own burgeoning relationship as well as Alex and Kristen's. "Things certainly did work out. With Kristen running Sew Fine, and the rest of my family working there, I can trust the business will continue into the future." Something she'd hoped for, and not just for the money it would make.

"So you're retired. What are you going to do?"

"Oh, teach a class now and then. Sew. Paint. Maybe lead a slightly more laid-back life."

And maybe do a little matchmaking for Heather if she could. Heather and her twins could use a man in their lives, though Margaret wasn't going to mention that to John.

"Hmm, laid-back, huh? Maybe you'll have time for a cruise."

"A cruise?" She perked up at the suggestion. "You mean on one of those big ships?"

"No. I was thinking a smaller type of boat. The kind two or three people can handle."

"You bought another boat?" Margaret had already realized that John had plenty of extra funds to play with, having been a successful businessman before moving to Sparrow Lake. "Like the one you had in Chicago?"

"Not yet. Besides, I'm at a new place in life. I'm starting over. I think one of those yachts with all the electronic thingamajigs might do the trick." He asked, "Are you interested?"

"Of course!" said Margaret, beaming at him. She might be retired, but she considered it a new phase in her life. She would never be too old for adventures. "Starting over is an art that everyone should embrace."

* * * * *

REQUEST YOUR FREE BOOKS!
2 FREE WHOLESOME ROMANCE NOVELS
IN LARGER PRINT
PLUS 2
FREE
MYSTERY GIFTS

HEARTWARMING™

Wholesome, tender romances

YES! Please send me 2 FREE Harlequin® Heartwarming Larger-Print novels and my 2 FREE mystery gifts (gifts worth about $10). After receiving them, if I don't wish to receive any more books, I can return the shipping statement marked "cancel." If I don't cancel, I will receive 4 brand-new larger-print novels every month and be billed just $4.99 per book in the U.S. or $5.74 per book in Canada. That's a savings of at least 23% off the cover price. It's quite a bargain! Shipping and handling is just 50¢ per book in the U.S. and 75¢ per book in Canada.* I understand that accepting the 2 free books and gifts places me under no obligation to buy anything. I can always return a shipment and cancel at any time. Even if I never buy another book, the two free books and gifts are mine to keep forever.

161/361 IDN F47N

Name _____ (PLEASE PRINT)

Address _____ Apt. #

City _____ State/Prov. _____ Zip/Postal Code

Signature (if under 18, a parent or guardian must sign)

Mail to the Harlequin® Reader Service:
IN U.S.A.: P.O. Box 1867, Buffalo, NY 14240-1867
IN CANADA: P.O. Box 609, Fort Erie, Ontario L2A 5X3

* Terms and prices subject to change without notice. Prices do not include applicable taxes. Sales tax applicable in N.Y. Canadian residents will be charged applicable taxes. Offer not valid in Quebec. This offer is limited to one order per household. Not valid for current subscribers to Harlequin Heartwarming larger-print books. All orders subject to credit approval. Credit or debit balances in a customer's account(s) may be offset by any other outstanding balance owed by or to the customer. Please allow 4 to 6 weeks for delivery. Offer available while quantities last.

Your Privacy—The Harlequin® Reader Service is committed to protecting your privacy. Our Privacy Policy is available online at www.ReaderService.com or upon request from the Harlequin Reader Service.

We make a portion of our mailing list available to reputable third parties that offer products we believe may interest you. If you prefer that we not exchange your name with third parties, or if you wish to clarify or modify your communication preferences, please visit us at www.ReaderService.com/consumerschoice or write to us at Harlequin Reader Service Preference Service, P.O. Box 9062, Buffalo, NY 14269. Include your complete name and address.

HWDIR13R

ReaderService.com

Manage your account online!

- Review your order history
- Manage your payments
- Update your address

---

*We've designed
the Harlequin® Reader Service
website just for you.*

Enjoy all the features!

- Reader excerpts from any series
- Respond to mailings and
  special monthly offers
- Discover new series available to you
- Browse the Bonus Bucks catalog
- Share your feedback

Visit us at:

ReaderService.com